LIZ MARCH: © SIOBHAN HARVEY

Witi Ihimaera has written thirteen novels, among them *The Whale Rider* in 1987, and six collections of short stories and works for children. His last novel was *The Parihaka Woman* in 2011, and *The Thrill of Falling* is his seventh short story collection.

Ihimaera has also had careers in teaching, theatre, opera, film and television. His work was set to music by well-known contemporary musicians in *Ihimaera*, commissioned for the 2011 Auckland Arts Festival. His words for *Kaitiaki*, composed by Gareth Farr, were presented at a Beethoven concert by the New Zealand Symphony Orchestra in September of the same year. He has travelled extensively, most recently to festivals and conferences in Britain, Germany and New Caledonia.

He lives in Auckland.

THE THRILL OF FALLING

VINTAGE

— FOR JESSICA, OLIVIA, JANE AND JAMIE —

A VINTAGE BOOK published by Random House New Zealand,
18 Poland Road, Glenfield, Auckland, New Zealand

For more information about our titles go to www.randomhouse.co.nz

A catalogue record for this book is available from the National Library
of New Zealand

Random House New Zealand is part of the Random House Group
New York London Sydney Auckland Delhi Johannesburg

First published 2012

© Witi Ihimaera 2012

The moral rights of the author have been asserted

ISBN 978 1 86979 920 5
eISBN 978 1 86979 921 2

Design: Megan van Staden
Cover illustration: Megan van Staden
Cover images: Getty images (feather); iStockphoto (paper texture)
Author photograph: Liz March, © Siobhan Harvey
The author photograph was taken by Liz March for the publication
of *Words Chosen Carefully: New Zealand Writers in Discussion*,
Cape Catley, 2010.

Printed in New Zealand by Printlink

This publication is printed on paper pulp sourced from sustainably
grown and managed forests, using Elemental Chlorine Free (EFC)
bleaching, and printed with 100% vegetable-based inks.

Also available as an ebook

CONTENTS —

MAGGIE DAWN

A GOOD DAY —

I t was Saturday, 8 a.m.

Maggie Dawn was awake before the alarm went off on her cellphone. She lay quietly in bed for a little while, looking at the patterns on the ceiling caused by the curtains drifting in the morning sun. Then she leant over and reached under the bed for her diary and pen.

Brushing her hair back from her eyes, she wrote:

LISTEN UP, WORLD, TODAY IS GOING TO BE A GOOD DAY

'You got that?' Maggie Dawn called out the window.

With that out of the way, she got up and smoothed the duvet. She slipped into the dressing gown with the dragon on the back and went down the hallway to the bathroom. Although she was only fifteen, Maggie Dawn was a big girl. Skinny people walked, but calorifically challenged individuals sashayed, a kind of sideways-frontways ambulation of her most prominent feature, as Maggie Dawn liked to call her butt, switching the weight from one cheek to the other.

The word 'sashayed' appealed to Maggie Dawn: it brought to mind sway, sidle and sass, which were good adjectives to describe the way she moved through the world.

From the front she knew that with the right amount of sass

people looked past her weight to how light she was on her toes. And, as long as she didn't dress in jeans that moved into the crack of her butt — yew, gross — she knew they wouldn't make any smart comments about the rest of her.

The bathroom was last down the hall on the right. There was one other bedroom in the tiny council flat, Gran's, which Maggie Dawn liked to air as often as possible to get rid of the smell of the old lady who sometimes, well, leaked.

Maggie Dawn crept in. Gran was still asleep after returning late from the casino. Her false teeth were fizzing in a glass of water beside the bed, and her wig was on the floor. Gran was in lala-land if she thought the wig made her look attractive; whenever she wore it, it looked like a very sick cat was sitting on her head. Maggie Dawn picked the wig up and put it on top of the wardrobe where it belonged. She also sneaked a look in Gran's purse. It was always good to know where matters stood.

Whaddya know? Gran had restrained herself! There was still a $50 and a $20 note plus some change, so she hadn't lost all her benefit money for the week on the pokies. Good girl, Gran.

Maggie Dawn sashayed into the bathroom. She took off the dressing gown, careful not to look at the person who had now appeared naked in the full-length mirror opposite her, and sidled into the shower.

Among Gran's cheap soaps and toiletries from the $2 Shop, with old use-by dates, she found her own personal bar of quality soap that she'd scored in the girls' changing room at college last week. She began to soap every roll and flap, every hollow, nook and cranny, singing her favourite rap song:

Tol' you once, tol' you twice
Keep outta ma face uh huh uh huh . . .

Humming and bopping and feeling much better, Maggie Dawn stepped out of the shower, wrapped a towel around her body and, now that she was fully composed, was able to look at herself in the mirror, posing this way and that.

'Oh-kay, bad girl,' she said, finally. Nothing had changed. Same old same old: a kinda pretty face on a kinda nice body which was — Maggie Dawn would never have used the 'f' word (f-a-t) or the horrendous 'o' word (o-b-e-s-e) — not thin.

Maggie Dawn knew that her weight made her unattractive, but there were compensations: she had lovely brown eyes, ger-reat skin, she would never go bald with all that frizzy hair and, although she had big juicy pillow lips (so did Angelina Jolie), her teeth were white and even. Not for her false teeth in a glass at forty.

As for the rest of her, well, there was No Hope of getting all that w-e-i-g-h-t off, but if she saved up hard enough, by the time she was in her twenties she could have a tummy tuck and breast reduction — which would mean that she wouldn't have to wait for reincarnation.

Maggie Dawn put on her XXXL bra and panties, and slipped into her XXXL jeans and pretty op-shop top. She shuffled her feet into the slip-on men-sized trainers bought from The Warehouse, snapped on her watch, rings and a couple of bangles, put some hoops into her ears and then sashayed to the kitchen.

Steeling herself against the inevitable, she opened the refrigerator door. The usual array greeted her: half a carton of milk, butter, bread, eggs, stringy piece of bacon (yay!). Not half empty: half full. It was enough to get by on.

Five or so minutes later, Maggie Dawn had Gran's breakfast tray ready. 'Gran,' she said as she went into the room, 'time for kai.' She put the tray on the bed and tried to shake Gran awake. 'Gran, knock, knock. Anybody home?' Gran suffered from sleep apnoea and sometimes didn't take a breath for ages. Her mouth was open and she looked like death.

Gingerly, Maggie Dawn poked her and Gran gave a deep gasp and her eyelids fluttered.

'Good,' Maggie Dawn said. 'So you're alive then.'

She had come to stay with Gran six years ago so that the old lady could look after her — it tended to work the other way round — and Mum could make a better job of looking after Chantelle and Roxanne Adorata.

'Here are your teeth, and I got you a *Woman's Weekly* when I was at the shop yesterday.'

Gran focused her rheumy eyes and smiled. 'Thank you, darling.' Her breath was stale as.

'I have to go to Mum's now,' Maggie Dawn continued. 'I'll do the supermarket shopping on my way back tonight.'

Gran reached for her purse and gave Maggie Dawn the $20 note. 'Can you buy me a scratch ticket?'

Maggie Dawn sighed. Scratch ticket, $3. That left $17 for the groceries. Ah well, so what else was new? She would, as usual, have to rely on the pocket money she got from Mr Singh at the local book and stationery store. He wasn't very good at English so paid her for two hours a week to mark the new stock.

'I'll see you later, Gran.' She kissed the old lady on the forehead. 'Be a good girl.'

WELCOME TO THE 'HOOD —

Maggie Dawn made a shortcut through the park.

Every Saturday she took the kids off Mum's hands for the day — Chantelle and Roxanne Adorata had been joined by a brother, now five, named Zoltan. They were all, including Maggie Dawn, from different fathers. Oh, why was Evelyn so indiscriminate? As for the names, well, Mum chose those to represent fantasy worlds she'd never live in herself. At least nobody could say that she didn't have any imagination. When you thought about it, not bad for a woman who didn't finish college.

But imagination can only get you so far. When it came to raising kids, Mum was worse than hopeless.

'Watch out,' called a voice.

Maggie Dawn was just passing the clothing bins where some nicely dressed Pakeha ladies were piling their discarded last-year fashions. It was one of the women who had given her the warning. Before Maggie Dawn could even think, three bikes whizzed past, in a flurry of shouts and screams. One of the cyclists gave her a kick as she passed by. Maggie Dawn stumbled and fell.

Her arch enemy from college, Candace Reynolds, with her mates Teresa Crosby and Rachel Williams. 'Whoops,' jeered Candace, 'did we just hit a cow?' Laughing, they rode on towards the mall.

Embarrassed, Maggie Dawn picked herself up and slunk past the Pakeha at the bin. 'Hey!' she yelled at the retreating girls. 'Can't you read the sign? "No dogs allowed!"' She felt anger building up inside her. Nothing could stop the thoughts that streamed through her mind:

'*Yeah think you're better than me Candace and you may be top of the class but I'm right behind you and I will mow you down you bitch so you may be queen of the heap right now with your legally blonde act but I got brains and you honey will always be a bimbo yeah you heard me you bitch so don't mess with me and think I don't know how you got that job at the mall that I shoulda got your daddy phoned up head office while I was standing there I had the job in my pocket but when Ron Simpson put the phone down he said the job was already taken I needed that job bitch . . .*'

'No, no, no,' Maggie Dawn said to herself. 'Be kind, think good thoughts. Don't let Candace Reynolds ruin your day. It's going to be a good day.'

'*But you're still pissed that you didn't get that job at the mall eh go on admit that you wanted to smash Candace Reynolds' head in.*'

'Shut the fuck up,' Maggie Dawn muttered to the voice in her head. Quickly, she plugged herself into her iPod. Into her ears went her earphones and, hey presto, zombieland. Blissed out, she joined the other living dead spasming and jerking around the park.

Mum's place was a state house on Pleasant Drive. Call living here pleasant? Ha ha funny ha ha. The street mainly comprised women like Evelyn on some benefit or another, saddled with kids and no dads. If there was somebody around who fitted that kind of description, well, he wasn't exactly getting ahead in his life.

As Maggie Dawn went around the back something lunged at her from the house next door: Granite, a big brown pitbull cross. She hated the dog, but at least it kept away bad muthafuckas who might want to do Evelyn and the kids over.

'Are you home, Mum?' Maggie Dawn yelled as she opened the back door and went in. Stupid question: of course Mum was home. All the mums round here were home unless — hey the sun does sometimes shine on (Un) Pleasant Drive — they scored the occasional job like Evelyn's at Pak'n'Save.

Maggie Dawn heard gunshots coming from the living room. There she found Chantelle, Roxanne Adorata and Zoltan all sitting on the sofa in front of the TV. 'Hey,' she called.

'Hey.' Their eyes were wide with fear as they watched the werewolf rip off a poor girl's head, chomp, chomp, chomp. They were dressed and all ready to be taken out for the day.

'Mum?' Maggie Dawn yelled up the stairs.

As Evelyn appeared Maggie Dawn felt her heart catch with love. Mum must have been on late shift. Her eyes were dazed but she smiled when she saw her eldest daughter. She pushed back her hair and fumbled in her dressing gown for her smokes. Lit one. Puffed. Sprinkled ash on the stairs.

'Honey,' she said, 'Dave's coming around this afternoon.'

Dave was the new boyfriend. He belonged to a gang. Worse, he sold dope. 'I thought you threw him out.' Maggie Dawn was angry. 'He's such a loser, Mum.'

'Yeah ... well ...' Evelyn continued, 'I'm giving him one more chance.' Pause. 'Could you ... uh ... keep the kids with you all day? Give me and him some space?'

'Mum, don't do this to yourself,' Maggie Dawn pleaded. 'He really isn't into you. He's a user.'

Evelyn started to cry. 'Baby, you just don't understand ...'

Understand? Why didn't people credit Maggie Dawn with some intelligence? All her life she had been told that she would never be able to escape the limitations of her life, blah blah blah ... Well, she refused to be a statistic. People put her down, but she was on her way up. She studied hard — sure, she was just average, but she tried. She did her homework on a kitchen table in Gran's flat and presented it to Mr Hawkins whenever he called for it. But did she get credit for it from her classmates? No way.

Just last week when she returned to her desk she overheard Candace Reynolds trying to put her down. 'Who does she think she is? Thinks she's better than the rest of us, dontcha, Maggie Dawn?' Mr Hawkins was in the middle of his lesson when Maggie Dawn, mad as hell at Candace's remark, stood up and sashayed to the front of the class. 'Yes, Maggie Dawn?' Mr Hawkins was startled that she had interrupted his teaching.

'Sir, there's something I want to say to everyone.' Then she turned to her goggle-eyed classmates and began: 'I know what some of you think about me, but if I do my homework and you don't do yours, don't blame me for you all sitting on your arses and letting your lives go down the shithole. I'm trying my best here for myself. And all your talking behind my back's not going to stop me, Candace Reynolds. You'll probably have three kids by the time you're twenty, but that's not gonna be my world. So don't you or any of you other bitches stand in my way cause I'm coming through. Stuff the lot of you. And Mr Hawkins, you have a nice day.'

Baby, you just don't understand?

Not only was Maggie Dawn doing her best at school, she was also trying to educate herself. Most of her friends, like Tawhi, avoided the public library but she knew that college would only get her so far. If she wanted to go further she'd have to help herself up the ladder.

When she felt the urge, she sashayed into the library for an hour or so. Every week she liked to deploy a new word and a new phrase picked up from her reading. This week's new word and new phrase were: 'autocratic' and 'taking everything into consideration'.

She'd lost quite a few opportunities already this morning to put them both into practice. Better make up for lost time.

Maggie Dawn had also discovered that the library had some really cool self-help shit. Books about how to improve your self-esteem, your confidence, your career prospects. Some weren't so great: about breaking the food cycle so that you would not get f-a-t.

And as for Evelyn, well, she was in a cycle too. Like the other mothers on Pleasant Drive, she was waiting for a man to take her away from all this.

Oh, Maggie Dawn understood all right.

'Come on, kids.' Maggie Dawn blew a kiss to Evelyn. 'Love you, Mum.'

'Do you need any dollars?' Mum asked. 'Here . . .' She threw a few miserable bucks down the stairs.

Gee, do people think I'm a bank? Maggie Dawn thought to herself. Ah well, more money was required from her own savings. Maybe she could ask Mr Singh for extra hours.

It wasn't until she and the kids were on the pavement that she realised that they hadn't come ay-lone. Zoltan had brought a pair of wicked-looking scissors. 'Don't you think you should leave those at home?' Maggie Dawn asked. He was busy cutting up the sky and snipping the sun in two. He shook his head.

Suddenly Dave turned up in his car, roaring up the road as if he owned it. He had two mates along with him. They started to take crates of beer out of the boot. 'Wotcha starin' at, bitch?' Dave asked Maggie Dawn.

'You're such a cliché,' she answered. Let him try to work that one out. 'And so auto-cratic,' she added.

'You always like to use big words, dontcha, bitch? You bettah watch yuself or I'll make that lip of yours even bigger.'

Maggie Dawn gave him the stare. She would have answered him back but, taking everything into consideration, she had the kids with her. She pulled them after her. Zoltan looked back, took aim and snip, off came Dave's head.

AT THE MALL

Midday and all was well. The kids were skipping and yelling in front of Maggie Dawn, glad to have escaped the werewolf; he was still hungry and wanted to bite their heads off.

'Where are you taking us, Maggie Dawn?' asked Chantelle.

'There's a movie we can go and see at the multiplex,' Maggie Dawn answered. 'Would you like that?'

'Can we get us some lollies first?' asked Roxanne Adorata.

'Sure.'

'Yay,' said Zoltan, snipping away at passers-by with his scissors.

At the mall Maggie Dawn saw Candace Reynolds helping Ron Simpson putting out the usual sign:

NO HOODIES
NO SKATEBOARDS
NO PATCHES

Ron Simpson was the mall's security officer and he had employed Candace to assist him in the office. When she saw Maggie Dawn approaching with the three children, she giggled and said to Ron Simpson, 'Maybe we should add No No-Hopers to the list.'

Maggie Dawn had always felt that attack was the best mode of defence. 'I do not appreciate the insinuation in your remark,' she said very loudly. 'I spend my money at this mall and will not be spoken to in such a way by . . . by . . . staff.' Then she added, 'Good afternoon, Mr Simpson.' He had the courtesy to look a bit sheepish. He knew she should have got the job.

The doors to the mall opened automatically, and Maggie Dawn couldn't stop Chantelle, Roxanne Adorata and Zoltan as they rushed inside. Quickly she followed them, the doors closing fast behind her, swish swish. The children ran in and out of the shops and up and down the mall. Unconcerned, Maggie Dawn headed for New World where she grabbed a trolley, then gave a loud whistle:

'Haere mai, ki te kai!'

Immediately the kids came running towards her. Maggie Dawn picked Zoltan up and put him in the trolley. Chantelle and Roxanne Adorata took turns pushing the trolley down the aisle towards the fruit section.

'Oooh, grapes,' Maggie Dawn said. 'Are they ripe?' She took a few in her hands and put them in her mouth. Then she turned to the others. 'What do you think?'

The kids took a bunch each and scoffed the lot. 'Too sour,' they agreed.

'Shall we try the plums?' Maggie Dawn asked.

Down the hatch. 'Ugh,' Chantelle said, 'they're off.'

Cutting a swathe through the fruit section, Maggie Dawn led

the charge to the confectionery aisle. The kids had a fantastic time filling up a plastic bag with their favourites: chocolate fish ('One for the bag and two for us'), wine gums ('Two for the bag and three for us'), peppermints ('Three for the bag and a handful for us') and liquorice allsorts ('Four in the bag and, whoops, too many, but we handled them so we'd better eat them, eh?').

Maggie Dawn headed for the checkout. There was a man in front of them, wearing a cap with his ponytail sticking out the back: lame.

Her cellphone ding-donged. It was her mate Tawhi texting her:

— W r u? Wt u doing?
— At th mll. Tking kds 2 mvies
— Cn I cm?
— C u 1pm mltiplx

Maggie Dawn closed her phone. The man with the ponytail hadn't been called to a checkout counter yet . . . but there was something strange about him now.

Uh oh. Where was his ponytail? Maggie Dawn stared at Zoltan. He was looking at her as if butter wouldn't melt in his mouth.

Then, behind her, Maggie Dawn heard the sound of an outraged old lady whose lovely long dress now had a huge cut in the back, showing her panties. And now a young girl discovered that somebody had cut the straps of her fake Louis Vuitton bag.

Zoltan had been busy with his bloody scissors, but when had he done the deeds? You had to keep an eye on that boy.

'Time to get outta here,' Maggie Dawn said to nobody in particular.

The man without the ponytail was called to a checkout

counter. And then it was Maggie Dawn's turn, to pay $1.50 for her plastic bag of sweets.

'What the fuck...' The man had discovered he'd been scalped. His ponytail was lying on the floor and people were gathering to look at it. Was it ... could it ... be a dead possum?

There were a couple of shrill whistles and Ron Simpson came speeding along with Candace in tow. He had a long pole in his hands and a baseball bat at the ready.

'Don't anybody go near it,' he said. 'It could be dangerous.' He stabbed at the ponytail, relieved that it did not stab back. Then he was alerted by another cry.

An old man who'd been snoring on one of the benches in the mall had woken up to discover that he now had only half a handlebar moustache.

Maggie Dawn gave the man without a ponytail a bright smile as she pulled the kids around the corner. Taking everything into consideration, he looked better without it anyway.

She bent down to Zoltan's level and gave him the look. 'I've noticed your interest in sharp things,' she said as she took away his scissors, 'but this is where it stops before you move on to pocket knives or samurai swords — and you're not going to become a member of any gang, you geddit?'

Zoltan looked alarmed. This was the Queen of Outer Space talkin'.

He goddit.

'Hey, Maggie Dawn!' A hand was waving. 'Over here.'

Tawhi was waiting at the entrance to the multiplex.

Gee, why did Tawhi have to wave? At over six foot, she stuck out like a sore thumb. But when you were like Maggie Dawn, not thin, you didn't exactly go with the glamour crowd. Nah, you were stuck with other odds and sods like Tawhi the tall one, Renee with the wooden leg, and Chan the Chinese boy, who was brilliant at maths.

'Hey,' said Maggie Dawn.

Tawhi was dressed to kill. She was looking for a boyfriend, preferably a fulla as tall as she was. She was ever hopeful: she'd read a magazine article that said it didn't matter what you looked like, there was always someone in the world who was into your type. The secret was to put yourself out there and wait till that someone turned up and, boingggg!, true lurv, baby. Not that such a boy would ever exist in this dump.

'I got us our tickets,' Tawhi said.

'Did you?' Maggie Dawn stiffened. 'I'm not a freeloader, Tawhi,' she continued as she paid her friend back — gloom, over thirty bucks. The way things were going, she'd soon be in the red.

'Okay,' she said finally, 'let's go to the movies.'

Shouting with glee, the kids dived through the door and went way down the front where they could see everything. They were so much fun to take to films. Maggie Dawn hadn't told them it was in 3-D. She couldn't help but feel so much love for them as, laughing with joy, they held up their arms to catch some of the stuff that was floating out from the screen at them. She looked at Tawhi — You'll be my best mate forever — and then she thought again about poor Mum, her arsehole boyfriend Dave and Gran away with the fairies.

And in the dark nobody could see her shivering.

Oh, kids, how are we all gonna to get outta here?

WE ARE FAMILY

After the movie, Maggie Dawn said goodbye to Tawhi who thought she might go and hang out at McDonald's; maybe the fulla of her dreams was there having a Quarter Pounder with cheese. The kids were jumping around and yelling, 'Can we go too and have a burger and fries? Puh-lease, Maggie Dawn, please!'

'No, we can't afford it.' More to the truth, she couldn't afford it. There were still the groceries to get and Gran's scratch ticket too. She had just enough cash left over for one ice cream they would have to share but, what was this? An old koro came over and told the candy-striped attendant, 'I'll take care of it.' He must have been a relation or somebody.

Okay, so the next problem was this: Mum had asked Maggie Dawn to keep the kids for the day so her and arsehole Dave could have some space. She knew what that meant, but she would never understand the sex thing and why people had to do you-know-what in the middle of the day.

Yuck, way too much information.

'Let's go to the marae,' she said. 'There's bound to be something happening down there . . . and kai too.'

The kids nodded enthusiastically but weren't so keen when they saw the groups of old people in black waiting at the gate. A funeral was underway, with the callers crying to each other, 'Aue te mamae me te aroha mo te kuia nei e!'

But Maggie Dawn looked sternly at the kids. 'Now that we're here we'll pay our respects and then we'll go.' Noticing some lovely white flowers in a garden across the road, she gave Zoltan back his scissors. 'Do something useful for a change,' she hissed at him. Happily he and his sisters sped across the road. When they returned they had a lovely bouquet with them.

The children accompanied the visitors onto the marae and waited with bowed heads as the old ladies wept for the old, old lady lying in the polished box. *One of these days Gran will be like that.* Maggie Dawn pushed the thought away quickly — no, no, no.

They waited to pay their respects, and, when it was their turn, Maggie Dawn led them up to the grieving family and gave them the flowers. One of the women beamed and addressed the dead woman: 'Anei, Hera, nga putiputi mo koe. Sarah, some flowers for you.' Maggie Dawn was smothered in kisses and wet tears, and the younger children were slobbered over.

Then Maggie Dawn jerked her head to a side door where they made their escape. They sprinkled water over their heads before leaving the meeting house behind.

'I'm very proud of you,' Maggie Dawn told them.

We didn't eat,' said Zoltan, 'and I'm really hungry.'
Well, they could go back to the food hall at the mall, but at that moment, Maggie Dawn saw that a wedding was taking place at the local Anglican chapel. The bride sparkled in the sun. Beside her was a handsome groom with white, white teeth. 'There's where we'll get our feed, kids,' she said.

But Roxanne Adorata, always one for making a fashion statement, said, 'We're not dressed for a wedding.'

Maggie Dawn remembered the Pakeha ladies who had been dropping off clothes. 'No worries,' she answered. Screaming and yelling, she chased the children back across the park. When they got to the bin, she upended Zoltan through the hole at the top of it; his legs kicked away as he slid inside. Next moment he started throwing things out.

'Look at these clothes!' Maggie Dawn said, shocked. 'Some are really nice!' Here was a cute button-up jacket for Zoltan, a pretty little jumper for Chantelle and what was this? A fake diamond tiara for Roxanne Adorata. And hey, a bonus: a purple silk scarf to take home for Gran.

The children raced back to the chapel where the wedding banquet was already starting. It was easy to slip in and, look, there was a table just for the little children! Seating them there, Maggie Dawn looked for an empty chair among the adults.

Ah, there was one.

Mrs Johnson, the woman next to Maggie Dawn, smiled at her, puzzled. This didn't look like Mayoress Kelly. Not only that, but this teenage girl was Maori, surely, or perhaps a not very nice-looking Italian.

Oh dear. Maggie Dawn hadn't realised that the wedding was full of Pakeha, not one Maori in sight.

'Are you Joshua's daughter?' asked Mrs Johnson. 'And are those charming little children your brothers and sisters?'

'Kaore,' Maggie Dawn replied. It meant no, but all that Mrs Johnson could tell was that it was foreign. Hmm, maybe Joshua's daughter was from some other Mediterranean country.

The waiter came with a lovely plate of turkey. 'Here we are then, dear,' Mrs Johnson said, articulating carefully so that the poor girl could understand.

One more task to do before Maggie Dawn took the children home.

They skipped and ran all the way back to the mall. Into New

World again to buy Gran's scratch ticket and milk, bread, butter, sugar, bananas, corned beef and baked beans.

On the way out, Maggie Dawn saw Candace Reynolds chalking an addition to the sign at the mall:

AND NO SIZZERS.

'I know it was you or your dirty little sisters or brother,' she said.

Dirty? Maggie Dawn saw red. A person was innocent until they were proven guilty. Not only that, but where was Candace's evidence?

She carefully put Zoltan's scissors into one of the plastic bags of groceries. 'Wait here,' she said to the children. Sweeping past Candace, Maggie Dawn knocked on Ron Simpson's office. When he appeared she pointed at the sign.

'I don't want to sound too autocratic,' she began, 'but taking everything into consideration I have to tell you that your staff person doesn't know how to spell. Sizzers, puh-lease! What's the use of a sign if people don't understand what it says? Have a nice day.'

PARTY TIME ON PLEASANT DRIVE

Bloody hell,' Maggie Dawn muttered.

She could hear the party from a block away. By the time she got to Mum's house she could tell that arsehole Dave and his gang mates had taken over. The noise was horrendous, with the stereo up loud and people screaming and yelling and coming and going and giving the fingers to the neighbours.

Even Granite, the coward, had decided to call it a night and was huddled in his kennel.

'Don't take the kids in there, Maggie Dawn,' one of the neighbours, Sally, called. 'The fuckin' animals have already had a coupla fights. The cops have been called. They'll be here in a few minutes.'

'The cops?' Maggie Dawn asked, alarmed. If they found any illegal substances in the house, Evelyn could be charged. And if that happened . . .

'Stay here, kids.' Chantelle and Roxanne Adorata were clinging to each other, whimpering, and Zoltan was scissoring frantically.

Maggie Dawn barged inside.

'Everybody out!' she screamed. 'Get the fuck out of my mum's house.'

But they were so out of it, did they even hear the big black fatty as she tried to push them out any opening? Nah, they pushed back and it was her own fault if she fell down and cut her hand on glass, the stupid cunt.

Up the crowded staircase Maggie Dawn went, like a tank on the rampage.

'Mum? Mum? Where are you?'

Not in the bedroom. There were four other people there and they looked like vampires sucking blood from each other. Nor in the kids' bedrooms, trashed already, and stinking with smoke and booze. Trashing the house was bad enough, yes, but nobody trashed her brother's and sisters' rooms.

Maggie Dawn heard Evelyn screaming. Left shoulder down, she slammed the locked bathroom door apart and went through.

Mum was sitting on the toilet, not screaming at all but laughing her head off, with white stuff all around her nose and mouth.

Oh, Mum.

Arsehole Dave was urinating all over her. He turned and looked at her. 'You want some of my piss, too, bitch?'

That was it, she completely lost it.

He was smirking, thinking he'd put Maggie Dawn in her place, stuffing his cock back in his jeans and buttoning up his flies when she hit him. 'You bastard,' she hissed.

Quick as a flash Dave slammed her back. He pinned her to the wall with his right arm against her throat. 'You like that, you little cunt?' He was groping in his pockets for something. Some pills.

Maggie Dawn tried to keep her lips shut as he attempted to force some down her throat. 'Come on, hon-ey, open up and belong to Daddy.'

Groggy and desperate for breath, Maggie Dawn tried to prise Dave's arm away but he shoved a knee into her groin.

Maggie Dawn cast a frightened look at Evelyn: Mum, help me.

Dave's face was right up against Maggie Dawn, his eyes red and wild, spittle spraying from his mouth. Frustrated that he couldn't get Maggie Dawn to swallow, he put the pills back in his pocket and raised his fist. 'You've been asking for this, bitch.'

He started on her. Smash, smash, smash, crunch.

Oh God. The pain. But, far away, there was the sound of sirens. The cops.

Yeah, big man, keep on hitting me, that's it, because every time you hit me will mean another year on your sentence when they send you to fuckin' prison, arsehole, arsehole, arse . . .

LISTEN UP, UNIVERSE

Today was going to be a good day?

'Are you feeling better now, darling?'

Still dazed, Maggie Dawn was bandaged up and on painkillers, waiting with Gran in outpatients for a taxi to take her home. The doctor had managed to patch her up pretty well with a few stitches to some cuts above her left eyebrow and her lips where Dave's fists had split them. But Dave was going to go down, big time. The cops had told her after she'd made her statement.

All in all, being beat up was worth it except for two scary moments. The first was when the cops said that Mum might also be up on a charge for having drugs at the house. And the second was when the social welfare lady at the hospital started to talk about putting Maggie Dawn and the kids into care. Meantime, however, they would be looked after by Gran.

'Evelyn's bound to lose the house, you know,' Gran said when the taxi arrived. 'If Housing throws her out, I don't know what we're going to do. I can't look after all of you.'

'We'll think of something,' Maggie Dawn answered.

At Gran's, Chantelle, Roxanne Adorata and Zoltan rushed out onto the street to meet them, clinging to Maggie Dawn and not wanting to let her go. 'Can I have a bandage on my head too?' Zoltan asked. Chantelle and Roxanne Adorata would sleep on the small couch in the sitting room, and Zoltan with Maggie Dawn in her bed.

'A lady from Social Welfare will be coming tomorrow,' Gran said. 'I don't think she's going to like the flat. It's too small.'

'I'm not going to let anybody take the kids, Gran,' Maggie Dawn replied. 'I'm just not.'

She remembered something that might make Gran stop worrying. 'Here's your scratch ticket, and I found you a nice scarf. You can wear it next time you go to the casino.' Maybe then people wouldn't notice her awful wig. 'And Gran, you mustn't let those Social Welfare people take us away, okay?'

Shaking her head, Gran went to join the kids in the sitting room where they had settled down to watch television. She must have bought fish 'n' chips for their tea, good old Gran.

Maggie Dawn sat for a while, and then cleared away the wrapping the fish 'n' chips had come in. She limped through the kitchen and out the back where the rubbish bin was. As she was putting on the lid, she looked up at the night sky:

'Are you trying to mess with me?' she asked.

She gave a deep, deep sigh, went back inside, turned off the television and told the girls to go to bed. She settled Zoltan, but he sat up and suddenly began to brandish the scissors like secateurs. Then he kissed Maggie Dawn. 'We're safe now.'

Maggie Dawn helped Gran to her bedroom.

'I didn't win anything on the scratch,' Gran said.

WE'LL ALWAYS HAVE PARIS

ONE —

'Is that you, Will?' asked the voice on the phone. 'It's Cousin Lamarr, ringing from Tauranga.'

'How did you know I was back in Gisborne?'

'I have spies among all the trolley dollies on the international airlines,' Lamarr chuckled. 'I've been tracking you ever since you left Canada. What are you doing in the old home town?'

'Visiting my sister,' I answered. 'Her husband died and she rang me in Toronto to let me know. His tangi was last week.'

'I'm sorry to hear that,' Lamarr answered. 'Well, look, cousin, I've had this brilliant idea.'

Uh oh, that sounded like trouble.

'When you're on your way back to Auckland, could you possibly do me a favour and bring Mother up?' Lamarr was close to tears. 'The old people's home doesn't want her any longer. She's being . . . difficult. So I'll have her stay with me for a while and surround her life with a little glam and fabulosity.'

That explanation changed the situation. 'Okay, I'll alter my air tickets and fly back to Auckland via Tauranga and drop her off.'

'Will, watch your common language! Mother on *public* transport?' Lamarr's voice had gone up a few decibels. 'No. You will bring her in the Bentley.'

I couldn't believe my ears. 'You still have the Bentley?'

'Mother may have sold everything else when Father died, but she always kept the Bentley. I've telephoned Joe at his garage where it's stored and he's promised to get it ready for you. You know Mother. One must . . .'

'. . . always have a Bentley,' I said.

He whispered, as if confidentially, 'The usual emergency kit is in the glove box.'

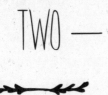

'Aunt Lulu?' my sister Kataraina said when I told her what Lamarr wanted me to do. 'Now there was a woman! One of the last of the taniwha ladies of the coast, eh. Isn't she in her nineties now?' Then she leant into me and whispered, 'I hear she's gone gaga.'

Aunt Lulu's real name was Ruru-i-te-marama, Owl of the Moon, but the Maori pronunciation of the 'r' sounded like an 'l' to unaware Pakeha, so Lulu she became. She and my father, Monty, had been brought up by their dowager spinster grand-aunt Wairangi, who, not having any children of her own, picked Dad from one litter and Lulu from another. Their respective parents didn't seem to mind; in those days before birth control Maori had twelve to fifteen children and one less ankle-biter must have been easier on the legs.

When she was young Aunt Lulu had been a devastatingly beautiful girl — I've seen the photographs — tall, thin, café au lait skin, honey-coloured eyes and hair that was dark red, probably the legacy of a Spaniard whose caravel had been blown off course — way off course. My dad was younger than Lulu and, though they may not have been blood siblings, they looked out for each other. From the sounds of it, Dad had his work cut out because Aunt Lulu was the kind of woman about whom men would say, 'If you think Lulu's beautiful now, man, you should have seen her in those days.'

By all accounts Aunt Lulu was virginal, but she looked like a voluptuary. The consequence was that young men mixed up the signals and Dad often had to protect her.

THREE —

When I turned up at the home in the Bentley I was puzzled that I had to sign so many papers for Aunt Lulu's release.

'What is this?' I asked, irritated. 'A jail?' I felt like a marshal come to take custody of some saloon girl who was being run out of town, like Claire Trevor in *Stagecoach*.

'Mrs Harrington has serious mental problems,' the matron said. 'Not to mention her medical issues. She's being discharged permanently. We can't keep her here when she's a danger to our other clients.'

Other clients? 'Don't worry,' I answered, and not in a civil way. 'Obviously, she's better out of here.'

I was so angry I didn't even bother to ask, or read the papers, to ascertain what Aunt Lulu's mental problems or medical issues were. And I didn't really have time because Aunt Lulu appeared at the doorway, looking like an innocent little old lady who was being unfairly ejected.

M emory plays tricks with you. I hadn't seen Aunt Lulu for a long time and, though it was clear that she'd seen better days, I would have recognised that hair any day. It was fire-engine red and, today, Aunt Lulu was channelling Lucille Ball in the movie of *Mame*.

'William *dah*ling, how lovely of you to come to collect me. Where's the chauffeur to take my bags?' She was pulling a poor arthritic-looking creature along behind her on a lead. 'Pooch? Come along now and give William a kiss.'

I thought quickly. 'The chaffeur didn't turn up for work today,' I answered, brushing both dry, powdered cheeks with my lips.

'I know what you mean . . .' said Aunt Lulu. 'Good staff . . .'

The matron stiffened, outraged.

'. . . are *not* easy to find.'

She flung her tatty fur over her shoulders, arched her neck and waited for me to proffer my elbow so that she could make a grand exit.

I escorted her to the car, where she turned and began to blow kisses to the other patients who had congregated to see her off. Some actually clapped as she stepped into the Bentley. 'Tell the hotel staff to send my suitcases on, won't you?' she said to me in a loud voice. 'And do tip the maid.'

Oh, the delight of digging into my pockets for a few dollars to push into the matron's hands.

Showing signs of intermittent life, Pooch gave a growl and snap of his teeth and then, all energy exhausted, settled into Aunt Lulu's arms when she picked him up.

I opened the door for Aunt Lulu and as she seated herself, all pretence fell away. 'I'm being kicked out, William,' she whispered, tears of humiliation in her eyes.

However, she revived enough of her savoir faire to shout out the window, as we drove from the kerb, Gloria Swanson's line from *Sunset Boulevard*:

'I am big. It's the pictures that got small.'

There was applause from the patients who apparently hadn't thought Aunt Lulu was a danger. Gratified, she whispered, 'One must always leave in the same manner as one came: as a star!'

And then she cradled the dog against her face, 'Okay, let's go to Lamarr, eh Pooch?'

When Aunt Lulu was a teenager, Wairangi realised she had an uncommon and intelligent beauty on her hands and, therefore, none of the young men around Gisborne was an appropriate suitor.

That discerning dowager grand-aunt came from a line of chiefs and must also have known that if she didn't get Lulu out of town her daughter would fall pregnant to some lucky but undistinguished Maori lad. Wairangi kept Dad behind to look after the land, but Lulu she sent up to Auckland to attend a convent school.

This was during the Second World War, and therefore, with all those American servicemen around, Aunt Lulu found a new kind of boy following her as she made her way from the convent dormitory a few blocks along the Remuera streets to the school classrooms.

To be frank, Aunt Lulu did not find the attention discomforting. By this time she was a functioning voluptuary who found her virginal status tiresome and wished to quickly rid herself of it. She had also discovered she liked everything American, in particular American movies, and she took to channelling film sirens like Lauren Bacall, Hedy Lamarr, Rita Hayworth or Rhonda Fleming, all of whom had titian hair; it's not a colour you see these days.

'Americans are best,' she would say. 'They smell so di*vine*. They have intelligence, but not too much, they're extremely good in bed, and the best thing is that they love to get up very early and go and play golf in the mornings. A girl must always be left alone in the mornings to freshen up.'

She would show us how to drape oneself seductively on a couch, in calculated dishabille, desirable and ready to be ravished ... again.

And she had made her own Hollywood dream come true when she married an American GI, Gardner Harrington.

I n his photographs at least, Uncle Gardner was a spunk. He looked like one of those blond, muscular lifeguards on Malibu Beach, and had all those even, white, teeth. He was the Burt Lancaster of Aunt Lulu's dreams, and he was as horny as.

He was eighteen when he was stationed in Auckland, and he

met Aunt Lulu at one of those dances that New Zealand matrons liked to organise for 'lonely GIs', though family legend says that he first caught a glimpse of her as she was going to Mass on Sunday. He followed her into the church where the choir was singing 'Ave Maria' and after another look, he was a goner.

At the time, Aunt Lulu was sixteen going on twenty-six, a mature head on a young girl's body, and fortunately Uncle Gardner's desire for her was reciprocated. And one thing about Aunt Lulu, she was never patient and all her whims required instant gratification. She knew what she wanted: Gardner. Nothing could stop her from having him. They fell madly in love and lust — though you weren't supposed to have sex until after you were married. Instead you necked or petted. Presumably Aunt Lulu either didn't go the whole way or, alternatively, was incredibly lucky.

If we take the benign view that Aunt Lulu and Uncle Gardner were virgins, the consequence was that Aunt Lulu, seeking consummation, climbed over the walls of the convent school and eloped with him. This brought the wrath of the American military down on them both and there were huge efforts to have the marriage annulled. Wairangi wasn't pleased either: an American as a son-in-law? She sent Dad up to Auckland to bring his sister back home. I understand that when Dad met Uncle Gardner, they had a huge fight in the middle of Queen Street. Dad went down to Uncle Gardner's uppercut, but it was to her brother that Aunt Lulu went to offer solace.

'I'll come home with you, Monty,' she wept. Yes, she was prepared to give her husband up because of her love for my father. I suspect that they'd always loved each other and, after all, they weren't brother and sister at all but, rather cousins, so they could have got together — but let's not go there, eh.

Nevertheless, Aunt Lulu did return to Gisborne with Dad and Gardner Harrington went back Stateside but — he didn't want to get divorced. Despite his parents' objections, he came back after the war to collect his wife.

'What took you so long, Gardner?' she asked, before she slapped him.

Thus did Uncle Gardner forsake the Land of Uncle Sam for New Zealand. He and Aunt Lulu must have been really hot for each other because they produced three children with glamorous Hollywood names — Viveca, Yolanda and then their precious son, Lamarr.

By that time, Dad had met Mum, married her, and had me and Kataraina. When I was born, it was only to be expected that Aunt Lulu would consider me her son too. But whereas Dad had taken to the Maori side and lived in a Maori world, Aunt Lulu, by virtue of her marriage to Uncle Gardner, existed in a spec-tac-ular world of her own.

To my boyhood eyes, Aunt Lulu was the most unlikely Maori you ever saw. She was tall, attractive, scandalised the aunties in Ruatoria by dyeing her red hair even redder, and she wore slingback high heels that went clickety click over their wooden floors.

And what made her world spectacular? Well, although at the time she married Gardner and swore that she was unaware 'he had all that money', it all came out in the end. He was actually Gardner Harrington III (and my Cousin Lamarr was Gardner Lamarr Harrington IV). No wonder the Harringtons were horrified when he married someone, well, dark.

Nevertheless, he was the heir to the family fortune. Minions of the Harrington empire were therefore dispatched to 'Noo Zeelin' ('Where the hell is that?') to tell Uncle Gardner that all was forgiven and he should bring his bride home. Aunt Lulu and the three kids were hauled off to meet the folks 'in some dull place called Washington DC,' she would tell us, airily. There, the Harrington rellies tried to parlay her suspect Maori blood into something more suitable: they liked the possible Spanish caravel link in her ancestry and began hinting to their social circle that Lulu's pedigree was Castilian.

Aunt Lulu soon put that little deception in its place when she appeared at the opera in a stunning Maori cloak and with feathers in her hair. 'Castilian, my ass,' she would tell us of this little incident.

Surprise, surprise, being Maori appeared to have more cachet in the Washington society set. Castilian nobility were a dime a dozen, but it wasn't every day that you had a Maori princess living in one of the best streets in Georgetown, with Rose Kennedy next door.

The Harringtons were in construction, mainly building malls throughout the US, and the plan was that Gardner was to take over board chairmanship. But they hadn't reckoned on Aunt Lulu. She persuaded Gardner that while their official residence might remain in the States, why not retain a 'residence by the sea', i.e. in 'Noo Zeelin', and commute to work?

Despite the enormous logistical problems, Gardner agreed. He ensconced Aunt Lulu in a big two-storey house on Riverside Road, the best street in Gisborne, gave her a cook, butler, nanny and chauffeur and then, as if he were any ordinary husband, got dressed, took the car to Gisborne airport, flew to Auckland and then by flying boat to Washington DC via San Francisco: one month there, two weeks back, one month there again, two weeks back and so on. Aunt Lulu, in consideration of his crazy schedule, took herself and the children off to Washington DC as regularly as she could, but also at Christmas, Easter and Thanksgiving Day.

How the marriage managed to sustain itself nobody will ever know. I'm sure that Gardner must have had tempting offers from Washington socialites only too willing to take him away from the wicked wiles of that wanton Maori woman, but it never happened.

No gossip ever attached itself to Aunt Lulu's reputation either. She would explain her and Gardner's astounding accomplishment by saying, 'Americans are as faithful as *dogs* —' I have news for you, Aunt Lulu '— and while they don't last the distance they *never* go off the boil. As for me, I've always loved Gardner. As long as he's in my life, he's the only man for me.'

But it was more than that. Aunt Lulu and Gardner Harrington were fascinated with each other and, as I was to realise, Uncle Gardner adored his daughters and Lamarr. There was no way he would ever jeopardise his love for them.

One more thing: Aunt Lulu always had an interesting way of speaking.

'If nothing else,' she would say, 'always speak *clear*ly and with in*ten*tion. It's the only way to get staff to understand what it is you wish.'

It's a pity her advice wasn't taken up by her dogs. Aunt Lulu always had a dog, always a male, always a pug and always — or at

least it's what I thought when I was introduced to the first one —
either Pooch or Bark or Wag.

'Pooch?' Aunt Lulu screamed. '*Pooch?* You ignorant young
boy, his name is Pu-ccini!' She then began to instruct me on the
Italian composer of *La Bohème, Madame Butterfly* and *Turandot.*
As for Bark, he was actually Bach as in Johann Sebastian, and Wag
was, of course, as in Richard Wagner.

She always insisted on calling me William. 'One never
shortens names. That is vulgar.'

FOUR —

We sped out of Gisborne.

Aunt Lulu and Pooch were happily sitting in the back and I
was still wearing the silly look — some might call it a maniacal
grin — I'd acquired since picking up the Bentley from Joe, the
garage owner. No doubt about it, he'd certainly kept the car safe
from all the ravages of weather and time — it was as handsome as
I remembered it. I mean . . . a Bentley? I'd been mesmerised by the
car since the day in 1956, when I was ten, that it was delivered to
Uncle Gardner. It was shipped straight from the factory in the UK
to small-town Gisborne and caused a sensation whenever it rolled
into rural Maoridom where most people saved really hard for a
second-hand car or rode the bus or went by horse to the marae.

Joe was in tears and kept polishing the Bentley even as I was driving it away from the garage. 'I will personally strangle you,' he called after me, 'if the car comes back with anything resembling a scratch.'

Man oh man, was I in Heaven? Was I what! Who wouldn't be, driving this beauty? She was a 1955 S-Type, six-cylinder sedan with an overhead inlet side exhaust valves type head delivering 4887cc horsepower. She had the distinctive two-tone colour scheme, and her simple lines bespoke wealth, good taste and the understated elegance of the very rich. She boasted a four-speed automatic gearbox, her top speed was 120 mph (that was a lot of grunt for a car from the 1950s) and, with no power steering, this was a car that had been built to be driven. Only a real man could drive her.

No wonder that I became an airline pilot and eventually a captain on Air Canada's Boeing 777-300ERs. As a bigger boy I'd needed a bigger toy.

'Oh, free at last!' said Aunt Lulu as we left the city limits. 'Now I must have one of my cigarettes. Do you have a lighter, dahling?'

'For you, Aunt Lulu, anything.' She'd taught me that every man carries a lighter and, even if he has difficulty turning to light her up while driving, he had to carry it off in the most masculine manner possible.

I took a quick squizz at my watch. It was nine o'clock and Tauranga was about six hours away: one hour to the Waioeka Gorge, two hours to Whakatane, where we could have lunch, and then a fast zoom around the coast to Tauranga would get us to Lamarr's place by late afternoon.

The car soon filled up with cigarette smoke, Aunt Lulu carefully tapping the ash into the Bentley's ashtray. Watching her in the rear-vision mirror, I couldn't help thinking that, given Aunt Lulu's influence on my boyhood, it was no wonder I'd developed a penchant for a career and wardrobe that had a bit of glamour: in my case, the four-star gold-embroidered epaulette that only captains of passenger aircraft can wear.

However, I had the suspicion that although I thought that way, Aunt Lulu and Cousin Lamarr probably just applauded the fact that I'd succeeded . . . within my own limitations.

Let me explain. In their world, there were some people who were stars and some people who weren't. I know now that I was in the latter category: always waiting in the wings, the boy in the film who's the best friend of the main actor, the one who doesn't get the girl and doesn't have the best songs to sing. Although Aunt Lulu and Lamarr both tried hard to bring Technicolor and widescreen into my life, I've always been the straight man.

As for me and Lamarr, we were the same age but, well, he was as spec-tac-ular as Aunt Lulu. It was only to be expected really: after all, Uncle Gardner wasn't around much to provide a male flavour to Lamarr's upbringing. ('God knows, I tried,' my father Monty confessed, 'but that sister of mine had him in buttons and bows from the moment he was born.')

In the absence of a father figure, Lamarr was doted on by Aunt Lulu and given everything he wanted by his proud mother and his sisters, who considered that he was one of their dolls. 'I grew up *dressing* up,' Lamarr would proclaim proudly.

'He's not different at all,' Aunt Lulu would always proclaim. 'It's just that he's, well, the*atr*ical.'

N ow, maybe Uncle Gardner wasn't very bright, but when Lamarr was around seven it clicked that his son wasn't particularly — masculine.

I remember the day clearly. There was some family hangi or something up the coast at Ruatoria, and Uncle Gardner was back for his usual fortnight at his 'residence by the sea'. While the adults were talking in the shade of the willows, the kids were playing in the sunlight — and I was involved in a game of football in the paddock among the cowpats with my barefooted rough and tumble mates.

Until then, I hadn't had much experience of Cousin Lamarr. None of us local boys had. Aunt Lulu had sent him down to boarding school in Wellington from a very early age. Maybe she thought lightning would strike twice and that, like her, Lamarr would eventually grow up and meet some nice rich American heiress — yeah, right. So that day was the first time any of us had ever seen Lamarr close up as it were. I mean he looked like a boy but something was a little off.

Uncle Gardner yelled out to me, 'Hey! Boy!' He waved me over. By that time the GI looks had faded and he'd begun to lose his hair, but he was still good-looking. 'See that kid over there under the trees?'

I shaded my eyes and saw three, well, girls, playing with a toy dinner set. 'You mean the boy —' I took a guess, but I knew all along it was Lamarr '— in the middle?'

Uncle Gardner nodded. 'That's him. I want you to invite Lamarr to play with you young fellers and, every chance you get, you throw the little sonofabitch into a cowpat.' He proffered me a few coins to sweeten the deal, so I spoke to the other boys and, well, money talks. With their agreement, I went over to the willows, where Lamarr was pouring tea for his sisters.

'Hello, cousin,' I said to him. 'Wanna play ball?' I couldn't help the slight sarcasm that crept into my voice. I was sure Lamarr wouldn't want to dirty his pretty little jumpsuit or whatever it was. Play with dolls maybe but . . . play ball?

Was I ever wrong! Lamarr looked at me, at the other boys, and he was off to join us like a rocket. When I dumped him in a cowpat he shrieked with glee and ran after me and dumped me! — and I wasn't even holding the ball.

'No, cousin, you have to go for the boy — on the other side,' I added, because he still hadn't got it. 'The one who's got the ball and wants to score a try.'

Well, that did it. Lamarr became the best tackler on the field. So I don't want you to think that he was afraid of getting hurt, because he wasn't. In fact he later made the first fifteen at his boarding school. He was a first five-eight, though he had desperately wanted to be a forward. One night when we were hanging out he told me why: 'I just loved getting in among those hairy thighs and *pushing*.' He'd never have done a Hopoate (Lamarr's standards were too high), but whenever he was in the scrum he was in, well, hog heaven.

Aunt Lulu and I reached Matawai, the Bentley cruising up all those hills like a dream. I was so busy driving that I hadn't realised the medication or whatever was keeping her, well, normal, was starting to wear off.

She looked at me, as if for the first time, and said, 'You know I have a nephew who works for the airlines just like you do. You might know him. His name's William.'

She took another look and her memory shifted again. She leant forward and gave me a sharp rap on the shoulder.

'And you know, Brown, that I always like you to wear your chauffeur's cap whenever we're in the Bentley. I won't tell you again.'

Uh oh.

Coward that I am, I rummaged in the front compartment and found the cap that had once belonged to Brown — he was Maori and his name was really Brownie.

'Yes, ma'am,' I said as I put it on.

'That's better,' Aunt Lulu said.

FIVE —

Silly boy, me, to think that driving Aunt Lulu to Tauranga would be that easy.

And so it was that from Matawai, approaching the long winding road through the Waioeka Gorge, I ceased to be Aunt Lulu's nephew, William, and became Brown, one of the long line of dogsbody-cum-drivers that Uncle Gardner had employed whenever he was home in New Zealand.

Why the chauffeurs? Well, being American, Uncle Gardner could never get accustomed to driving on the left side of the road. And he never did like the Bentley. 'What kind of goddamn country is this,' he would grumble, 'when an American citizen can't buy a goddamn Chrysler because the steering wheel's on the *wrong goddamn side?*'

I actually didn't mind that Aunt Lulu assumed I was Brownie. I'd liked him, especially since he would sometimes let me drive the Bentley (I was thirteen the first time I got behind the wheel) when he was sent to the grocery store to get something important like more cigarettes or confectionery. And, after all, playacting had been such an important part of growing up with Lulu and Lamarr: if she wanted to do a *Driving Miss Daisy*, that was fine by me. I'd do anything to keep her happy.

Sitting in the Bentley, with Aunt Lulu nodding off and then rapping on my shoulder to say, 'Brown, you're travelling too *slow*! What is this, a hearse?' and the wild bush standing in for Alabama, I couldn't help but think back on those times when Uncle Gardner, after that first football game, would send Brownie around to pick me up and take me to the house.

My father concurred in what amounted to a game to stop Lamarr from turning from a sissy into something even more horrible and nameless. So the word was put on me: I was to be Lamarr's daytime playmate and his best friend.

'Lamarr's such a girl,' I complained to Dad.

'It's only for a few hours a week,' he reprimanded me, 'and you're whanau, for Chrissake.'

Yeah, Dad, well thank you for putting that number on me. Fat chance, too, that he would sweeten the deal with some cash, like Uncle Gardner. No, this time I'd have to take on Lamarr as if he was some kind of social welfare project.

However, there was a ray of sunshine. I had become a randy teenager and I secretly had the hots for my cousin Viveca, who herself was interested in experimenting with a boy, even if it was her cousin. My seeming reluctance to be her brother's best friend actually hid a scheming heart.

This was how the involvement in Aunt Lulu and Lamarr's channelling games began.

'Don't take the boy home yet, Brown,' Aunt Lulu would call from the living room. 'We need somebody *mas*culine to play the hero.'

Aunt Lulu's love of American movies had persisted and she'd managed to pass on her passion to Lamarr. To assuage her love, Uncle Gardner had built a huge home cinema in the basement with a huge screen and projector. On would go a movie, 16mm film mostly . . . I suspect Uncle Gardner was relieved that I would supplant him in the male starring roles he'd had to play, out of love for Aunt Lulu, until I came along. And Aunt Lulu particularly loved either Vivien Leigh and Clark Gable in *Gone With the Wind* or Bette Davis and Paul Henreid in *Now, Voyager* or, her particular favourite, Humphrey Bogart and Ingrid Bergman in *Casablanca*.

I learnt to smoke at Aunt Lulu's, trying to light two cigarettes and pass one to Aunt Lulu or Viveca or Yolanda or Lamarr — whoever had won the lottery to play the female part that night — and uttering, between coughs, 'May I sometimes come here?' However, I did develop muscles when I had to carry any of them as Scarlett O'Hara, but especially Lamarr, up the stairs where, like Clark Gable, I was supposed to ravish her — or him.

I liked *Casablanca* much better, especially if I was playing the Humphrey Bogart role as the gruff Rick, owner of the Café

Américain. All I had to do was to be madly in love with Ilsa —
usually Aunt Lulu, who always insisted on the Ingrid Bergman
role — as she came into my place in Nazi-controlled Casablanca,
looking beautiful in a simple white gown.

Ilsa had never been Rick's, having married the Czech
resistance leader Victor Laszlo — but we were once lovers in Paris.
While Sam the piano player plays 'As Time Goes By' we remember
our bittersweet relationship:

et's see,' Ilsa says. 'The last time we met . . .'

'It was "La Belle Aurore".'

'How nice,' Ilsa smiles. 'You remembered. But of course that
was the day the Germans marched into Paris.'

'Not an easy day to forget.'

'No,' Ilsa says.

'I remember every detail,' Rick goes on. 'The Germans wore
grey, you wore blue.'

'Yes. I put that dress away. When the Germans march out, I'll
wear it again.'

f course Rick realises that he still loves Ilsa, even though she's
married. In the famous last scene, as the German villain, Major
Strasser, is closing in on Casablanca airport, Rick forces Ilsa to
get on a plane which will carry her and Laszlo to freedom. 'We'll
always have Paris,' he says to her.

It's one of the great farewell scenes in film, and to this day I
can still remember every word of it.

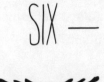

SIX —

I drove fast through the Waioeka Gorge.

I had purposely turned up the heating and, thank goodness, Aunt Lulu began to wilt and sag and, very soon, was snoring her head off. Pooch followed suit, whimpering and snuffling and shivering as if he was having a canine nightmare.

To be frank, I was getting worried. What had Aunt Lulu done to warrant her ejection from the home? What were her 'medical issues'?

I tried to reach into the glove box to get out her medical file, but every time I did that the Bentley swerved dangerously. No, I'd just have to make the best of it. I drove more carefully but still as fast as I could, hoping to get as much mileage as possible behind us before Aunt Lulu woke up.

And after all, I owed Lamarr.

Sometimes I hadn't been a very supportive cousin. In fact, growing up with Lamarr and being forced to be his best friend was pretty tough on us both, even if his father was an American and his mother was a Maori princess. Whenever he returned from boarding school — after Wellington he went to a more select school in Sydney — he was always worse rather than better. His brand of theatrical behaviour, as Aunt Lulu called it, didn't go down in Gisborne and, once, when I saw him across the street, I snuck off in the other direction.

The trouble was that my defection had been witnessed.

The next time I was at Uncle Gardner's, Aunt Lulu called me to her bedroom. She had on her dark glasses and was puffing furiously on a cigarette. She stubbed it out and folded her arms. 'So when did you turn out to be pure arsehole, William?'

I blushed red and looked at the floor.

'Don't look away from me, you little shit,' she continued. 'Lamarr is your cousin. Just as Monty and I were close, you owe each other to be back to back against the world. Apart from which the world is too full of *dull* people who have no colour and who *conform* to the lowest common denominator. People like me and Lamarr are the only solution to making sure the world doesn't become boring and conventional.'

She was really going for me.

'I'm sorry, Aunt Lulu,' I muttered.

'Sorry?' she screamed. 'Sorry doesn't cut it. After all I've done for you, what Lamarr has done for you, William? Get out of here, you little piece of pathetic trash, and go back to where you belong.'

Well, I learnt my lesson. From that moment on I started becoming a better cousin and friend to Lamarr. I often found myself having to protect him, beating up other boys who laughed at him.

Not that he always appreciated it.

'You have to stop being my shadow,' Lamarr sobbed after one such occasion.

'If I don't do it, who will?'

'I'll do it myself, damn it,' Lamarr answered. 'I may be helpless but I'm not entirely hopeless. I'll get by.' He tried to look like Vivien Leigh in *A Streetcar Named Desire*. 'And if I don't, I'll rely on the kindness of strangers.' Then he added, 'And I know you only started to be friends with me because Dad paid you.'

Lamarr knew? That was the lowest ebb of our relationship,

and I realised I didn't want it to go any lower. I put my arm around his shoulders.

We were always trading lines from the movies. 'Hey kid, you don't have to say anything and you don't have to do anything. Maybe just whistle, ' I said, repeating lines from *To Have and To Have Not*. 'You know how to whistle, don't you?'

He looked at me, offended. 'You're asking *me* how to *whistle*? Honey, I've already had a lot of practice!'

He struck a pose. 'You just put your lips together and blow!'

With an attitude like that, he survived.

SEVEN —

We were approaching Opotiki when I went over a pothole and the sudden thump woke Aunt Lulu.

She peered at me. 'Who are you?' she asked.

She clutched Pooch in front of her for protection. There was fear in her eyes.

I stopped the car and put on my best smile. After all, the smile had worked when I'd had to pacify distraught passengers on various flights over the years so it should do the trick with Aunt Lulu. 'I'm your nephew,' I said kindly. 'William.'

'William? No, you're not,' she whimpered. 'You're too old for William.'

Then she really went to lala-land.

'Oh my God, what have you done with William? What are you doing driving the Bentley? Have you murdered my nephew and put him in the boot?'

In desperation, I made a mistake. 'All right, Aunt Lulu, I'm not William. I'm Brown. Remember?'

But Aunt Lulu's memory had made a hyper space jump since then. She stared at me, said, 'You're not Brown either,' and she struck a pose worthy of Joan Crawford in *Whatever Happened to Baby Jane*. 'Have you murdered Brown too? Oh no! Are you after my pearls?'

She started to scream.

'Please Aunt Lulu, don't do that,' I pleaded.

What could I go except try to drive with one hand on the steering wheel and reach over and pat her with the other hand? But that outreaching hand caused another reality shift. She pressed herself back against the seat and I could see her eyes blinking fast.

Was she going into cardiac arrest?

No. After a short while she drew herself up, glared at me and said, 'Matron? Matron! I have to go weewees.'

As I discovered later, one of her medical conditions was that her bladder was shot to pieces. I should have counted myself lucky that she'd lasted *this* far. Ger-*reat*: why was there never a toilet in sight when there was an emergency? I looked for the nearest clump of trees.

'Not them, you fool,' said Aunt Lulu, noting my gaze. 'They're too far away and I'm wearing my best heels.'

I slowed the Bentley and stopped. When I opened the door Aunt Lulu cast a commanding eye over me. 'You'll have to carry me,' she ordered, surveying the fence, paddock and trees beyond.

As for Pooch, he leapt out, trembled, took a few doddery steps and sprayed one of the rear tyres before collapsing with the effort.

Not only did I have to carry Aunt Lulu, but when we got to the safety of the bushes she refused to squat.

'Don't just stand there,' she growled.

I held her off the ground as she gathered up her skirts and let fly.

This wasn't something they taught you at flight school.

'Lamarr,' I muttered, 'you owe me one.'

The nightmare, however, had only just begun. Pooch was waiting beside the Bentley, and although Aunt Lulu picked him up she refused to get in the car.

'Please, Aunt Lulu, let's get going.'

She saw a big ute booming down the road. It must have belonged to pig hunters — it had spotlights for night work and a huge dead porker across the bonnet.

Before I could stop her Aunt Lulu made a run for it. 'Help! Help!' she screamed.

The ute screeched to a halt.

Aunt Lulu tottered towards it. 'Oh, thank you,' she told the three burly men inside, who looked as if they ate four sides of pork each for breakfast, dinner and tea. 'There's a strange man, he stole my Bentley, he's after my body and my pearls, and he's held me captive all morning.'

Well, what would you do if a little old lady carrying a small dog stopped you in the middle of the road and told you she'd been kidnapped?

'Look, I can explain,' I bleated, wearing my best smile, as they advanced on me.

Pity I wasn't wearing a captain's cap and jacket with epaulettes. The last thing I saw was somebody's fist in my face and I went down.

EIGHT —

I woke up in the Opotiki police station. I was lying on a small couch being attended to by a doctor. In the back, a nurse with a nametag that read 'Simpson' was looking after Aunt Lulu.

Three somewhat shamefaced pig hunters were sitting in a corner.

'Listen, mate,' one of them said, 'sorry we hit you, eh.'

'Oh, that's okay,' I answered.

'You don't want to press charges?' the police constable asked. I suspected he'd been trying to arrest these blokes for some other misdemeanour, probably to do with an illegal marijuana plantation.

'No, it's really not their fault. Is my Aunt Lulu all right?'

'Nurse Simpson has given her some medication,' the constable said. 'She actually remembers your aunt from a television panel show she was on, answering questions live.'

'I've been a fan of Lulu's for years.' Nurse Simpson's tone was reverent. 'She and the other ladies on *Roses and Your Thorns*. Your aunt was marvellous.'

'We found her medical details in the glove box,' the constable added. 'Hopefully the medication will last until you get to . . . Tauranga, is it? If you like, Nurse Simpson will be glad to go along with you.'

I considered the offer seriously. The adoration would keep Aunt Lulu safe in fantasyland but . . . 'No, it's okay,' I replied. 'Just . . . what is her condition?'

'Don't you know?' Nurse Simpson asked, startled. 'Your aunt has dementia. She caused quite a few incidents at the rest home.'

She went through Aunt Lulu's misdemeanours.

At first I was alarmed because they appeared so wilful: Aunt Lulu believing the rest home was called Tara and belonged to her; Aunt Lulu accusing the matron of being a wicked aunt who was keeping her there under false pretences; Aunt Lulu telling the staff they were Nazis and trying to get to the airport to escape them.

Then it dawned on me. Most of her misdemeanours were based on the movie scenarios we'd acted out so often. 'Gosh, anybody would think she was an axe murderer,' I muttered.

What she'd really done was to go to Hollywood heaven.

Aunt Lulu was released back into my care. Before we left Opotiki, she posed for a few photographs and gave Nurse Simpson a shaky autograph.

I stopped the car at a petrol station to fill up and then said, 'Let's find a restaurant and have some lunch, eh, Aunt Lulu?'

'I'm sorry, William,' she said when we were seated. 'For a moment there, I just didn't remember who you were. Old age, nephew, it's not much fun.' She touched my cheek tenderly. 'I'm so glad you're not still the same uptight little prick you were when you were younger.'

'None of those years was wasted, Aunt Lulu,' I answered. 'Something finally rubbed off on me, eh?'

She gave a gasp of grief and huge tears began to spill from her eyes and down every crack and crevice in her face.

'Aunt Lulu, you'll spoil your make-up.'

That stopped her fast. 'Oh, my public,' she said. 'They must never see what we stars are like in the daylight.'

She was worrying about *her* appearance? I'd wondered why people in the restaurant were looking at me strangely.

It wasn't until later that I saw the shiner.

The daylight was fading as I drove from Opotiki to Whakatane and then along the beautiful stretch of coast road to Tauranga.

I was in a mellow, nostalgic mood. At that moment, there was no better place to be than in the Bentley, driving my aunt to her son, while the sun was going down.

I suddenly remembered Lamarr's emergency kit. I reached into the glove box and found the tapes of old movie songs to which, during all our long trips in the Bentley, we — Lamarr, Viveca, Yolanda, me and even Uncle Gardner — would sing along.

I put the first tape on, a Victor Young standard, and Aunt Lulu gave a shiver of delight and began to join in:

> When I fall in love, it will be forever,
> or I'll never fall in love . . .

Her voice had been a beautiful lyric soprano. Over the years, afflicted by cigarettes, it had descended and was now a splendid basso profondo.

It had always been in the cards that Lamarr would join the Harrington family business but, when his father was kicked out of the firm — I can just imagining the board muttering about the 'bad blood' in that side of the family what with Gardner going troppo and Lamarr going gay — he had to rethink.

For a while he flirted with a number of careers. Of course they were all in the entertainment business. He tried acting and had a mild success in *Boys in the Band* where he was playing to type, but roles as heterosexual heroes were simply beyond him. Nevertheless he felt New York and the Great White Way beckoning and decided, when he was twenty-two, to try his luck in the Big Apple. He landed at the airport, told the taxi driver, 'Take me to Times Square.' When he arrived he struck his best pose, flung open his coat (it was freezing) and roared, 'I'm hee-rrr-eee!'

Alas stardom was on holiday, so he upped sticks and flew to Los Angeles, where he hung out in West Hollywood. There, he found his own kind of adoration along Sunset Boulevard.

By that time I was flying for Qantas. I remember one time being in Los Angeles on stopover and I got a telephone call from Lamarr, who decided to come on by.

Now, the thing about Lamarr was that he slept during the day and only came alive at night. He took one look at my single hotel room and immediately pronounced, 'Where's your bed? You can't possibly sleep on the floor,' and checked us into the Hollywood Hilton.

Fortunately for Lamarr, he had actually turned out to be a hunk like his dad. Even so, he was a hunk who looked somehow askew. You know, you looked at him and you thought, Handsome as. Then he moved and you thought, Huh? Maybe it was the slight sway, or the all-knowing preen, or the combinations of colour: blue jeans, orange shirt, purple socks. So first of all, girls would look — and then shut off. And then their boyfriends would look — and nod, 'Uh huh.'

We went out to some cowboy bars that he knew about and frequented, all of them gay. He didn't mind being pawed and petted, but he could see I was uncomfortable. 'Cousin William,' he said, 'this is *not* your scene. But thank you for trying. We'll always be there for each other, though, won't we?'

There was such an aching sense of panic and love between us as if, after all, the kindness of strangers wasn't quite enough and would never be enough, for either of us. 'Yes,' I promised as I hugged him. 'Just whistle, right?'

In the end, the US of A was not Lamarr's scene either and,

flamboyant as ever, he returned the next year to New Zealand. He was thirty when fortune favoured him and he met Harry, an Australian restaurateur who pursued him to Tauranga and didn't mind watching old Hollywood movies.

And then I heard Aunt Lulu give a little chuckle and when I looked into the rear-vision mirror she was looking at me and she said:

'Oh Gardner, you got that shiner all for me?'

To tell you the truth, I didn't mind that Aunt Lulu thought I was Uncle Gardner.

In fact, I suspect that he's who this story is really about. From the first time he had asked me to 'throw the little sonofabitch into a cowpat', Uncle Gardner and I had been on the same side. He was the iconic hero, someone like Alan Ladd in *Shane*: decent, disarming, moral. He wore his heart on his sleeve and he unreservedly loved Aunt Lulu and his family.

I remember one occasion when Uncle Gardner had come to see me play indoor basketball during a high school tournament. Lamarr was watching from the sidelines and I should have known, when the game was over and Uncle Gardner was congratulating me, that my sporting prowess cast him in a shadow. He came over to offer his congratulations too. 'You should have been Father's son,' he said. 'Not me.'

Forgive me, but all I could feel was elation. All my life I had felt the same thing: my own father regardless, Uncle Gardner and I could have been made from the same flesh.

But the blood drained from Uncle Gardner's face. 'What the Hell are you talking about, Lamarr? *You're* my son.' He pulled Lamarr towards him and shook him. 'I love *you*.'

Just before Uncle Gardner died, fifteen years ago now, he called me to see him. Those blond good looks of his had completely faded and he'd put on quite a bit of weight, but he was still as charming and as concerned about Aunt Lulu and his family as ever.

'Those daughters of mine are in the USA and I've left Lulu in good hands but, William, I would like to make you the executor of my will.'

I was floored.

He began to weep. 'Look after them all, won't you? Particularly your Cousin Lamarr. He needs a masculine brother, you know what I mean? Damn it, I don't mind his predilections and peccadilloes because he's my own flesh and blood. And it was his mother's fault that he turned out the way he has and, no matter, I still love him, you hear? But every now and then, throw the sonofabitch into a cowpat.'

And so I assumed Uncle Gardner's persona.

I looked into the rear-view mirror. Tried to smile with that same awkward, lopsided but sexy grin. Crinkled my eyes. Imitated that slow Southern drawl of his.

'Ever since I saw you as a schoolgirl, I've loved you, Lulu. For you, I'd grab all the stars in the sky and one by one strew them at your feet.'

Uncle Gardner, this one is for you.

TEN —

Finally, I delivered Aunt Lulu, the great Ruru-i-te-marama, to her son and heir.

As soon as I turned into the driveway of Lamarr's house he came running out crying, 'Mother? Mother!'

'Hello, Lamarr,' said Aunt Lulu as he yanked open the door to the Bentley. She looked him up and down. 'You're putting on weight,' she said, as Marlene Dietrich did to Orson Welles in *Touch of Evil*. 'Time to lay off the candy bars.'

Lamarr blew me kisses. I waited to one side as he gathered his mother in his arms. 'How dare they do this to you.'

'Out on the street, Lamarr,' she sobbed. 'They threw me away as if I was of no use to anybody.'

And then she stopped in her tracks.

'I will not go a step further,' she cried. 'William? Take me back! Take me anywhere! I will not be a burden to Lamarr!'

At first I thought it was one of her usual melodramatic outbursts. Then I started to worry. This was real.

'No! No! No!' she cried as Lamarr forced her onward. She was kicking at him and trying to claw at his face. 'Let me go back!'

'Harry!' Lamarr shouted. 'Help!'

Harry waddled out but, try as they both might, Aunt Lulu would not go into the house. She began to scream — 'Oh, Gardner! Gardner!'

And she fell to the ground.

don't know why I did what I did.

I walked towards Aunt Lulu and pulled her up. She gave a slight cry of fear and fought against my enfolding arms.

The moon came out and Sam began to play 'As Time Goes By' and I was Rick, owner of the Café Américain, and here I was with Ilsa at the fog-enshrouded airport, just ten minutes to spare before the plane to Lisbon was to depart.

put my soul into my acting. 'You said I was to do the thinking for both of us,' I said to Aunt Lulu. 'Well, I've done a lot of it since then and it all adds up to one thing. You're getting on that plane with Victor where you belong.'

Pooch began to bark. No Pooch, I thought to myself, this is not your scene. I was worried that Aunt Lulu might not respond as she looked at me, puzzled, but then she recognised the script. Good girl that she was, she immediately stepped into Ilsa's character. 'But Richard, no, I, I —'

'You've got to listen to me,' I said roughly. 'Do you have any idea what you'd have to look forward to if you stayed here? Nine chances out of ten we'd both wind up in a concentration camp. Isn't that true, Louis?'

Lamarr pretended to countersign the papers. 'I'm afraid Major Strasser would insist.'

'You're saying this only to make me go,' Aunt Lulu cried. The plane's propellers were already turning, roaring loudly in the night.

'I'm saying it because it's true,' I answered, grabbing her arms and forcing her to accept what I was telling her. 'Inside of us we both know you belong to Victor. You're part of his work, the thing that keeps him going. If that plane leaves the ground and you're not with him, you'll regret it.'

'No,' Aunt Lulu cried again.

'Maybe not today, maybe not tomorrow, but soon, and for the rest of your life.'

'But what about us?'

Her question lingered in the air.

I'd forgotten the line.

Aunt Lulu stiffened and glared at me. 'Amateurs!' she declared. 'Why am I always surrounded by people from . . . central casting! And look at the lighting! Where's the make-up girl? How can I possibly appear before my public looking like this?'

She pointed at me. 'As for you — all of you — call yourselves act*ors*? Where are Humphrey Bogart, John Wayne and Jimmy Stewart when you need them!'

She drew herself up and, head tossed back, made her exit.

Lamarr turned to me. We were grinning like maniacs.

'Here's looking at you, kid,' he said.

ONE MORE NIGHT

PART ONE —
IN SEARCH OF
EMERALD CITY

1 /

LONDON

So here we are, me and my mate Whero, and I can feel that beautiful hot white spotlight on our faces. I look across at her, the way the light reflects off those cheekbones of hers and all those sparks come to nest in her hair. How did she ever get to be so gorgeous? She's a rock diva, queen of the club, and I ramp up the sound on my guitar. Although she frowns, she takes up the challenge.

'Come on, Whero, honey,' I urge her, 'let it out . . .'

I hear the volcano purr of it, that clear rumbling big voice, no sides to it, man, a Milky Way of sound pouring across the darkness:

Once there was a nest . . .
floating on the sea at summer solstice . . .

Here in the darkness the punters are loving it. Some of them must be bloody Kiwis come to see a New Zealand girl making good in London.

I'm hyped up, proud to be Whero's mate. People say we look like sistahs . . . and it's freakin' true, you can't tell us apart. And we are smokin', man! But we haven't even reached the climax of the song and . . . then what happens? Whero walks off the stage! Without a word. Stops singing. Leaves me stranded there.

Just. Like. That. Yup.

Shit.

2 /

ENTER PETERA

The back room is dingy and dull.

'So what the freakin' fuck was that all about?' I ask Whero.

She has the gall to pretend that nothing happened. 'What?' She shrugs, plucking at her guitar, defiant, trying to stare me down.

'Unbelievable.' I shake my head. 'Did you see the audience? Did you hear them? They were loving our ass.' Not that they're happy any more. I can hear them baying for our blood. 'And you just walk off. You, Whero Davies, the Kiwi wannabe queen of music and lyrics. You left me, Red, your mate, to the lions. What's your damn problem?'

It sounds like the punters are breaking up the place. Dermot, our manager, must be tearing his red Irish hair out trying to placate them.

Is Whero concerned? Na. 'Maybe I don't wanna be the queen of music,' she says.

I laugh, incredulous. 'But you can't do that. Walk off. This is London, not Eketahuna or Gore, for fuck's sake. We're this close —' I hold up the fingers of my right hand '— we were this close to signing up.'

'Red, I gotta love your confidence,' she says.

I gasp for air. Man oh man, there are times . . . 'The record label guy — Bob, Ben . . . Benjamin . . .' I shake her, trying to force her to get a grip.

'Karl. His name's Karl Jeffs.'

'He was out there tonight. And he saw you walk off the stage!' I try to explain in words the bitch will understand. 'Isn't this what we came to London for? Sistah, I dragged your ass here. I was the one who had the balls to get us on the plane, got you to leave the comfort zone of Auckland so you could be a rock chick in London.'

Oh, I give up. Let Whero explain her actions herself to our faggoty little manager.

At that moment, over all the ruckus, I hear a knock at the door. Maybe it's Dermot himself. I open the door. 'She's all yours,' and a loud blast of angry noise follows him in.

ut it isn't Dermot.

It's some guy, dark, and at first I think he's Arab or Hindu but then he steps out of the shadows and looks right into me. I know he's Maori and that he means trouble.

'Fuck off,' I snarl at him. 'Whero's mine.'

'Oh, is she now?' he replies before pushing me aside. He's dressed in a slightly awkward colonial-boy-come-to-the-big-smoke kind of way, like he's a cow cocky from Te Awamutu. The look he gives Whero speaks of charm and humility but I know it's all bullshit. Bull. Shit.

'Hello Whero,' he begins, 'my name's Petera.' He waves his hands in a friendly manner. 'Buggah me, you had that crowd in the palms of your hands, girl. God knows where you took them, but you had them all right. And then, well, there was that bit where you walked out. You left the place a war zone, eh.'

I try to warn Whero against him. 'Don't let him get to you, mate.'

It's too late. 'What do you want?' she asks.

'I want to know you better, eh, shake your hand and—'

'Why? Cause we're from New Zealand? Cause we're both Maori?' She says the words with sarcasm and my heart leaps: maybe she's onto him. 'You need a place to crash, eh. You heard a Kiwi accent over the microphone, saw a brown face and thought, "Sweet as", two Maoris got themselves lost in Europe, and maybe she'll help me out. Think I'll just take advantage of some good old Kiwi hospitality. Well, that ain't gonna happen. Cause I ain't a Kiwi, I'm an Aucklander, and Aucklanders eat Kiwis for fuckin' breakfast.'

Oh, but he's a snake, this Petera.

'Kia ora for that,' he answers, 'but I already got myself a hotel so I will politely decline your invitation.' Then he moves in. 'Look,

I haven't been completely honest with you. My last name's Davies. I'm related to you on your dad's side. And since I've been here in London I've been looking . . . for you . . . mostly.'

Whero backs away. 'What for?'

I can tell she's scared. I mean, fuck, I'm scared too.

'Your mother, my Auntie Anahera, told me to look you up. After all, your dad only died last month, eh.'

Whero's eyes brim with tears. 'I rang her. By the time I got the message that he'd died, it was too late. I wanted to get on the plane and go to the tangi but when I phoned Mum she said, "No, stay in London. Kotare would have wanted it that way. His little girl . . . trying to make it as a singer."'

'Kei te pai,' Petera answers, 'I'm not here to judge you. Your mum loves you and the whanau understood. Anyway, I said I was coming over to London and Auntie Anahera asked me to see how you're coping.' Awkwardly he hugs Whero. 'You play a mean guitar — the ole fulla would've been proud.'

'You play?'

'Hey, I'm Maori, aren't I?' He laughs, oozing more charm and pretending that he's offended. 'I'm staying at the Sanderson on Oxford Street — pretty flash, eh?' He takes out a pen and small notepad and writes on it. 'It's um — it's a cab ride from here. I'll be in London for a bit, taking in the scenery. It would be choice to catch up.' He tears the page out of the notepad. 'Till next time, eh?'

I step in his path. I'm not going to let him get away without making sure he knows I'm ready to take him on. But he looks at me as if I'm of no consequence, as if I'm not even there. 'I'll deal with you later,' he says.

When he's gone, it takes me a while to get my breath back.

'I don't like him,' I tell Whero. 'He could come between us.'

3 /

OVER THE RAINBOW

Next morning, I'm breathing easier.

Whero's asleep, completely out to it, and Dermot appears to have forgiven her. But I'm still worried about last night: her walking off the stage and, of course, Petera.

What does he want?

I slip out of bed and, tiptoeing to the window, open it slightly. Not enough to let the whole world in, but just enough so that I can take out a ciggy and have a smoke. God, I wish we had enough dollars so that we could have our own flat. Still, we were lucky that Dermot came up with a solution.

'Why don't you come and stay with me and Tupou?' he'd said. 'We've got a spare room. We could split the rent. It would make it easier on all our pockets, eh?'

Earl's fuckin' Court. We come to London and where do we end up? The Aussies could claim it as the next Australian state. And Kiwis could do the same, raising the Tino Rangatiratanga flag. All you hear around here are the colonial accents:

'Gidday, mate. Kia ora, cuz. Put a shrimp on the barbie. All Blacks forever.'

Yeah, you can tell I'm still in a mood, but no wonder Whero and me tried to lose our accents when we got here. However, at least you gotta say one thing about Antipodeans. When you're on the tube and strap-holding with all those hairy armpits at nose level, it's not the colonials who give you a whiff: Londoners stink.

And, after all, those colonials — even the ones from Canada, India, Scotland and Ireland — they're our punters. There's plenty of them.

The empire is ster-riking back. Chur, bro.

Just as I'm finishing my ciggy I hear Tupou coming in from his late shift at Heathrow. God, how did a Polynesian prince like him ever end up with a faggoty little Irishman? To women Dermot looks like a . . . well . . . dork, but he must have some mysterious appeal to men. Though God knows I've caught a glimpse of him in the shower and you can hardly see it.

I stub out the cigarette, throw it out the window and sneak over to the door to listen in to their conversation. Open the door a crack and I see that Dermot is making breakfast. 'You gonna help me,' Dermot asks Tupou, 'or are you just goin' to stand there fantasisin' over my arse?'

Gee, he's ever fuckin' hopeful.

'So? Do you want some breakfast or not? And what's with the smile?'

Tupou is just standing there with an idiotic look on his gob. 'I smile, Dermot, thank you for asking, because I am hot shit. Take a guess at what you're looking at.'

'Apparently I'm lookin' at one Mister Tupou Ihaka,' Dermot answers, 'who has the uncanny ability of shootin' lava from his arse.' He edges around the table with two plates and ladles out baked beans.

'Ugh,' says Tupou. 'I was hoping for something like spaghetti and meatballs but . . .' he takes a spoonful and returns to the point '. . . not lava: sunshine!'

'Sunshine?'

'I got the promotion. I walked into that room, pointed my rear at Barry, bent over and music be-gan to play.' He demonstrates, shaking his backside and shimmying. "Let the sun shine, let the sun shine in, the suuun shine iiin." Lo and behold, team leader.'

Behind the door I'm trying to stop from laughing. I mean, shut *up*, sometimes Dermot and Tupou are like *Saturday Night Live*.

Breakfast is forgotten now. 'Put a niggah in a suit,' Dermot claps sardonically. 'and he thinks he's goin' places.'

'Actually — yeah,' Tupou answers, flaring. 'Stick with me, kid. We'll be in New York before you know it.'

'New York?' Dermot asks. 'Who wants to go to feckin' New York! My yellow brick road leads to Sydney. From the Emerald Isles to Oz, geddit? The best shows on telly in Dublin were reruns of Aussie soap operas. And Ramsay Street and Summer Bay made me determined to click my heels together and escape the shite grey chill of a Dublin winter.'

Tupou pouts. 'I never knew Sydney meant that much to you.' But he's not about to give in quite yet. 'So you came to . . . er . . . London?' he adds with barely concealed sarcasm.

'At least it was the first step on the way south.'

'Flying into Heathrow with nothing but a suitcase full of dreams,' Tupou continues, exaggerating. He pretends to be a television interviewer: 'Sir, have you got the balls for London?'

'You should count yourself lucky that I stopped over,' Dermot says. 'If I hadn't, we'd never have met.'

'Yeah, right,' Tupou says sneakily. 'There you were, hanging in the urinals between flights. You thought I was a Polynesian prince . . .'

'In your dreams.'

'And I saw you . . . and, yes, Dermot, I heard music.' He coughs, pulls Dermot up from the breakfast table and starts dancing with him. '"You know we belong together — you and I forever and ever."' It's the theme song to *Home and Away*.

Dermot doesn't find it funny. 'Piss off.'

'"No matter where you are,"' Tupou continues, '"you're my shining star."'

'I said, shove it!' Dermot yells. 'Don't dump on my dreams.'

'I'm just playing.' Tupou knows he's gone a bit far.

'Well, I've had enough games today, from you . . . and Whero too. Stupid moo walked off stage last night before finishin' her set. I busted m'ballocks getting the record label guy to come see her and the bitch does that to me.'

Tupou looks towards the bedroom door; I hide behind it. 'You reckon she'll be all right?' he asks. 'She's been acting very weird lately. What is it with her?'

'Maybe it has to do with her dad,' Dermot answers. 'And her mum too. Maybe she's feelin' guilty about not goin' home to the tangi. And maybe there's stuff about them she hasn't dealt with yet.'

4 /

KOTARE

Now listen to me, Whero, you mustn't feel guilty, bub.
You know I'll always love you . . . and your mother. Have I ever told you how I met her? A thousand times eh! Well tough, I'll tell you again.

was at the reef, just around the bay from our marae where it fronts onto the sea. Tamanui Te Ra had risen and Tangaroa, God of the Sea, was calling — who was I to ignore his voice?

Aue, if only I'd known what Tangaroa had waiting for me, I'd have jumped out of bed, grown wings and flown to the seashore much earlier.

'Oy, you, ya buggah.'

Who me? I had just come up the beach with a sack of paua. Shit, I thought, Tangaroa himself must be on patrol and wants me to put some back.

'Yeah, you, ya sad buggah, nicking all the kai moana.'

But would Tangaroa talk in such bad-ass language? No. And apart from that, he must have had a sex change as the voice sounded mighty like a female. Uh oh, maybe the voice belonged to a kehua! 'Is that . . . is that you . . . Nan?'

'Umm . . .' the voice hesitated. 'Yeah, except that I'm younger. That's what happens when you get to heaven, boy, you get young again. Now you make sure you get that sack to the marae on your way back home. That will make up for all your greed, ya blimm'n poaka.'

I saw movement in the scrubby bushes on the sand dunes. I crept up on the voice, zeroing in. 'Yes, Nan. Sorry, Nan.'

Whoever it was could barely contain her amusement. 'Don't apologise to me. It's Tangaroa you're hurting.'

'Gotcha!' The voice belonged to a young girl, and she squealed as I pulled her out. 'I don't think I'll be apologising to anybody.' She was wearing a bright red bathing costume. I took a long look and then, 'Gee, Nan, you've changed,' I said. I must admit my heart was already going pitter patter, hubba hubba. 'So who the hell are you? You oughta be out there —' I gestured to all the women in their

ballooning dresses, like ducks' bums as they put their heads in the water '— collecting pipi and gossiping with all the other wahine.'

The girl looked at them and down at herself. 'Wearing this?'

'Well . . . maybe . . . maybe not.' I began to be unsure about what to do next. 'My name's Kotare — Kotare Davies.'

She looked at my outstretched hand. 'Unbelievable,' she said, shaking her head.

'Well, I can't kiss you on a first date!' I replied. 'How come I haven't seen you around here before?'

'Maybe I'm just visiting. And stop looking at me like that!'

'From where?'

'You take that sack to the marae and I'll tell you. Look at all your paua! At least those old nans out there treat Tangaroa with respect and leave some kai moana for tomorrow.'

'Okay, I'll keep half a sack for me and I'll donate the other half to the marae.' Gee, she'd better be worth it.

'Auckland — I'm from Auckland.'

'Phew-wee! Pretty flash, girl, pretty flash! That's where you got your costume from.'

'You're a blimmin' genius.'

'Don't treat me like an idiot.' Couldn't she see I was trying to be serious?

'I'm sorry,' she answered. 'So . . . half a sack to the marae? I'm worth at least that, although some boys I know would . . .'

'Okay! The whole sack.' And I was rewarded with a big smile that made the sun shine in my heart.

'Anahera, my name's Anahera.'

Yeah, but Anahera who? 'Anahera Grace?' I asked. Shake of the head. 'Anahera Manuera?' Another no. 'Anahera Kaa?' Nuhnuh. This was getting up my nose. 'Anahera Rumple-fuckin'-stiltskin?'

'Anahera McLean.'

'We're not related!' I almost punched the air.

'No,' she smiled, 'we're not even remotely whanaunga.'

I was dancing on the inside. 'Will you be here tomorrow?'

'Maybe, maybe not. All right, yes,' she replied. 'Bring your guitar, eh? I'll teach you how to play until your fingers bleed.' Then she was off and over the sandhills.

'And don't forget,' came her voice. 'The whole sack.'

That's how I met your mother, bub. But I knew I had to work fast because a girl like her, new in the neighbourhood, wasn't going to be without a fulla for long. Not only that, but there were better-looking boys down at the marae.

Next day, I pulled a sickie from the meatworks — reckoned all that meat could wait to be chopped another day. I phoned the boss: 'I'm really crook, boss' — cough, splutter, cough. Then I drove fast to the reef to get some serious fishing in. Other whanaunga were down there, and I joined them in the water.

'Hmmmn,' said Auntie Polly, who was with some kuia, 'the early kingfisher catches the . . .' She gestured to Anahera, who'd just arrived, and the other aunties roared with laughter.

I must have broken the record, Whero, for the fastest time to fill a sack with paua. Once the sack was chock full, I pulled it after me up the beach, sucking in my stomach. Anahera was playing my guitar, pretending that she hadn't seen me, my rippling muscles, my tight ribs, my sexy thighs. Then she looked up. 'Oh, it's you.'

I kept my pose a while longer before collapsing into my usual sloping shoulders, sunken chest and bony legs. 'One sack of kai moana,' I began, 'for the marae . . .'

'Oh?' she asked. 'And what do I get?'

I scrabbled for the other koha I had hidden, beforehand, in the sand. 'Um, I found this kowhai floating in the ocean.' I blew the sand off the yellow blossom. A bit wilted, but it couldn't be helped.

'I wonder what it was doing . . .' Anahera answered, rolling her eyes, 'floating out there?'

'Well, it must have known Christmas is coming . . .' I raised the kowhai above her head.

Anahera laughed at me gently. 'Wait your patience, boy. Your kowhai should be a mistletoe. You kiss under a mistletoe.'

'Yeah, I know.' What did she think I was: entirely stupid? 'But where am I going to find any mistletoe around here?' I sidled in for the king hit. 'Oh come on, let's give those old aunties out there something to gossip about.'

'Maybe tomorrow,' she giggled, escaping my arms and running away.

Your mother sure played hard to get with all her 'tomorrows'!

Luckily it was the weekend so I didn't have to pull a sickie the next day. But I was a bit late arriving at the reef and, although it was crowded with the rellies and the whanau and the few Pakeha trying to poach our kai, what was this? Everybody was packing up to go home.

I sat beside Auntie Polly on the sand. 'What's wrong, Auntie?'

'Today, the world has changed, boy.' She motioned to a sign that hadn't been there yesterday. I walked over to look at it. This time, I couldn't help swearing. 'Fuckin' bastards.'

Anahera, coming over the sand dunes, heard me. 'Kotare, wash your mouth.' Then she realised something bad had happened. She looked nervously at Auntie Polly and watched as the trucks revved up and headed back to town. And I was so obviously angry, my fists clenched, looking out to the ocean.

'What's the matter?' Anahera asked. 'Is there a shark out there?' She tried a joke. 'Is the water too cold?'

'First they take our land,' I answered, 'and now our fuckin' ocean.' I pointed to the sign. 'It says the water's polluted — sewage pipe. We can't use our beach.' I dunno, something just got to me. I dropped to my knees and . . . I couldn't help it . . . I began to cry.

'It's all right, Kotare,' Auntie Polly called. 'You'll find another place to fish. There's always another place.'

'Is there, Auntie?' I asked her as I stood up. 'And we go there and catch kai moana until the next sign tells us to move on?' I felt I had to say something to Tangaroa. 'Sea, we've been unkind to you. We've poisoned the land and now we feed our poison into your waters. We've lost our aroha for you, and our respect for life. Forgive us . . . Haere ra, e rangatira.'

I felt Anahera take my hand in hers and lean her head against my shoulder. Then at long last, she kissed me.

'You're a sweet man,' she said.

It was on that day, Anahera told me later, that she fell in love with me, bub.

All because I was a sweet man.

I couldn't believe my luck when I asked her to marry me, and she said yes. After the wedding, we went up to Auckland to make our lives and, for a while, we stayed with her folks.

Your mother, Anahera, became my angel.

Even when my troubles began.

5 /

CALL TO THE MINSTREL BOY

So here we are, me and my mate Whero, onstage again.

How come? Dermot got us a second chance at another club, Delilah's. *Nobody* gets a second chance in this town, but the faggoty Irishman pulled some strings and, fucking amazing, Delilah came through!

'How did you manage it?' Whero asks him.

'Told some lies. Shite, I'm goin' straight to hell. Said the reason you walked off the stage was because you had food poisonin' and needed to spew ... and, you know, Delilah's been wantin' a chance at you. So for feck's sake, Whero, when you get out there on the stage and in the spotlight, stay there. If you don't, and you walk, you and me are finished. Got that?'

But there's always a moment, just before we take the stage, when girlfriend turns to me, panicking, her eyes wide with fear. 'I can't do it, Red,' she says. 'Not without you.'

Hell, I live for those moments. 'That's what I'm here for, babe,' I tell her. 'It's me and you forever, remember? Womb to tomb, birth to earth and all that shit. So let's get out there, bitch, and rock this es-tablish-ment.'

There's something about Whero. If she wasn't heading for rock-chick stardom she could make it on Broadway or even Hollywood — a bit of Barbra, a dash of Judy, something of Janis and, when she really lets out the throttle, Jennifer Holliday.

If you're standing in the way, watch out.

But it's more than that. When she takes the stage tonight there's a deep moan. And then she begins to sing:

The nest is gone now . . .
drifting away on the tides . . .
But somewhere, somewhere . . .

Oh, the punters, mostly Kiwis again, I know they want to fuck her.

'Open up,' I yell at Whero, 'time to show what ya got.'

The sound crew — well, the sound man — who's trying to control Whero's huge voice just gives up as it rockets into the stratosphere. And there am I, not wanting him to do that, forcing her on and higher and louder and no don't stop, don't stop, don't . . .

Zowee. Fireworks, climax time.

Backstage, everyone's happy with Whero, kissface, kissy kissy.

'I could never do it without you,' she says to me.

'And that's the friggin' truth,' I grin.

Is Dermot relieved? He's drinking straight from a bottle of Southern Comfort, blissing out but . . . uh oh, I see that he's brought a suitcase. Maybe that argument he had with Tupou earlier has tipped the scales. He doesn't want to go to New York so . . . time to move on out? Or maybe he was serious about him and Whero going their separate ways if she didn't work out tonight.

Here comes Tupou with bubbly in his hands. He takes Dermot's bourbon from him and switches it with a glass of champers.

This I gotta hear!

What y'doin'?' Dermot asks as Tupou leans in and cops a feel. 'I'm celebrating my extremely hot boyfriend 'cause he's a cracker.'

'I love that word,' Dermot sighs. 'For me, it's up there with "struth" and "flamin' heck" and "cobber" and "digger" . . .'

Tupou looks at him askance. 'Are you trying to get a rise out of me when I'm trying to say sorry? And wanting to congratulate you for tonight? Whero was fabulous! The audience went apeshit.'

But nobody's home at Dermot's tonight. 'Alf Stewart,' he says, lifting his bubbly in a toast, 'he's the lucky bugger who gets to say all them words. Aussie words. *Home and Away* words. Ray Meagher, he plays Alf Stewart.'

Tupou gives Dermot a long, sarcastic look. 'Struth,' he mouths. 'I think a dingo took me boyfriend.'

Dermot eyeballs him. 'You're a genuine stand-up comic. I'd do anything to be a stranger in your land.'

'Aw, fair go, mate. Aussie ain't my land.'

'Australia, New Zealand, same old, same old.'

'You'd make a terrible Australian,' Tupou taunts. 'You get sunburnt too easily. England, Ireland, same old, same old.'

'Take that back, y'filthy bitch.'

Oh, for goodness sake, guys, make up. Whero and me like living with you and don't want to be back on the fuckin' street.

Tupou sees Dermot's suitcase and, before Dermot can stop him, picks it up and opens it. 'Oh, I see. You don't want to come with me to New York so you're going to Australia?'

'Don't jump to conclusions.'

'You're leaving me?' Tupou's voice is cracking. He takes out one of Dermot's shirts to underline his point. 'You were going to tell me, of course, and Whero.' He begins to sing 'Tie Me Kangaroo Down, Sport'.

Dermot grabs him. 'No, I'm not leavin' you — or Whero, not now that she's back on feckin' track with her career. And if you look closer, you'll see that my suitcase is only half packed.' He pauses. 'I'm not goin' to Aussie.'

Well, that's fuckin' good to know! So where then?

'My uncle rang from Ireland,' Dermot tells Tupou. 'Seamus, my mother's older brother. It's his birthday and he wants me to go back for it.'

'Can I come too?' Tupou asks, and then he sees a look pass over Dermot's face. 'Oh, right, this faggot niggah isn't good enough to take back to your people.'

'I'm not goin' to be gone for that long. But maybe . . .' He begins to do a bit of a rant. Is it the booze talking? 'Look, what the feck are we all doin' in London anyway!'

'Catholic sonofabitch, and just when I was about to tell you that I told the boss to stuff the job in New York.'

'But that would be just exchangin' one —' Dermot makes signs with his fingers '— "metropolitan capital" for another. Why don't we try somethin' new? What's wrong with succeedin' in . . . Dublin?'

He's got to be joking. Even Tupou is startled.

But Dermot raves on. 'Look, we all come to feckin' London because we think that's what we're supposed to do. If we can make it here, we can make it anywhere. But what if we don't fall for that shite?'

'Er . . .' Tupou begins, 'so you want to go back to Dublin? To the same Irish family that told their queer son to piss off? Like my family found out, so I hightailed it out of New Zealand to London?

Dermot, just a while ago you talked about going to Australia.'

Dermot clenches the champagne glass so tight it's a wonder it doesn't break.

'Feck, feck, feck. Sometimes I just don't know where I belong, Tupou. Or where I'm supposed to get to from here.'

Tupou hugs him close.

'Dermot, you belong to me. And we're each other's country, each other's family.' He takes a breath. 'Listen, you go back to Ireland to your uncle's birthday, I'll keep the home fires burning here, and then, you bastard, come back and let's sort this out. UK, Oz, Ireland, Aotearoa or even Apia, what the fuck does it matter as long as we're together.'

Two weeks later, Dermot's gone to Ireland and Tupou's mooning around the flat. Sometimes Whero and I take him to a bar to cheer him up and we all have a couple of drinks and dances — and man oh man, the number of posh British gentlemen who come on to Tupou. After all, he's a Polynesian prince.

Dermot, if I was you, I wouldn't stay away too long.

But that freakin' Petera and the memories of New Zealand that he brought with him are causing havoc. Worse, he's got Whero thinking of her dad again.

6 /

THE KIDS DOWNSTAIRS

Whero, you must understand that the way you are isn't your fault.

Sure you were a difficult baby, up most nights bawling your head off. Maybe you sensed the change coming when your mother told her folks we were moving out and would find our own place in Auckland city itself.

Aue, and my job packing batteries at a car factory died on me when they laid me off. And I was missing the sea.

Tangaroa, don't desert me . . .

It was your mother who found a place for us to look at in Mount Albert.

That was when she began to realise the truth about me, her sweet man.

The landlord was waiting at the gate when we walked up to the address. He had a BMW, real flash, and we'd come with you on the bus. 'I have to admit,' he said, 'when I saw your name listed on the rent form I was expecting something different.' He was one of those guys who had read a 'How to Make Money' manual and decided that having low-rent flats was a good way to get a fast return.

'Different?' Your mother went stiff. You had to watch that girl when she got her back up.

'With a name like Davies, love . . .' He lit his pipe, puff puff puff.

I don't think he was being deliberately offensive. He probably had Maori and Pacific Islanders in his other flats but was disappointed that we weren't Pakeha and therefore, well, an improvement.

'What's wrong with Davies?' Anahera asked. 'And you are Mr . . . ?'

'Papadopoulos,' he answered. 'Third generation Kiwi, though, so don't go thinking I'm fresh off the boat. I wasn't expecting Maoris is all.'

'And I wasn't expecting a . . . a Greek,' Anahera flared.

The landlord ignored her remark. 'Ah well,' he continued, as if he was doing us a favour, 'seeing as you're here . . .'

He opened the gate and was just about to lead us in when Anahera stepped quickly in front of him. He remembered his manners and let her through first.

'Thank you,' she said.

We followed your mother up a narrow and dark side pathway to a double doorway. One doorway was for the top flat, which we were hoping to rent. The other was for a bottom flat, which I thought the man at the letting agency had said was empty but I could swear I saw some Maori kids — teenagers — looking out from behind the curtains at us. Perhaps I hadn't heard him properly.

If Mr Papadopoulos assumed Anahera and I would give the place a quick once-over and then take it, man oh man, was he wrong. 'There's no need to accompany us while we take a look,' she began. Then, to make sure he didn't: 'Here, take care of baby for a moment, will you? And please don't smoke while you're holding her. We won't be long.'

Mr Papadopoulos was a bit startled, but we'd already walked off so what else could he do?

The flat was to be let furnished and, although the furnishings were a bit tatty — double bed in one room, single bed in another, sofa and chairs in the sitting room and table and chairs in the kitchen — the place was clean enough.

'At least there are no rats or cockroaches,' Anahera said, loud and clear, so that Mr Papadopoulos could hear. We went into a quick huddle, running over the pros and cons, and decided to take the flat. By the time we joined him — he was glad to hand you, Whero, back to us — he was looking at his watch. Anahera's eyes gleamed. 'Aha, a man who's in a hurry,' she whispered to me, 'is a man who wants to close a deal fast and can be beaten down.'

Not quite. 'You are married, aren'tcha, love?' Mr Papadopoulos asked. He'd noticed Anahera wasn't wearing a ring.

Maybe we were, maybe we weren't. 'The pregnancy caused my fingers to swell,' she said.

'Got the ring around y'neck, I s'pose,' Mr Papadopoulos said with sarcasm.

'I did have,' Anahera continued, 'on a chain, but I've put it away for a while. Unfortunately bub's wandering fingers tore it off in her scramble for the breast.'

I could tell that this detail was a bit gross for Mr Papadopoulos.

Anahera changed the topic. 'Could you tell us what the neighbours are like?'

'This is Mount Albert, love. There's lots of different cultures around here now. New immigrants from all over the place, all mixing in with each other. Did you see the Sikh temple along the road? I rented out one of my flats just last week to some Somalis . . . I like to do my part for refugees. And you want to see St Luke's Mall on the weekend . . . lots of smiling people getting on together. You Maori people should smile more often too — would make getting on with ya a lot easier, eh.'

Jeez, was the arsehole begging for a fight? Anahera saw my flash of anger and gave me a look: settle down.

Mr Papadopoulos looked at his watch again. Made up his mind: we were probably the only name on his fuckin' list. 'Righto, love, y'like the flat then? It would be good to get a married couple in it. It makes for more stability.'

'The walls need painting,' Anahera said, beginning the negotiation.

'Yeah, I'll get to that.'

'The carpet in the sitting room's got big holes. It seems very damp and that's bad news for babies.'

'Love, Auckland was built in the middle of a swamp and across a coupla harbours. You'll be hard pressed to find a flat that isn't damp.'

I spoke up. 'I think the rent's too high for what the flat is.'

Mr Papadopoulos looked at me, astonished. 'By crikey,' he said, 'it speaks.'

But Anahera came in fast. 'Kotare's right.'

'The boards on the stairs need work,' I began. 'There's mould on the ceiling of the bathroom, and there's a heap of junk downstairs needing to be taken to the tip. Also, the walls are thin as hell — and I can already hear the kids downstairs.'

Mr Papadopoulos gave me a strange, puzzled, look. So did Anahera. 'It's on a good bus route, hon,' she said after a while, 'so I can get to Onehunga when I want to see my folks.'

The landlord recovered. 'Look, the rent's three hundred and fifty dollars a week, plus two weeks' rent in advance, and a bond of two hundred. You'll get that back, of course.'

'Make it three hundred a week,' said Anahera, 'plus two weeks' rent in advance, no bond, and we'll wallpaper and repaint.'

'Three forty, one week in advance, no bond, I'll get rid of the junk out the back.'

'Three fifteen, new fridge.'

'Three thirty-five. No bond,' said Mr Papadopoulos.

'Three twenty.'

'Three thirty.'

I chipped in, spoiling their rhythm. 'Three twenty-five.'

'Done.' Surprised, Mr Papadopoulos gave me a respectful nod. When it comes down to it, a man likes to negotiate with another man. 'There we are then,' he continued, relieved. 'Oh, by the way, you're not planning any big parties, are ya? Just, I know you Maoris and your guitars.'

I couldn't resist. 'Been to a few, have ya?'

'I'm not bloody joking. You can move in this Saturday, I s'pose. I'll be here nine o'clock in the morning with your keys.'

Outside Mr Papadopoulos shook my hand. 'Right you are — cheerio.' And then I heard him whisper in Anahera's ear, 'You've got a right one there.'

We settled into our flat and Anahera made it look fuckin' awesome, given the little amount of money we had. Took up all our savings to move to Auckland in the first place, and, now Anahera had you to look after, she couldn't work.

It was up to me. Get off your ass, Kotare Davies, and get a job.

Fuck this place, fuck Auckland. Why wouldn't anybody give me a job? They looked at me, asked for my qualifications. Where the hell did they think I could go to on the coast to get qualifications! I showed them that I had strength, good hands and could handle any job they threw at me: I tried a coupla builders, the council, the harbour board . . .

I knew I had to get a job, and I prayed:

'Tangaroa, help me . . .'

I miss the healing sun and sea. I'm going out to Westfield meatworks to see if they'll put me on their waiting list . . . It's near the sea . . .

*A*nd *I did it, bub, I did it!*

I was smiling so much on the bus back from Westfield that even the other passengers started smiling. Well, a few didn't — they thought I might be one of those loonies who smile all the time. I got off at St Luke's and walked the rest of the way to our flat. Hey, I saw this fish 'n' chip shop. By the time I got back to the flat it was getting a bit dark but . . . there it was . . . and a light shining in the upstairs window, like the Star of fuckin' Bethlehem where my angel was waiting with you.

I opened the door and ran up the stairs. One of the kids in the downstairs flat — I think his name was Barney — waved to me from the window. The kids had a habit of playing their music a bit loud. I decided to talk to them about it soon. 'Ana! Ana!' I called as I went up, two steps at a time.

She appeared. Man oh man, I thought, Kotare Davies, you are one goddamn lucky sonofabitch.

'Would you keep it down, Kotare? I just managed to get bub to sleep.'

'Wake her up again. I got fish 'n' chips.'

'But I've made our tea,' Anahera said, 'and we gotta save our money. The rent's due this Friday.' She was near to tears. 'Hon, what am I going to do with you?'

'All sorted,' I told her. 'From next week I'm gonna be bringing home the dollars!'

Your mother's eyes lit up. 'You got a job? My hon's got a job?'

I whirled her around in my arms. It was so good to see her happy. 'Wasn't that hard,' I told her. 'I just walked into Westfield meatworks, told them what I been doing back home, asked them to put me on the waiting list — and it was my lucky day because there was a vacancy! And you know what the best part is? Westfield's right on the Manukau Harbour, which means I can go fishing after work. Tangaroa will look after us too.'

Anahera looked at me tenderly. 'Kotare Davies, I swear I've got a rival.'

'Eh?'

'The ocean.'

I thought about that for a moment. 'But can the ocean keep me warm?' I asked Anahera, as I kissed her. 'And does the ocean have lips as sweet as yours or hair as soft?' She began to melt against me. 'Can the ocean play music as sweet as my Anahera? Does it have fingers as delicate?'

'If you're trying to get around me,' she murmured, 'you're going the right way.'

'Is the ocean as playful or as deep as my Anahera? Kaore, kaore, kaore . . .'

'You're a silver-tongued kingfisher, Kotare Davies.'

I made my mournful face. 'And is the ocean as forgiving as my Anahera . . .'

She stiffened, searched my face, became frightened. 'Kotare, please don't do this to me. To us.'

I laughed, glad to fool her. 'I only had enough money for one crabstick!'

I grabbed it and put it in my mouth. But the joke was on me. She wasn't laughing. And when you started to cry in your bedroom, bub, and I said I'd go and look after you my Anahera said:

'No, Kotare. Not you.'

7 /

WHO ART THOU?

onder of wonders, I've persuaded Whero to stop thinking about her dad and come for a walk.

'Where you off to?' Tupou asks as she opens the door. Dermot will be home soon, thank Christ, and that will get him off our case.

'Oh . . . Oxford Street,' she answers him.

He thinks for a moment. 'Hey, why don't I meet you there later? We could go to a pub for lunch?'

'Okay.'

Meanwhile, I'm getting suspicious. You'd think that with all of London to choose from . . . I mean, who'd want to fuckin' hang out on Oxford Street! First of all you have to take the tube, and no sooner do you get up to street level . . . where are the Brits? Instead it's Russians in fur coats come to spend up large, or the French across the Channel for the day and Arabs going into Marks & Spencers.

We wander along for a while and, bingo, the light comes on in my stoo-pid brain and I see why Whero wanted to come here: The Sanderson Hotel. Yup, Red, you've gone from the frying pan into the fire. This is where that arsehole Petera Davies said he was staying.

'Won't be long,' Whero says as she walks in.

I could kick her. I watch as she approaches the reception desk. She talks to the receptionist. He looks in a computer, frowns and shakes his head. She talks to him again. He tries his computer a second time. Again no luck.

'There's no Petera Davies booked into the hotel,' she says to me when she comes out. Hell, I could have told her that.

W hero tries phoning the number that Petera gave her.

Along comes Tupou. 'Don't stand here too long,' he smiles, 'otherwise the cops will think you're doing the street.'

'I've got a cousin who said he was staying here,' Whero explains as she stows the phone. 'Except that he's not registered. And his mobile must be switched off.'

'Really?' Tupou asks as we push through the tourists and around the corner away from Oxford Street. 'Why the hell would he give you false details?'

'You might have met him,' Whero insists. 'He came to the club that night when I had my . . . er . . . moment.'

Tupou shudders. 'Thank God I wasn't there . . . and, no, I don't think I ever met your cousin.' He stops at a small doorway. 'Aha, here we are. This will do us.'

This is not my day. A fucking Irish pub. At least it's not crowded. Tupou finds a table in a corner. 'Okay, the reason why we're having lunch . . . is that Dermot's been in touch. I've got a letter from him. Shall I read it?'

'Go ahead,' says Whero.

'Hmm, some of this stuff is per-son-al,' Tupou begins, 'so I'll only read the part that clears Customs, okay? Now . . . ah, here's the paragraph that affects you. "Please tell Whero that I've made contact again with Karl Jeffs — he's still pissed she walked off the stage but I told him she had a virus. Since then he's heard about her gig at Delilah's and he's asked me to send a demo tape."'

Tupou opens his arms. 'Is my boyfriend good . . . or is he good? When he gets back, I'm gonna throw him on his back and show him your appreciation.'

Oh my God, a bulge is starting to grow in his pants in anticipation.

Kippers and chips and Irish beer are on the menu for lunch, and then Tupou has to leave. 'See you back home,' he says as he disappears down the street.

As we exit, what the fuck — Petera. Now I really know that someone is shitting on my day.

He ignores me. His eyes are liquid, pouring an intense, frightening glance into Whero's soul. 'Hey, cuz,' he greets her.

Whero looks at him with suspicion. 'Why would a bro tell me he's staying at the Sanderson when he's not?'

The prick's got all the answers. 'Aw, hell. Moved hotels is why. Living the nomadic lifestyle, so to speak. Just came this way to pick my gears up.' Then he stares me down, down, down. 'I see Red's tagging along?'

'What about your phone?' Whero asks, giving Petera a run for his money. 'I rang the number . . . nothing.'

Petera shakes his head, looking disappointed with himself. 'Global bloody roaming. Didn't realise I'd need it . . .' He's like quicksilver, circling Whero, confusing her. 'You know there's no buggah around these parts selling hokey-pokey ice cream? Enough to make you wanna go home, eh?' Then he moves in for the kill. 'You reckon you got the strength to survive London . . . alone?'

'Alone?' I ask him. 'You bastard, Whero has me.'

He ignores me. 'You don't miss home? What about your mother?'

'That's none of your business.'

'She's worried about you. Like father, like daughter . . .'

'Fuck off.' Whero is causing a scene. People are looking at her, giving her a wide berth.

Petera backs off, his hands up in the air. 'Okay, Whero, okay. But you've been wishing you had somebody like me for a long time. That's why I'm here. I'm overdue, I know that, but I'm here now. How 'bout we meet at your flat? Oxford Street's not really the place to hold a family reunion, eh? You need me, Whero.'

And then he grabs my chin, his fingers digging into my cheeks, and forces me against a pane of glass.

'You, Red, you're not invited, geddit?'

8 /

WE'LL ALWAYS HAVE AUCKLAND

Nope, not my freakin' day at all. Nor does it get any better when Whero and I return to the flat. Why? Because Dermot's back and we can hear the thunk, thunk, thunk in the front bedroom and, well, why should he and Tupou be happy when I have to deal with fuckin' Petera coming back into our lives?

They both come out of the bedroom with silly grins on their faces and pretend that they haven't been at it. Tupou starts a celebratory glass of bourbon and, as Whero enters the room, passes her a fat spliff of hash.

'Gee, am I a lucky sonofabitch Irishman?' Dermot says as he

cuddles her. 'Two beautiful Polynesians welcoming me home? Let me give you a hug, darlin', we're all on the up and up.'

'What are ya?' Whero asks with a smile. 'My mother? You get a kick out of dictating my life?'

'I ain't dictatin' shite. I'm just . . . cuddlin' up to my investment.'

Suddenly we hear something vibrating. 'What the hell is that?' Tupou asks drunkenly. He points accusingly at Dermot. 'Your pants are moving, hon.'

'Aw, feck,' Dermot dips into a pocket and pulls out his phone.

Tupou giggles. 'And there was I, thinking you were getting horny . . . again.'

Dermot ignores him. 'Yeah? Dermot here . . . yeah, that's me. Karl! How you doin'? What are you wantin', pal?' His eyes light up with excitement and he makes a thumbs-up sign to us. 'Yeah — yeah, for sure. That sounds grand. Maybe we could meet up later this week? Discuss the details further, yeah? Lovely, Karl. You're a feckin' legend.'

'Well?' Whero asks.

Dermot feigns ignorance, so Whero and Tupou pile on top of him. 'That was Karl Jeffs, wasn't it? What did he say?'

'He loves your feckin' demo tape!' Dermot yells with glee. 'Says that your voice is phonogenic. That it takes to recordin' as if it was made for it. Says that sometimes singers in bars and clubs don't sound as great when they're recorded but you, girlfriend, you only sound better. And he really loves your original songs. So, he wants to talk serious talk with me about . . . a recordin' contract.'

'Woo-hoo!' Whero yells. She gives Dermot a massive hug and pulls him up and into a dance.

'Does this mean we'll stay in London?' Tupou asks.

'You bet your beautiful ass,' Dermot answers. 'Soon we'll be snortin' coke through gold-plated straws. But . . .' His eyes get that faggoty Irish grin: '. . . if there's an album, wouldn't the primo place to launch it be . . .'

'Please don't say Dublin,' Tupou groans.

'Oh ye of little feckin' faith,' Dermot sighs as he begins again. 'Wouldn't it be . . . Auckland?'

t takes a while for Dermot's idea to sink in.

Then, 'Yay,' Tupou says, 'the dingo hasn't stolen my baby.'

And Whero, grooving on the idea, says, 'Everybody there would love your accent. Everything Irish is fuckin' sexy.' Then the bitch gets weepy. 'It's as good as it gets. It's home.'

Tupou restores some realism. 'I was going to say that it's constantly overcast and it's surrounded by about fifty big fuckin' volcanoes. Big . . . and, well, dead.'

'And y'play football with your hands, eh.'

'Are you demeaning our national sport?' Tupou yells. 'It's not football, it's rugby, you dumb Irish piece of shit.' He takes off his shirt. 'Stand up.'

Dermot is already standing but, hey, who's being pedantic. 'What for?'

'Gonna show you how to do a haka, the way the All Blacks do it,' Tupou answers. He takes off Dermot's shirt too — skinny Irishman, Jeez, put the shirt back on. 'Now, bend your legs like this, Grasshopper.' Tupou goes into the classic haka stance and Dermot tries to imitate him.

'Kia rite!' Tupou shouts, scaring the shit out of all of us. 'Waewae takahia!' He starts to stamp his feet. And then he's away. 'Ka mate, ka mate, ka ora, ka ora!'

And it's so funny to see Dermot following Tupou's directions:

'Cross trainer, cross trainer! Ski, ski! And cross trainer again!'

Tongue poking, knee slapping, chest pounding, it's comedy time, which turns into something gruesome as they sex it up together. At the end of it, we all fall about laughing.

'That was primo,' Whero says.

'I'll make a haka boogie man out of you yet, Dermot,' Tupou tells him.

And Dermot beams like a fuckin' Irish elf.

'Auckland it is.'

9 /

FAREWELL MY LOVELY

Here we are in the middle of Heathrow meeting Tupou before we go to see Karl Jeffs. Dermot is also due soon; Jeffs doesn't live far from Heathrow.

When Tupou arrives, he's eating an ice cream. 'Hey,' he says to Whero in between licks, 'how are you feeling about signing the contract?'

'Okay, I guess,' she answers. 'Is that hokey-pokey?'

'Actually, Heathrow is one of the few places outside New Zealand you can get it.' He sees Whero looking at the ice cream and edges away from her. 'And you can't have it.' Then he remembers something. 'Oh, Dermot gave me something this morning — it's for you. Can I give it to you now?'

He pulls a large package from his backpack. As soon as I see the wrapping I know immediately what's in it. Pills. I've been hiding them away from Whero for months. How the fuck did Dermot find them?

Whero looks at the package, uncertain, and then takes it. 'Thanks,' she says.

'Dermot was all secretive about it. You know me and secrets! So I opened it. What are they for?'

'Nothing.' Whero turns away.

'Nothing?' Tupou says. 'Dermot tells me that you haven't been taking them, you naughty girl, you.' Slurp, lick. Watch out, Tupou, curiosity can kill a cat.

'That's none of your business.'

'My sometimes intolerable boyfriend won't tell me what's going on, and now I'm in the company of a sometimes intolerable bitch.' Whero remains tightlipped and Tupou gives up. 'Okay, don't tell me anything. It's not like I need to know anyway.'

And after that outburst, Dermot arrives and sits down next to Whero. 'He's given you the pills already? Please take one before we go to see Karl. Will you do that for me?'

'Fuck off.'

But Dermot is insistent. He sees Whero looking for me and his eyes narrow. 'Red can't help you, girlfriend. So you won't take a pill now? Ah well . . . promise me, Whero, you'll start takin' them soon. I mean it, Whero, soon.'

10 /

DANGEROUS MOONLIGHT

And hey, the contract's signed, sealed and delivered.

Excitedly, we catch the train back to London. But all the way in, I'm plotting how to get those pills away from Whero . . .

Damn, Dermot's watching her with hawk eyes.

Worse is to come.

Dermot and Tupou go out for a beer, but Whero is tired so begs off and, instead, we come on home to find somebody waiting.

Petera, in the darkness, with only the moon coming through the window.

'Didn't I tell you,' he begins, looking at me dangerously, 'that you're not invited?'

I cuddle against Whero, she'll protect me from him. 'What do you want?' she asks him. 'How did you get in? Who gave you a key?'

'You gave me one,' he lies. 'Don't you remember?' Then he says, 'What about the pills?'

'She doesn't want to take them any more,' I say.

'Why not?' He turns to Whero. 'It's not Red's right to steal your pills from you.'

Whero defends me. 'Red's my best mate. She's only looking

after me. We both know what the pills do. They make me . . . go back.' She begins to sob and, before I can stop him, Petera folds her in his arms.

'There, there,' he whispers. 'I know you don't want to think of home . . .' he moves in closer '. . . and it's hurting you because the closer you get to the truth the more it's killing you.'

Whero moans and slides to the ground. Petera kneels on his haunches, lowering himself to her level. He gently places a hand on her shoulder.

I try to warn her, 'Whero, no!' but she instinctively leans into him for support.

I turn on the bastard. 'I'm the one she needs, the one who always helps her when she calls out. I'm the one with balls who can look after her, and I'm the one who brought her here from all her memories of New Zealand so that she could start a new life in London.'

'Is that so?' He stands and casually approaches me. 'Well, it's my turn now.'

I look at Whero, pleading for her to help me, but she's finding it difficult to breathe. And then Petera takes a swing at me. The back of his hand smashes into my jaw, sending me flying some distance across the room.

He's calm and clinical as, methodically, he begins to beat me up.

'Red's not right for you,' he says to Whero. She tries to get up and stop him but it's almost as if his blows are also raining on her.

'Please,' she says to him, 'you can't do that to her . . . to us.'

This time Petera punches me in the guts. Whero howls with pain. 'Leave her,' he says to me.

He's split my lip. My stomach really hurts. Another punch.

'Fuck you,' I tell him as I go down. I'm on the verge of blacking out.

Petera kicks my skull. Whero holds her face in her hands.

'Leave!' he shouts at me again, his spittle spraying. 'Leave us. Leave her.'

He kicks me again and again and I lose consciousness.

And all is darkness.

— — INTERMISSION — —

PART TWO —
AT THE SAME TIME
AS THE SPIRAL IS
GOING FORWARD,
IT IS RETURNING

11 /
RED

My eyes flicker, and I see Whero staring into them. She has put me in bed and we're lying side by side, covered with a quilt.

Oh, Whero, we've seen a lot of the world since we met as children, haven't we? Of course I haven't been with you all the time but, somewhere, somehow, we've always met up and, hey, girlfriend, we've always been there for each other, right?

'Are you okay?' Whero asks, tenderly stroking my face. 'Petera gave you a bad beating. I should have called the cops.'

'I'll be all right,' I answer. 'Hold me close, girlfriend?'

She does so and I wince. 'Well, not too close.' And as she settles against me I remember the first time we met.

Oh, how I've always loved that girl!

She must have been about eight — I was the same age — and she and her mum, Anahera, had come back to the East Coast over the school holidays so that Whero could spend time with Kotare's kin.

The day was hot, the sky blue as the sea, and Whero was playing in the water, not too far out, where the reef was. It was low tide, foam sweeping before the wind from the sea, and the shoreward part of the reef was exposed. Whero saw a seahorse, flashing through seaweed in one of the pools and she got so excited, running up the beach yelling, 'Mummy, Mummy!' She was like her father: he loved Tangaroa's domain too.

Anahera was asleep in the shade of some bushes, so Whero decided not to wake her up. Instead, she sat down beside her mother and then, seeing her father's guitar, carefully picked it up and began to strum it.

Ouch. She strummed badly. She hurt my ears. She must have hurt Anahera's ears too because she stirred and woke up.

'Oh, sorry, Mummy. I was trying to play the tune but I can't hit the right chords.'

Smiling, Anahera held Whero from behind and guided her fingers on the guitar:

Kingfisher come home . . .
Never too far, too far to roam . . .

She put the guitar aside, leant back and looked out at the sea. 'This was where your father and I first met,' she told Whero. 'Right here, nine years ago now. We had our romance, here in the sand. Oh, he was a handsome boy, your dad — don't you ever listen to people who say otherwise. He hated it when the beach was polluted. Him and all the people from the marae, including his Auntie Polly, had a tangi here — such a sad sound for such a beautiful day. They respected Tangaroa. Since then, nobody comes here. Just me and you.'

'Will Daddy ever be back with us?' Whero asked.

'We have to hope so,' Anahera replied. 'When we return to Auckland we'll go out to the hospital to see him, eh? I know he will be looking forward to seeing you. We can take him fish 'n' chips, eh? He always liked fish 'n' chips!' She hugged Whero. 'In the meantime, you and me have each other. This is where we belong . . . together.'

Then Whero remembered. 'Mummy, I saw a seahorse!' With that, she ran ahead of Anahera, splashing quickly across the shallow water to a low rocky staircase in the lagoon. She searched for a moment in one of the pools and, 'There it is!'

In a trice, Anahera had the seahorse fluttering in her hands. 'It got stranded here when the tide went out,' she said. She cradled it carefully and, swiftly, motioning to Whero to follow her, went to the edge of the reef where the sea turned blue. 'Here we go,' she said.

The seahorse was delicate and luminescent. It whirred and scintillated in the sunlit sea and then, slowly, began to descend into its depths.

'Haere ra, seahorse,' Whero whispered. She was so sad, so sad.

The sky was a mirror and so was the sea. When Whero looked into the water I looked back. As she returned to the beach her mother didn't see me coming up behind Whero and slipping my hand in hers.

'Kia ora,' I said. 'My name's Red.'

12 /

TIDES OF TIME

Of course, Whero, when I first met your father, all I could see was a sweet, sweet man.

He was pulling a sack of kai moana up the beach and, at the time, I thought he was a bit of all right. In fact, he was one of the best-looking boys I'd ever seen, and very different from the city boys of Onehunga, always so sure of themselves. He was a country boy, living on the marae, and so he had a natural goodness that attracted me to him. He loved the sea, he was always respectful to Tangaroa. He was cheeky too and innocent and I don't think he knew that I was planning to get him for my very own.

I guess you don't see people the right way when they're in their own environment. Even when we were married, and he came with me to Auckland, I still attributed his happy-go-lucky ways to a tender heart. But it soon became apparent that he wasn't cut out to be a city boy. Even worse, he couldn't handle stress. And when you were born, and there was pressure from Mum and Dad for him to get a job — he really did try, my darling Kotare — that's when I began to notice troubling things about him.

He would retreat into a world that existed only in his mind. Physically, whenever he was really stressed out, he would repeat various actions, like turning around and around, and talking to himself. The lying came later, and I suppose he did this to sustain the stories he told me.

In the end, Mum and Dad were arguing so much with Kotare that I decided we had to move out with you, bub. So we came into the city and found a flat. At first Kotare was fine, and he managed to find a job at Westfield meatworks. He loved the idea that it was close to the sea. He used to talk about the kids downstairs — we lived in the upstairs part of the house — which bothered me a bit, but I let it go. Meanwhile, I found a part-time job at a local greengrocer where the owner, Mr Chattopadhyay, from Bengal, didn't mind having a baby behind the counter.

Kotare was very good at giving me his pay packet. But, about five weeks after he took the meatworks job, he told me that his pay wasn't coming in until the next week.

That's when the lying began. When that week came around,

Kotare said he lost the money on the way home. So we had to start budgeting and watching our money, and that distressed him — especially when he thought you were hungry, bub, and crying because of this. I now know that he was beginning to feel guilty about not being a good provider. Whenever I mentioned our money worries, he took my comments personally.

The following week he should have come home with money in his pocket. Instead, he brought fish 'n' chips. It was always fish 'n' chips whenever things were going wrong inside him.

He started to snap at both of us. He would never have meant to hurt you and me, and he never raised a hand . . . but after a while we were shouting at each other, and I knew it was only a matter of time. It wasn't his fault. He just didn't want to tell me what was really happening to him.

I found out in the end. He'd been fired in his fifth week for what they said was erratic emotional behaviour. But what had he been doing during the day? I telephoned one of the men I knew worked with him, and he told me that my darling liked to go to the beach close to the meatworks. One afternoon, in desperation, I put you in your pushchair and we went out to Manukau Harbour on the bus.

I saw him. He was sitting with his head in his hands. I could hear him talking to himself. 'How am I going to tell my angel about my job? She's already got enough trouble looking after baby.'

I sat down beside him. I touched him. He was shocked to see us. 'What are you doing here?' he cried.

He was so confused and upset. Next moment he got up and started to run away, flapping his hands like a mad man. I watched him while the wind sighed over the beach and the water lapped against the shore.

I wheeled the pushchair after him. He was standing in the mud, staring dully over the mudflats. He was making strange scratching movements and saying something:

'I can smell the fucking rotten smell of the meatworks. It's poisoning the sea.'

'Kotare,' I asked him, 'is this where you've been spending your days? The whole time?'

'Yup,' he answered. 'Playing hide 'n' seek. You and baby want to play with me? You go and hide and I'll find you.' Then his head snapped up. 'Can't work for the abattoir any more. They poison the ocean. Won't do that. Tangaroa doesn't like it. Auckland's not the place for us, angel.'

I hugged him. 'Kotare, what are we gonna do? Bub's gotta eat. We gotta pay the rent too.'

He was all over the place. 'There's five kids living below us. I hear them playing their music. Sometimes I go down and visit them.'

'I guess I could see if I could make my job full-time?'

He nodded vigorously. 'Thelma works in a sewing factory, Rose is getting a job at Mr Chips down the road, Sambo works in a bakery, sing a song of sixpence a pocketful of rye, four and twenty blackbirds baked in a pie.'

'Thelma? Rose?'

'And Koro and Johnny Mack. But they don't have jobs. They keep wanting to come fishing with me, but I told them you can't do that any more because there's a sign gone up, and they laughed and laughed. Five hundred bucks the kids are paying Mr Papadopoulos for a flat smaller than ours. We got us a good deal, angel.'

You started to cry, Whero.

As for Kotare, he was frightening me. I didn't want him to talk about the kids downstairs any more, but he wouldn't stop.

'They got no furniture, just mattresses,' he went on. 'Thelma

reckons she can spruce it up. She'll nick some material from the sewing factory, make them some new curtains. They're pretty hard case . . . when they're not too pissed. They get angry when I talk about the ocean.' He was shaking his head so hard I thought it might snap off.

'Kotare!' I shouted to get his attention. 'Listen to me — promise me . . .' In desperation, I bent down to the water, cupped some in my hands and flicked the water over his face. 'Do you love me? Do you love me, hon?'

'I would do anything for my Anahera.' He was wiping the sea water away from his eyes, weeping, and his nose was running.

'Don't visit the kids downstairs any more. Don't visit them. Promise me, hon?'

He thought this through, frowning at first. Then he gave a giggle. 'What if they visit me?'

And this time I was really frightened. 'Then don't let them in . . . Lock the door, Kotare . . . shut them out.'

13 /

YELLOW BRICK ROAD

wake up with a start. I see that Whero has dozed off.

I feel much, much better! 'Hey-ee, matey,' I say as I shake her awake, 'time to get up and play.'

'Fuck off, Red,' she moans.

I'm insistent, but before I can get anything more out of her, there's a knock at the door. Uh oh, it's Tupou, and I don't want him to see me like this, still all bruised and bashed up from Petera's assault. Better find a place to hide away. After all, a girl has some pride.

Tupou sticks his head around the door. 'Whero?' he asks.

She sits up. 'God,' she tells him, 'I feel as if somebody's done my head in.'

Tupou is still hesitant.

'You gonna come in?' Whero asks. 'And where's Red gone?'

'Red? I dunno.' He mutters something under his breath. Something like, 'Damn you, Dermot.' Then edges into the room and sits on the bed, stroking Whero's hair. 'God,' he shudders, 'I can still remember how awful it was when I came home and found you . . . Did you know I had to call the doctor?'

'You did what?'

'When I came back from the pub,' Tupou explains. 'Dermot stayed on with some friends but I wish he'd been with me as I've never been so scared in my life. I really freaked out when I saw you . . . lying on the floor . . . comatose. I thought you'd OD'd — but I'd seen enough ODs to know it wasn't that — and then I thought you'd had a heart attack or been assaulted or something. I called the doctor and, shit, then I realised that if I called the cops, they might find some of the drugs and stuff in the flat . . . Anyway when the doctor came you called him Petera and you were screaming and yelling your head off . . . but he gave you something and, thank God, you calmed down. Went out like a light.'

'Thank you, Tupou,' Whero says in a little-girl voice.

'Anyway,' Tupou continues, 'the doctor's just rung. He asked if you've signed those papers he left for you.'

'What papers?'

Bugger. From behind the door, I see I've been outed: I hid

those papers so Whero wouldn't find them.

'Does the doctor want to commit me or something?' Whero asks, as if it's a joke.

'No, he thinks he knows what your condition is . . .'

'My con-dition?' The way Whero says it sounds like she's shit scared. I'm scared too. Why the fuck can't people leave us alone?

'He wants you to sign the papers so that he can get your medical records released to him.'

'Thanks,' Whero says, 'but no thanks.'

'No isn't an option,' Tupou says firmly. He seems to be enjoying being masterly. 'Give a dog a bone, Whero . . . I'm trying to give a damn. And are those your pills on the bedside table? Good, there's a glass of water too.'

Tupou is firm. He puts two tablets in the water and gives the glass to Whero. 'Bottoms up. Take all of it down. God, that sounds so sexy! Now show me your tongue. Good girl!' Satisfied, he gets up. 'Right. I'll leave you to get dressed. Dermot wants to see you at Karl Jeffs' recording studio. He and Karl want to run through your songs and choose some for an album. Here's the address. Take the Hammersmith line.'

When Tupou leaves, I sneak back to Whero.

'Some friend you are,' I say. 'You could have pretended to take the pills.'

'I can't stop to argue with you, Red. I'm not going to miss a second chance to redeem myself.' She looks at me tenderly. 'After all, aren't you the one who got pissed off when I walked off the stage?' She takes a serious look at me. 'Listen, you'd better stay here.'

'Are you out of your cotton-picking mind?' I ask. 'You and me, we're a team. I'm your back-up girl. We always do this together.'

'Not today,' she continues. 'I can't have you around looking like Madam Death. I'll take along the backing tape and sing along to that. And I can accompany myself on the guitar.'

'No,' I protest. But the world is going round and around, and Whero leads me firmly to the bed. 'Stay there. Rest.'

She goes to the bathroom. I hear her showering. Shortly afterwards she's back in bra and panties, slipping on her jeans, a sexy top and a leather jacket. To top it off, she puts on six-inch stilettos. 'What d'ya reckon?' she asks.

'You're fuckable,' I reply. I'm panicking. I can feel her slipping away.

'See ya,' she says in a flippant tone.

'No, wait . . .' But it's too late. She's out the door and gone.

14 /

SOMETHING DOWNSTAIRS

A few days after I found Kotare out at Manukau, I managed to convince Mr Chattopadhyay to take me on full-time.

I rang my folks and asked them for a loan to pay Mr Papadopoulos the rent we owed him and sorted that out so that we would still have a roof over our heads. Of course, the main problem after that was who was going to look after you, bub, during the day? I couldn't trust Kotare to do that, and, anyway, despite his problems he was hunting for a new job.

There was a lovely Pacific Island lady who lived just a bit down the street and she said I could leave you with her — she was looking after her grandchildren. Oh, Mrs Fitisimanu adored you, Whero!

I thought everything was coming right, but, one evening, when I got home after work, Mrs Fitisimanu was waiting at the front gate with you wrapped up in blankets in her arms. Some of the other neighbours were around. Something was happening in the flat. All the lights were on and there was a huge racket coming from upstairs. Downstairs, the windows were, as usual, dark.

I placated the neighbours. They were grumpy. 'Tell your husband to stop all this noise. If he keeps this up, we're calling the cops.'

I asked Mrs Fitisimanu to take you back to her place. I walked along the pathway, opened the door and started to go up the stairs.

'Hon?' I called. 'Are you up there?'

When I went into the sitting room it was a shambles. It looked like an explosion had happened and all the furniture had been thrown to the sides of the room. In the middle, walking round and round in circles was Kotare. Round and round. Whimpering. Agitated. His hands were cutting up the air. Then he stood stock still, thinking a moment, before looking through the furniture for two large sound speakers.

'Hon, what are you doing?'

He looked at me, but he didn't really see me. 'This will show them,' he said. He placed the speakers downwards pointing at the floor, and then hooked them up to the hi-fi.

'Who?' I asked again.

'The kids downstairs.' He put a CD into the hi-fi and let rip at full volume. 'I'll show them! I'll give them a piece of my mind.'

I went over to him, managed to get past, but he held me back from switching the hi-fi off. 'Please, Kotare,' I pleaded, 'what about the other neighbours?'

'If those kids are gonna keep their music on all night, then I'm gonna turn up mine.'

'What music?'

'Their music,' he answered. He was having difficulty breathing, the way you do, Whero, when you're stressed out. 'They make fun of me, playing their songs. And when I went down to talk to them, they just laughed in my face. Well, who has the last laugh now, eh?'

I was still wrestling with him. 'You went downstairs? Visited the kids?' I managed to pull the cord from the wall.

'Fuck you, Anahera,' he said, bunching his fists. His eyeballs were bulging out of their sockets. The look of a crazy man was written all over his red, perspiring face. 'Put the fuckin' plug back in.'

'You promised you wouldn't go down there,' I cried. My heart was thudding. Oh, what was happening to my darling?

'Put the music back on!' Kotare roared. 'Can't you hear them? They've put their volume up. We have to fix them, drown them out, fix them good.'

That's when I began to sob. I crumpled to my knees.

'I can hear them even louder now, Anahera. Rose, Thelma, Sambo, Koro and Johnny Mack. They're laughing at me.' And he jumped up and down on the floor. 'Shut the fuck up!' He put the plug back into the socket. The CD fired up again.

I stumbled to the hi-fi, pulled the CD out and threw it to the other side of the room.

'What did ya do that for?' Kotare asked.

'Hon, there are no kids downstairs.'

He tried to take this in. Then, 'They moved out?'

I went up to him and held him tight. 'There's never been anyone down there, hon.'

'Never? But I've spoken to them, I've drunk with them, I've sat in their sitting room.' He thrust me away. 'Bull-shit, Anahera. They're there all right. They've gone all quiet now, gone all fuckin' quiet, playin' possum, but they're there. I'll wake them up. They want to play games? I'll wake the bastards up.'

I grabbed him again. 'Hon, you're tired. We're both tired. Let me make us a kai, eh? Or you can go and get us a feed of fish 'n' chips? And then we'll just clear up the place and have an early night? Eh?'

But I couldn't stop him. He went down the stairs and, next moment, I could hear him smashing the windows of the downstairs flat. 'Wake up, you bastards! I can wait all fuckin' night! You hear me? I got . . . I got all the time in the world.'

At that moment, I heard the police siren. Can't blame the neighbours really. One of them must've called the cops. I heard the commotion as they restrained him.

'What the fuck? Lemme go-o-o-o-o-o-o.'

I heard one of the neighbours saying, 'It's not handcuffs you need. Get a straitjacket. Take him to the loony bin.'

I waited upstairs. Mrs Fitisimanu joined me and gave you to me. I was rocking you in my arms when the cops came upstairs with my darling between them. He was frightened, bewildered, crying.

'What's happening, Anahera? What's happening to me?'

15 /

REVELATION STUFF

I wake up to a huge noise — it's Whero, Dermot and Tupou returned from Karl Jeff's studio. I tiptoe to the door to see Tupou opening a bottle of champagne and pouring into three glasses. And I can hear Whero singing one of her songs:

Come home before the dark of night . . .
Come home before you lose the light . . .

Why the feck didn't you sing it like that when we recorded you?' Dermot teases. I'm so jealous. We always do things together, me and my mate, always.

Time to make my entrance.

But someone pushes through the door and closes it after him. My nemesis. The one and only Petera. 'Now see what you're doing?' I growl at him.

He won't let me pass. His prodding fingers hurt.

'I would die for Whero,' I tell him. 'Leave us alone.'

'Why do you think she called me?' he asks. 'She wants to go back.'

'She never called you!'

'She does it every time she remembers . . . her dad . . . her mother . . . every time she looks in the mirror . . .'

'She doesn't want you, Petera.'

'Then tell her to stop remembering . . . Tell her to stop feeling guilty that she has become a burden, like her father was, to her mother.'

He pushes me again and, whoa, I am falling.

'This is it, Red. It really is time to go.'

16 /

NOT YET THE DARKNESS

I manage to cry out 'Whero!' through the open door of the bedroom. As soon as she sees me fighting with Petera she comes running.

'Dermot!' she cries. 'Help me!' She pushes Petera away. 'Let her go, you bastard!'

And I fall into her arms, I'm really hanging on to her by my fucking fingernails. She collapses with a groan.

'Okay,' Dermot says. 'I gotcha, girl . . . I gotcha . . . I'm here now . . . Nothin' matters any more — just you, babe.'

'Oh, Dermot . . .'

He consoles her. 'D'ya remember the first time we met? Y'played y'music for me — I fell in love with it the moment I heard it, swore I'd be your manager. My God . . . you sounded — looked — feckin' amazin', grit and tears and blood and spit like all the rock divas reborn.'

All the time Dermot's talking to Whero, I can see him scanning her. He's looking for me. And he sees me inside Whero and whips her face close up to his.

'Red's here, isn't she?' he says to Whero, shaking her. 'You're off your pills again, aren'tcha? Did she take them away? Has she been talkin' to you?'

'No, that was Petera.'

Tupou's gone bug-eyed. He swivels around, looking for ghosts.

'Oh, the other one,' Dermot says.

Whero begins to weep. 'Please don't do this to me, Dermot. I've been a good girl, haven't I? Since that time I walked off the stage I've been okay. I . . .'

'Yeah, but as long as you're not takin' your pills, you are still a feckin' liability, you stupid bitch.' Dermot turns to Tupou. 'Start lookin', will ya? The pills must be here somewhere. They're not very far away.'

Tupou begins a frantic search around the bed, drawers and cabinet.

'If you don't tell me where they are,' Dermot continues, 'I'll get the doctors in and tell them everythin'. No need for them to wait for your medical papers from New Zealand. I'll tell them exactly what your mother told me.'

Tupou starts to hunt on the bed, under the pillows and, damn it, he zeroes in on the wastepaper basket where I've hidden the pills.

Whero's shocked. 'My mother told you?'

'Yes,' says Dermot. 'About when it started for you. Around the time you were eight. You were comin' back from the beach and you introduced her to a little girl called Red.'

And then Dermot tells my Whero the truth.

'Your father was in a mental institution in New Zealand. Your mother went to visit him every week until he died. And you, Whero, you're sick too.'

'And Red?'

'She doesn't exist.'

'But I can see her,' Whero wails.

Tupou joins Dermot on the bed, cradling and rocking Whero.

'I know,' Dermot says. 'I know . . .'

He spills some pills into the palm of his left hand and signals to Tupou to get a glass of water.

Whero looks at me. She's struggling with her tears, aching with pain. 'Give me one more night with Red. Please . . . one more night.'

Dermot isn't without sympathy. He places the right dosage of pills beside the glass of water. 'Okay, one more night . . . but take the pills by the morning. Promise me.'

Whero nods. 'Okay.'

'Good, but if you haven't taken the pills, I kid you not, I'll ram them down your feckin' throat myself.'

That night, I lie down beside Whero, *we* lie within each other's warmth. I am her and she is me.

And Whero dreams.

17 /

TIME TO SAY GOODBYE

And now the dawn has come and the time for Whero to kill me, softly, in the glow of morning.

The weak bitch can't do it. Ahh, fuck. So I'm the one who

reaches over for the pills and puts them into the palm of one hand. I give her the glass of water. 'Down the hatch,' I tell her.

But she hesitates.

'Do you want me to show you how to do it?' I ask. 'You've got the balls now, bitch.' I mime myself drinking from the glass as if it was poison and then thrash around in the bed, my eyes crossed and tongue lolling out. By the time I've finished my little performance, Whero is laughing her head off. And then she gives a quick, tearful nod.

'I love you, Red,' she says. 'You're everything that's brave — the guts to chase a dream. I'm gonna miss you so much.'

Before I can even stop her, she's upended the glass and swallowed the pills.

No, no, no.

At the last moment I see Petera. I give him the fingers. At least I have the consolation of knowing that he'll be murdered too. Fuck you, Petera.

With the last of my life I kiss Whero. 'Girlfriend, be happy.'

18 /

AUCKLAND, A GOOD PLACE TO BEGIN FROM

Hey, see that Maori girl getting ready to take the stage? Her name's Whero Davies. Surely you've heard of her? And her hit album, *One More Night*? Everywhere you go on the London tube you see her poster. She's got a new album out now, and it's at the top of the charts.

Those two guys waiting with her? The skinny Pakeha is her manager and the other guy is his partner. They once had dreams of their own but Whero is now their dream.

Did you know Whero's come back to New Zealand to kick off a world tour? Isn't that great for a Kiwi girl to do that? From here she goes to Sydney, Singapore, and they want her to guest-star on *American Idol* in Los Angeles on her way to New York.

Her agent also wants her to go to Dublin. Why Dublin, for goodness sake?

Man oh man, the stadium is filled to capacity. The tickets for Whero's first concert sold out in minutes and there are some people still out there hoping for a cancellation. The prime minister is here, and I saw some of the *Shortland Street* stars coming in. Anybody who's a somebody is here. She's a hometown girl who's made good. Her dad died last year, but her mother has come to the concert. That's her, the woman in the green dress.

Hey, Whero's about to begin. The warm-up act has left the stage. The audience is screaming her name: 'Whero! Whero! Whero!' The strobe lights are going crazy in the sky.

Whero strides into the light, into the huge engulfing roar. And she smiles at everybody and opens her arms to them as she introduces her first song:

'This one's for Red.'

PURITY
OF ICE

1 /

LOOMINGS

Water promises to be to the 21st century what oil was
to the 20th century: the precious commodity that
determines the wealth of nations — *Fortune*

He was asleep, dreaming of a hotel, like a mirage, on a tropical
island in a beautiful azure sea. The sun was shining in a clear
blue sky *change that, move a cloud over the sun to cut down the
glare, ah, that's good* and the wind was coming cool across the
waves.

Where the tropical island came from, he didn't know. Maybe
he'd seen it in some ancient fantasy film shown by Bazza to tease
him, yeah, that's it: *South Pacific.* He frowned, didn't want to think
of Bazza right now *where the hell has that island got to?* Bring it back!

Ah, there it was again. *Most people long for another island . . .*
a voice sang, teasing, haunting. And there he was lying on a
lounger on the beach right in the front of the hotel, where he would
like to be. Only a few other people around. Smiling, smelling rich,
privileged. Tropical breezes were coming off the shore, bending
the palm trees along the golden strand of beach. A special place
where sun met the sea.

Aha! The waiter in the white suit had returned, bringing his mai tai in a tall glass with pure ice on top. 'Just as you ordered, sir.' The drink was so cool, delicious, oh oh oh, hitting the back of his throat and shivering through his dream.

Now bring on the dancing girls.

At his bidding seven dusky maidens came surfing across the lagoon, all dressed in grass skirts and holding leis out to him *sweet leilani, heavenly flower*, beaching prettily in front of the hotel. They waved and began to dance a hula *just for me*? Their hips swayed to a jaunty ukulele as they came up the beach towards him, onto the hotel terrace and, when they arrived, they took him by the hand and led him to the pool.

But what was this? Freeze frame? *Nononono.* Another woman was coming out of the waves. Short spiky red hair. Skinny ass. *Colby, get outta my dream. This ain't your party.*

Too late. He felt a shivering blast of cold. Somebody shook him awake. When he opened his eyes it was Colby all right, holding a cup of coffee. She was dressed in tracksuit and sneakers.

He was back in his bunk, freezing his butt off in the helicopter base deep in the fiords.

Colby rolled her eyes. 'Dreaming of hula girls again, are we?'

'What else am I to do on these cold lonely nights?'

'It's a wonder you're not braindead. Try something warm that moves,' she said.

'What about you?' he asked, reaching up to grab her.

She evaded his arms. 'The last time, you farted in bed.' She handed him the cup. 'Okay Maori boy, I'll give you five minutes to drink your coffee, and then up and at 'em.'

2 /

ALL ASTIR

Drake scratched himself, yawned, put on some music and, sitting up, sipped his coffee. 'All right, all right,' he said finally to the clock on the wall.

He swung his legs over the side of the bed and slipped on T-shirt, pants and running shoes. He wondered if he was losing his touch with Colby, but his confidence was restored when, towelling himself, he looked at his reflection in the mirror.

'Still a good-looking sonofabitch at thirty,' he said to himself. Black curly hair. Caramel complexion and, most interesting, eyes that were different colours: one ice blue, the other light brown. This often caused people to do a double take but, hey, not his fault if mixed Maori and Pakeha ancestry resulted in such an ocular oddity. A good physique — tall and muscular — that he owed to his father, Hemi. And, in homage to his father's warlike ancestors, a body tattoo of a taniwha, head resting on his left pectoral and scaly carapace hugging his back as if protecting him, the tail wrapping around his right calf.

Drake stretched, and made for the door. As always, he did a check of his room before he left. He took great pride in it, and his eyes lingered on a new acquisition in his bookshelf: beside *The Worst Journey in the World*, the copy of *Moby Dick* which he'd bought from an antiquarian bookshop during a recent trip to Wellington. In a world where novels were now available online, it had been aberrant behaviour to buy the book.

But ever since his grandfather had read it to him as a boy he'd loved it.

Call me Ishmael . . . Whenever I find myself growing grim about the mouth; whenever it is a damp, drizzly November in my soul; whenever I find myself involuntarily pausing before coffin warehouses, and bringing up the rear of every funeral I meet . . . then, I account it high time to get to sea as soon as I can.

As for his tidiness, Drake owed that to his mother, Phyllis. She had been a small, no-nonsense woman. *You should always leave your room the way you want to come back to it*, she used to say. And she was right: how great it was to be able to return and wrap the cocoon of familiarity around you and let the day drain away.

They were both dead now, Mum and Dad. They'd been in what qualified as an essential industry: a dairy farm in the Waikato. China had replaced the US as the world's leading economy, with Japan in third place, so most of the milk products went to Asia. Drake had expected to take over the dairy farm but, instead, ten years ago during compulsory military service — he'd chosen the air force and, in particular, helicopter pilot training — he'd gone to the top of his flight class. That had meant a diversion to 'military operations' and immediate assignment to what was known as the Hot Zone — the area straddling the equator — to help with the evacuation of VIP civilians.

Hemi and Phyllis hadn't seemed to mind that, from now on, he wasn't going to be close to home. Thinking that eventually he would return to the farm, they'd waved him goodbye at Auckland airport, saying, 'We'll see you when you get back.' They'd looked like your regular cow cocky and his missus, dressed up in their Sunday best to farewell him. Drake hadn't expected to be away for six years and, when he had returned to New Zealand, he assumed they'd be there to greet him, Mum in her blue jersey top, skirt and sensible low-heeled shoes and Dad in his ill-fitting suit and crumpled hat.

They weren't.

'We can't keep meeting like this,' Colby said when Drake came out of his room. She had already stretched and warmed up. 'Shall we run this morning or do you want to lift weights?'

Drake squinted into the pearl-grey light. 'What's the weather like?'

'Another beautiful day in Costa Del Fiord-ay,' she answered. Actually, though, you could never tell from inside the complex; inside was nice and warm all the time, and sealed against cold and rain.

At that moment, Starbuck, Flask, Samurai Sam, Czar and Hari, who was a Parsee, came loping along the hallway. 'Don't be a pussy, sir!' Starbuck yelled. 'The squadron that runs together . . .'

'Yeah, yeah, yeah,' Drake nodded. 'Okay, Colby,' he said as the boys joined him at the end of the corridor, where they were all getting into cold weather gear, thermals, hoodies, gloves and eye goggles, 'lead on. Let's do the whole circuit.'

'All the way?' Samurai Sam asked, looking suggestively at Colby.

'Why is it,' she responded, 'that you can make anything sound filthy?' She put on a sun visor against the morning glare and punched the exit button. Immediately the temperature dropped to almost freezing point and Samurai Sam was gasping for breath.

'You meant to do that,' Drake said. The vapour from his mouth was already creating crystals around his lips. He led the squad, scrambling out into the cold, running along the circuit track away from the Tangaroa Consortium.

Just another day at the office.

Seniority required that Drake get out in front and set the pace. He would have liked it leisurely except that Colby kept pushing him from behind. Starbuck was abreast, and Drake managed to mutter to him, 'Now I know why harpoonists are mainly women.'

It was a standard joke. 'Yes, sir,' Starbuck answered.

Drake concentrated on the run. When he'd spoken to Starbuck the air had invaded his lungs; ice caves with stalactites and stalagmites forming in their interior — not a pretty thought. He headed clockwise along the cluttered rooftop walkway of the main complex, jogging on the spot while the security guard looked him over. Once the check was done, he surged away from the complex.

Sheathed with sun reflectors, the base hugged the sheer sides of one of the deepest fiords at the bottom of New Zealand's South Island. It wasn't pretty: a Monty Pythonesque assemblage of cumbersome concrete blocks seven storeys high — headquarters, communications, personnel quarters — all connected by a dizzying array of walkways, elevators and lifts and topped off with an odd crown of flimsy communications antennae. Tumbled into the neck of the fiord, the base looked as if some giant's kid — a wannabe engineer with bad balance and no idea of perspective — had made it from Lego, got bored and abandoned it.

By the time the team reached the security road, Drake's breath was coming in huge, tortuous, ragged gasps and his eyes were stinging from the cold. The road took them past the remote defensive armament installations that ringed the fiord. The last attack had been made about two weeks ago, nothing major; since then, all was quiet on the southern front.

Five kilometres later, they came to the massive iron double-locked gateway at the entrance to the fiord, which separated it from the sea. It was closed; they dashed across.

'Let's rest a bit,' Drake ordered the others as he dived into the warmth of the gateway controller's station, startling Silas, the engineer on duty.

'Christ,' Silas said. 'Shut the freezer door, willya?' He quickly switched off the porno download on his tablet before Colby could see it. The office was a mess.

'Okay everyone?' Drake asked. 'Maybe we should have done weights this morning.'

Colby cocked an eye. 'You're not going to be like you are in bed, are you?' she enquired. 'Good at the start but can't go the distance?'

Starbuck and Czar roared with laughter. They appreciated Colby's acidic humour and the way she dished it to the boss.

Drake took it all in good humour. 'I thought you liked the hundred-metre dash.'

From Silas's place, the view was to die for. Within the high walls of the fiord the air was perfectly still — freezing, but still — and the water calm, but outside the gateway, the sea was storming up from the south, mountainous waves chasing squalls before them.

Time to get going again. 'Vengeance is mine,' Drake said. The laughter was cut short by oaths and curses as he led the squad back out into the freezing cold. Their breath jetted and curled in the air.

Approaching the base, they jogged past the submarine pens, still lit from the fleet's late-night operations. One of the subs was in dry dock. So were a couple of water-powered jet boats, used as tugs. On the hills the wind turbines were spinning hard. The ground shook with their rhythmic force; they were like Maori gods doing a haka.

'How're you all doing?' Drake asked everyone as they approached the elevator to the skyline water processing operations centre. Elevator? Well, it was more like an antiquated ski lift, but it did the job.

By now the squad was loping along, happy to be on the home straight, but Samurai Sam was flagging, taking twice as many steps as everyone else. Not that he would admit it.

Starbuck spoke for the group. 'Don't worry about us, sir,' he said. 'We've got your back.'

Suddenly, Drake saw something silver flashing through the air and hovering above him: a remote drone, come to check.

'Drake Haapu,' the drone said, 'you naughty boy. Why didn't you tell me you were going for a lovely walk in the park?'

'Morning, Sally.'

Sally was the communications officer at the base, fifty if she was a day. 'And is that the delectable Colby?' she asked. 'No wonder I've been stood up by you Drake . . . again. Ah well, lover boy, don't forget you and your squadron are due to lift off at 0100 hours. See you later, honey.'

The drone whizzed off, skimming the water of the fiord. By this time, the team had reached the point overlooking the helicopter pad, close to the water.

'Almost there,' Drake said to Samurai Sam. He saw Bazza, the air controller, coming out onto the helipad.

'Queequeeg and the early shift must be coming in,' Flask said.

Colby looked at her watch.

'Running on empty as usual,' she added.

Even as she was speaking, Drake heard the distant familiar thump-thump-*thump* of rotors and over the lock appeared a group of small specks like mosquitoes come to suck blood.

Colby counted: 'One, two, three, four, five . . .'

Drake shaded his eyes against the rising sun. He saw the familiar insignias on the approaching squad of Mad Max pilots — there was no other name for them really — Johnno, Slava, Oscar Bravo, Gayhead and Jenkins, and their outdated helicopters. As each chopper circled, Bazza waved them in. Mechanics were out, pulling one chopper off the helipad and into the hangar so that the next could land.

'Where the hell's Queequeeg?' Colby asked.

'He may have long-range fuel tanks,' Czar calculated, 'but he's cutting it fine.' Chopper pilots liked to dice with death and take the fuel gauge all the way down to the red when they landed. Judging by the earlier arrivals, however, Queequeeg was definitely running on fumes.

'I think I hear him now,' Harry said.

Bazza still had Jenkins on the helipad when, with relief, Drake saw a small spot in the distance: Queequeeg at last, riding *Daedalus*, but trailing a plume of black smoke, weaving a bit, nursing the engine along. A drama began to develop down on the helipad; Bazza had struck trouble stacking Jenkins into the hangar. Drake watched him frantically trying to wave *Daedalus* away to give him some time to sort the problem. But Queequeeg was coming in on a wing and a prayer, couldn't wait for the all-clear, saw a space close by Jenkins that he just might be able to squeeze into, wiggled, began to descend . . . and his motor cut out.

Daedalus dropped like a stricken angel. Bazza threw himself clear, and bang, Queequeeg hit the deck.

'Not the most elegant of landings,' Starbuck said.

'Good enough,' Drake replied.

When Queequeeg stepped out, Bazza was apoplectic, doing a song and dance. Queequeeg laughed at the little man, pointed down the fiord and then, looking up, saw Drake, Colby and the guys on the circuit. Forgetting Bazza, he gave a thumbs-up sign.

'Hunting must be good,' Colby said.

Not long afterwards, the fiord's double-locked gateway opened and two tugs entered, towing between them what looked like a large, uncut sparkling diamond.

3 /

THE CABIN TABLE

Drake hit the showers.

The run was a bonding thing. Showering together, too, allowed the squad to be easy in their skins with each other. The guys were good mates, always looking after each other. Such things mattered, especially when they were on patrol where anything could happen.

Flask, Starbuck and Samurai Sam were horsing around, pressing into Colby as she made for the women's shower room. 'Hey, Colby, save some water and shower with friends,' they laughed.

'You guys are all macho, penis-oriented, honcho shits,' she answered, slipping easily past them and slamming the door.

'We love it when you talk dirty,' Czar and Hari called. 'Wa-hey!'

'Wa-ho!' came the bellowing response.

The infra-red came on, the aged pipes wheezed and coughed, and the fine steam whooshed at them from all angles for the sixty-second max timing reserved for airmen; everyone else at the base got forty-five seconds. And why shouldn't airmen be privileged? After all, they were the reason why the base existed; without them, the Tangaroa Consortium wouldn't have anything to sell to the international community.

As the men dressed, Drake checked them for dings and bangs that they might not have reported to the medic after their last operation. He was worried at Samurai Sam's limp. 'Better tell him to get that checked.' Most of all, he was pleased by the men's good mood as they zipped themselves into their black overalls and leather flying jackets. Sixty seconds of steam was just enough to warm and *sting* them all a little, to remind them of their humanity.

And that they were still alive.

In the cafeteria, Drake picked up a tray and headed for the breakfast counter. Matilda was on duty.

'Bacon and eggs?' Drake asked. Well, the soggy yellow, white and brown concoction looked like it had once had poultry and pig origin.

'Rank has privileges,' she answered. 'Do you want coffee with that? Real beans today, all the way from Chile.'

'Thanks.' He, Starbuck and Flask moved to their usual table near the window where he sipped at the coffee and thought back to his Pacific island dream. Even the notion was problematic.

Did anybody live in Hawaii any more? Ha, with climate change, anywhere within 20 degrees latitude north or south of the equator was too hot to live in now.

'Hey, Matilda,' he called, 'is Hawaii still alive?'

She looked at him, puzzled. 'Yeah, just,' she said.

'The military airbase at Hickam's still operable,' Czar added, 'for long-range military.'

'Thanks.' No locals. *Sweet leilani, heavenly flower?* No palm trees. No golden strand of beach. Certainly no mai tais and dancing hula girls. Definitely in your dreams, mate.

But a memory welled up. His aged Maori grandfather, whom he called Huppapuppa — from childhood days when he couldn't quite say Wharepapa, which was Grandad's name. The old man helped Hemi and Phyllis with the cows. He had his own small bach on the farm — didn't want to take up space in the farmhouse — and as a teenager Drake loved to go over and have a yarn after dinner.

Huppapuppa was a mine of information about the world before the Big Burn. During one rambling talk, his eyes had lit up at the mention of the Hawaiian Islands. 'Oh, Honolulu . . .' he had coughed, catching his breath on his roll your own, 'that was one lulu of a place. Met myself a cute local girl on the beach . . . they had beaches then . . . and we went swimming at Hanauma Bay . . . it was paradise.'

Paradise wasn't a word you could associate with the Tangaroa Consortium, where the sky was always grey, the personnel were ex-military and the wind could freeze your balls off. Here, the locals were just a bunch of flying buccaneers and base personnel, with an equal contingent of women thrown in like Colby, Sally and Matilda, to maintain equity between the sexes. This core contingent was supplemented by mercenaries like Samurai Sam, Starbuck and Flask, all drawing pay from the consortium, one of many in the lucrative business of capturing the best water in the world for the commercial market:

Antarctic 100% Pure, the finest water on the planet.

When Colby came into the cafeteria Drake excused himself and went to join her.

'Fixing her up for a date tonight, boss?' Hari kidded him.

'Don't you mean an*other* date?' Flask added with a wink.

Colby overheard them. When Drake sat down beside her, she was smouldering. 'I'm no trophy,' she warned him. 'You know that, don't you?' Then, abruptly, she said, 'I've been meaning to ask you for ages now, how did you get your name?'

'It's really Francis but after too many punch-ups on the marae I changed it. And Drake went with Francis. My grandfather was really disappointed in me because he had given me boxing lessons and thought I was wimping out.'

Not only did Huppapuppa teach Drake boxing: it was from him that Drake had developed his love of books. And it was from his lips, as they milked the cows one day and the milk spurted, rich and foaming into the cups, that Drake as a teenager had learnt about the opening up of Antarctica to the water trade.

Huppapuppa told him that, with climate change, the ice shelves of Antarctica had begun calving. Huge icebergs broke off, filling the air with a constant crack crack crack as they split away, creating huge waves when they crashed into the sea. The original Antarctic Treaty partners had tried to maintain ownership of the giant bergs when they hit the warmer northern currents, but because they were no longer part of the continental mass, the UN said no. They decreed a Free International Zone (FIZ) that allowed any nation to capture what had become unexpected bounty: the pure, fresh, glacial water of the bergs. Any ice that made its way from the frozen continent could belong to anybody who hoisted a flag on it.

The Maori-owned Tangaroa Consortium dated from the days when the government returned Maori land under the Treaty of Waitangi. They didn't think the fiord would be of use to anyone, let alone have strategic value someday.

Were they ever wrong.

Drake watched as more bergs came up the narrow neck of the fiord, sliding serenely through the still water. Not only had they been towed; forward sails had been attached to them and, belling in the wild wind, had brought them faster to the fiord. However, as soon as they entered the double-locked gateway, the sails immediately fell limp, gathered in by tug personnel. From the gateway, the bergs moved through a carefully controlled system of locks, one opening while the other behind it was closing; the purpose was to progressively diminish the amount of saltwater that might have come through the gateway with the bergs.

The Tangaroa Consortium preferred to harvest tabulars, the colossi of the iceberg world. These floating frozen islands scraped both sky and earth. Below the surface they carried keels a massive two-thirds of their mass, often skidding along the bottom of the fiord. There the natural contours had been deepened and engineered to capture the bergs on automatic rails that took them to melting positions.

And so they advanced, some like aircraft carriers, others like tall white towers. Trussed up and tied, guided by the tugs and mini-subs and pulled forward by underwater winches, they made stately procession up the fiord. Jetskiers whizzed around them checking their progress.

The air resounded with celebratory music — today it was Handel's *The Arrival of the Queen of Sheba* — piped through speakers surrounding the fiord. 'Bloody Bazza.' Drake shook his head admiringly.

The sun came out. All of a sudden the fleet of bergs flashed and sparkled and glowed, radiating shimmering colours: delicate pink, luminous pounamu green, indigo blue, deep mauve.

The bergs filled the morning sky with rainbows.

D rake turned back to Colby. 'And what about your name?' he asked.

She looked at him sharply. 'It's not my real name, of course. In civvy street I had another life and another identity.'

Ah yes, Drake thought, civvy street. History was now marked, not by BC and AD but, rather, BB and AB: Before and After the Big Burn. BB many at the consortium had different names, simpler names, to go with their simpler lives. But AB, orphaned, they had chosen to hide behind new identities, had taken up new names, the more fanciful the better — anything to escape the memories of the world before.

Something must have got into Colby today; she opened up. 'You won't believe it,' she continued, 'but I was living in South Africa at the time. I went to college in New Johannesburg. I met a guy in the air force. He was in navigation but, man oh man, he should have been a Maori like you 'cause he couldn't hold a course even when the stars were out. So I took over and found I was good at it.'

'You married him, didn't you?'

Colby immediately shut down. 'You're getting a bit up close and personal, aren't you?'

In a flurry of noise Queequeg and the pilots who had flown with him on the morning shift entered the cafeteria.

Queequeg began kicking the furniture around. 'I almost ditched out there,' he said. 'We're flying death traps, tin cans with rotors. Can't you talk to the consortium, Drake, and get some real flying machines? Take it up with Kuia? I got into a dogfight out there with the *Red Baron* . . .'

'Gonzalez?' Drake asked, naming their main rival. He and Gonzalez had had a number of major battles as each tried to plant their flag of ownership on a berg, shooting down each other's flags mid-sky with lasers before they could spear the ice.

'Yeah,' Queequeg nodded his head, 'but my engine started smokin' and I had to hightail it out of there with my tail between my legs. Luckily, though, I'd bagged a beauty but I tell ya, if we want to cut it with the competition we gotta have modern choppers and not the second-hand stuff that the consortium buys from Japan.'

Drake had to admit that the base's fleet was pretty dismal. But it was better than most: since the Big Burn, the consortium had purchased anything that flew, from gas-guzzling jet aircraft to planes with, ye Gods, rotors and propellers. Similarly, it had ransacked the world for a suitable fleet of ships and mini-subs and converted them to waterpower, either in its jetted form or as steam.

Welcome to the retro world of the future.

'Who else did you see out there in iceberg alley?' Drake asked. The bergs from Antarctica came up a corridor to the east of the undersea Campbell Plateau, northward past Macquarie Island, squeezing between Auckland Island and Campbell Island and along the east coast of the South Island.

'Hard to say,' said Queequeg. 'Visibility was low, with the cloud cover down to sea level, so we were wave hopping for most of the time. Apart from Gonzalez, the Germans were operating from their carrier fleet, the Chinese off Bounty Island, and the usual assortment of cowboys sniping at the smaller stuff from their bases on Stewart Island.'

Drake realised that Queequeg had hesitated. 'I saw something else out there,' he continued. His eyes glowed and his voice became hushed with awe. 'I saw Moby Dick.'

4 /

THE WHITENESS OF THE WHALE

'There she breaches! There she breaches!' was the cry, as in his immeasurable bravadoes the White Whale tossed himself salmon-like to Heaven. So suddenly seen in the blue plain of the sea, and relieved against the still bluer margin of the sky, the spray that he raised, for the moment, intolerably glittered and glared like a glacier; and stood there gradually fading and fading away from its first sparkling intensity, to the dim mistiness of an advancing shower in a vale.

At Queequeeg's words, Drake was drenched with a fearful sweat. His hand went to his shoulder and the disfiguring scars and thick welts from his long ago encounter with the giant berg.

In those days, new to the squadron, he had scoffed at the existence of such a creation, something that defied all logic. But he understood the impulse to imagine such an entity into the world: it was only to be expected that the airmen would create a myth, not of a great white whale but of an icy counterpart which roamed the Antarctic Ocean, malevolent, dedicated only to the destruction of man.

The legend told of a huge iceberg that had existed since antediluvian times, created in the womb of Antarctica and birthed from a glacier canal to fall, slippery, into the sea. Millions of years later, cruelly sculpted by wind and sea, it had become an unholy nemesis in the shape of a whale.

'Watch yourself, young feller,' Bazza had warned Drake when he laughed at the story. 'Moby Dick can hear you challenging him. He'll be after you now. And if he gets you in his death roll, you're a goner.'

It was not long after this that Drake had his first encounter with Moby Dick. Young Anders Yates had been his harpoonist in those days, a boy with down on his chubby cheeks, eager to prove himself in the company of older men; he liked to call Drake 'Captain'.

One clouded dawn, the base's klaxon began to wail and all the pilots scrambled for their choppers. Rangi, the Tangaroa Consortium's own satellite positioned above Antarctica, had sent pictures back of bergs which it had been monitoring since they broke away from the Ross Shelf. Huge monsters, some more than eighty kilometres long, they had been gradually moving north with the Humboldt Stream. Now, having broken into smaller bergs, a large cluster of them had arrived at the borders of the FIZ.

The squadron leader at the time was Crozier Dalrymple, and Drake had already been assigned an ancient chopper that he immediately dubbed *Pequod*. The wind was blowing hard and squally, and the squadron was already at its maximum fuel range when, suddenly, ahead, were the bergs, dazzling in the sunlight.

Crozier Dalrymple radioed, 'They're the right size, so take your pick, boys.'

They were soon at it, flagging the catch to their hearts' delight.

'Harpoon away!' cried Anders Yates as he sent the standard pennant of ownership whizzing down to the berg and then, with his harpoon, took the shot. Rocket-assisted, the harpoon sizzled through the air and through the berg's skin.

Drake watched the computer as it read out the harpoon's course through the berg. 'Thirty, sixty, ninety . . .' The harpoon zigzagged slightly as it tried to find the berg's gravitational centre, then— there!— on target.

'Got it, Captain!' yelled Anders as he guided the harpoon through the rest of the berg to three hundred and sixty metres. 'We're through,' he confirmed, as he tapped the keyboard and sent horizontal stabilisers snaking along the bottom of the berg.

It was while he was radioing the position to the tugs and mini-subs that Drake spied, in the distance, another iceberg, shining spectral white, boiling up and out of the sea. 'So it's true then,' he whispered. He knew it was the legendary Moby Dick and he cursed himself that he could not unhitch himself and go after it.

Like some ancient artefact, the berg climbed into the sky.

Its shimmering skin had been tattooed, pitted and whorled by aeons of scouring waves and wind. Black or indigo patches on its enormous white bulk indicated cavities that created its unstable buoyancy.

Crozier Dalrymple had not made a catch. 'I've got him,' he radioed.

It all happened so quickly. Moby Dick floating there, seeming benign, and Dalrymple approaching in textbook fashion. And then the berg turned as if casting a backward glance, showing a cyclopean eye. Suddenly it reared above the chopper, tipped and in plunging, grabbed the machine in the downdraft. Then came the death roll, the turning and turning, before Moby Dick took Crozier Dalrymple with it into the depths.

Had he awoken the monster? Was that when the vendetta between them both had begun?

Drake looked at Queequeeg, his mouth dry. 'You saw Moby Dick?'

Queequeeg nodded. 'As God is my witness, aye Sir, I saw the monster. He came up right beneath me. Breaching the surface, he was ready to snatch me out of the air and roll me back down with him to my death in the briny sea below.'

'How did you know it was him?' Drake asked.

'By the single eye and the battering ram of the bastard's icy head,' Queequeeg swore. 'And also by the gigantic profile, the hump of the beast which rose ever upward, endeavouring to buck me into the air. Then, in sounding, he showed me his peculiar yellow underbelly and the cluster of harpoons embedded in his flukes. Oh, it was him all right.'

On Crozier Dalrymple's death, Drake took over the squadron. His age hadn't told against him, or his lack of experience. Kuia, CEO of the consortium, saw in him an utter fearlessness and an ability to lead men. Even more telling, pilots followed him and trusted in him.

Drake, for his part, couldn't wait for his second meeting with the rogue berg. He studied the reports of other pilots who had tried to capture Moby Dick. Some had successfully harpooned the berg, but the cables had been too short or they'd had to wheel away from his implacable rage. Even when he was harpooned and in tow, the death roll could wrap towing tugs and mini-subs in flailing hawser lines and down they would go with him.

Drake's obsession with Moby Dick grew. How could the berg appear and disappear at will? Was it because of that freak buoyancy mass, those chambers which, sometimes filled with air and sometimes with water, enabled the entire berg to tilt, flick at the sky, plunge fathoms deep and stay there? From where, then, did the air come to allow Moby Dick to surface again? And how could he appear in places where he should never have been? How could he get there if he hadn't swum against the tide?

The fact was that anything, even the impossible, could happen in a world where climate change played havoc with the sea. Traditional ocean movements could no longer be counted upon. The Antarctic Ocean had turned into a place driven by solar bursts one moment and icy weather fronts the next. In the early days, confused pods of whales had trapped themselves, circling around and around within the clashing tides. Later, entire fleets of ships found themselves unable to break free of immense tsunami, rushes of waves that drove them into huge whirlpools until they sank with the other detritus of a decaying world.

It was not to be wondered at, therefore, that an iceberg could float, at the whim of sun and wind, along corridors of clashing currents and even against the prevailing tides.

And it was only a matter of time before Drake encountered Moby Dick again.

The sun had been a cartwheel in the sky and the sea was black. But the water was sending frost-smoke across the surface and, as the *Pequod* flew deeper into the mass, all vision was lost.

'Captain?' young Anders Yates asked.

'We can't turn back,' said Drake. Nobody returned to the base empty-handed. Somewhere out there, Rangi had sighted bergs. Somewhere . . .

Vicious hail began to fall, rapping at the windscreen of the chopper. It was in the middle of the hailstorm that Moby Dick chose his moment to attack.

If Drake hadn't been alert he would not have seen the dark mass lurking below the surface of the sea. Only good fortune made him look down and there— there!— was that huge baleful eye staring back at him.

Moby Dick leapt into the sky.

'Hold tight!' Drake cried to Anders Yates as he threw the chopper away from the ascending berg. Sweat beaded his brow as Moby Dick showed an underbelly ghastly with embedded ropes and hawsers, evidence of earlier encounters. 'Take the shot!'

The harpoon zinged through the air, but somehow, while the chopper bucked, Anders Yates was caught in the cable and yanked out of his seat. 'Oh Captain, my captain!' he screamed.

All Drake could do was to watch, helpless, as the young boy disappeared into the hail.

In that same moment, a contrary current created a perilous downdraught. The *Pequod* slid against one of Moby Dick's icy sides and would have plunged into the sea had not the chopper, with a sudden loud explosion of metal and glass, lodged on a jutting fluke, which punctured it — and that was when Drake's shoulder had been scored. Screaming with shock and fear, he managed to lever the helicopter off the fin before Moby Dick could take him in the death roll. He lifted the chopper into a shuddering climb and away.

Next time, e hoa.

Liftoff at 0100; two hours away.

Rather than go back to his room, Drake decided to take the elevator to the water processing operations centre on the skyline. No sooner had he pressed the button than the old lift began to shake, rattle and roll.

'Welcome to Lubjanka by the Sea,' he muttered to himself as he held on for dear life. This was more like some deteriorating base on the Gulag Peninsula than a supposedly high-tech operation in New Zealand.

Kuia, otherwise known as Boss Lady, was in the main operations room, wearing dark glasses and looking down at the fiord, now crowded with icebergs, glowing in the southern light. 'Kia ora, Francis,' she said, greeting him by his real name.

Whenever Drake was with Kuia, he felt an incredible sense of peace. 'Kia ora,' he returned. Kuia was his substitute Huppapuppa — maybe his Huppamama.

'You be careful out there today,' she warned. 'The weather looks as if it's closing in.' Above, the sky was heavy and grey with boiling clouds; within the fiord, everything was still.

For a while, Drake and Kuia watched in silence as, below, the crews of the tugs and mini-subs — the consortium's honcho group of young thrill-seeking wave surfers, hang gliders, bungy jumpers and kamikaze scuba divers — continued disengaging the last tow lines of kites and sails from the bergs. Everybody at the base affectionately called them the Yahoos, this being their favourite word. Danger was their desire, as they winged their ways over the bergs checking out the cables, skimmed around them like butterflies to ensure trim, or even dived beneath them to secure them even further from rolling.

The guys are complaining about the helicopters,' Drake said.

'That doesn't surprise me,' Kuia sighed. 'I saw Queequeeg almost crash on the helipad. Okay, I'll put in another requisition order, but it's hard enough getting black market fuel these days to keep you all flying, let alone purchase modern air support.'

She turned to Ralph, the chief technician. 'Looks like the Yahoos have finished their job.'

'On with the show?' asked Ralph.

'Yes.' Kuia nodded.

'Goody,' said Ralph as he turned to the comms system: 'Clear the processing area.' The Yahoos scattered like flies.

Ralph started to do a dance around the mainframe, whizzing from one control panel to the next. Immediately, the whole operations centre began to jiggle and jump. 'Better hold on to something,' Kuia said. 'And here, you might need this.' She gave Drake a sun visor.

'Come on, baby,' Ralph said to the computer. 'Give me more power to the grid.'

Drake heard the huge, protesting whine of turbines as the

platforms on which the icebergs were resting ascended from the waters of the fiord. Each platform was lined with siphons leading to reservoirs deep within the surrounding hills.

Next moment huge solar reflectors, designed to concentrate every beam of available light like a row of silver plates, slid up from all sides of the fiord. Ralph manoeuvred them so that their power was focused onto the icebergs at rest. 'I need more, baby,' he yelled to his turbines.

He jabbed the button to increase the power from the wind farm. Christ, thought Drake, as the rotors went into overdrive and things started to shake and quake around him.

'Let there be light!' Ralph screamed above the din.

With a sudden, bright flare the mirrors sparked into action, solenoid panels shaking. The landscape dissolved into whiteness as the melting began.

And Drake remembered a day when he was helping Hemi and Phyllis to take the cows back to their underground silos and his grandfather was with them.

Huppapuppa looked up in the sky. 'That storm we've been warned about, it's coming.' The herd, sensing the oncoming danger, set up a loud bellowing and lowing. They couldn't wait to get safely inside. Drake was closing the gates when there was a blinding flare, followed by a withdrawal of air, as if it was being sucked up. The birds, what few there were, were circling madly, trying to find a way, it seemed, away from and out of the sky. Some of them managed to flutter into the silo before it was sealed.

'That came on fast,' Huppapuppa said. 'Are you all okay?' He had Drake's face in his hands, looking into the boy's eyes to see if his retinas had been burnt. 'Better take the boy home,' he said to

Hemi and Phyllis, 'and batten down the hatches.'

They'd made their way back to the farmhouse, and by the time they arrived, the temperature had already climbed 20 degrees. Quickly, they went into the underground shelter.

'Thank God,' Huppapuppa said, 'we still live in New Zealand, and in the world's good lung.'

'What do you mean?' Drake asked him.

'Well, New Zealand, Antarctica, Australia and the Pacific, we're in the part of the world that's still okay after the Big Burn. The rest of the world, that's the bad lung,' he said, as the extraordinary heat storm burst around them. 'We should be thankful we don't live there because they get these storms all the time.'

Huppapuppa had explained that for most of the world's peoples, global warming was a death sentence, bringing flood and drought, crop failure and mass starvation. 'At first world governments tried to save everyone, but as more and more people needed food, and there were more cataclysmic natural disasters, it all became too much. By the middle of the millennium, it was too late. Continuing greenhouse gas emissions completely destroyed the ozone layer and, without it, solar destruction began. One year After the Burn, wars began in India, the Eastern Archipelago and Central America. But those who survived concentrated on their own survival, and you couldn't blame them. Let's face it, it was easier now that most of the poor had been incinerated. And water became the new oil, especially the top grade stuff from Antarctica, which only the very rich could afford.'

Icebergs: the pure, crystalline essence, a million years in the making.

The purity of ice.

5 /

THE SPIRIT SPOUT

Suddenly the klaxons started to wail.

At first, Drake thought the fiord was under attack. The industry was so lucrative that rival consortiums were not above warring with each other — on land or sea. Just three months ago, an unknown party had tried an air strike on the consortium's operation; and two weeks ago security forces had been under fire from snipers coming overland. Each ocean operation required armed protection too: all vessels of the fleet — choppers included — were armed. That didn't completely stop the poachers, who weren't averse to attempting to snipe at a berg while it was under tow or trying to unhook it from the tow and claim it for themselves. With so much money riding on a berg, an easy capture was preferable to the difficult task of hooking one yourself. Some of the most desperate battles occurred underwater, as rivals tried to 'skin' the berg, puncturing its amniotic sac and siphoning it from below.

No, the klaxon was for something else. 'I'd better see what the trouble is,' Drake said to Kuia.

She restrained him for a moment. 'Be careful out there, e hoa,' she said. 'I've had a bad feeling all day.'

He winked. 'You know me, the least bit of trouble and I'm coming straight home to Mama.'

As he was descending in the elevator he saw a remote drone

whiz up to him. It was Sally again, scolding him. 'So there you are, Drake, you naughty boy! Where have you been?'

'Talking to Kuia,' Drake answered. 'What's up?'

'Ah well,' Sally sighed, 'stood up by yet another woman.' Then her voice became businesslike. 'All pilots are to report to the helipad. You're to lift off as soon as you can.'

No sooner had Drake arrived at the helipad than Bazza was onto him. 'Rangi has revealed that there's an almighty storm coming out of nowhere. It could last for days. We want the entire squadron up and at 'em, flagging what bergs are out there before the storm hits and closes us down. Bring them home. It's going to be a free-for-all as rival companies are scrambling too.'

'Round-up time,' Drake told everyone.

'Wa-hey,' Drake's men chorused in the traditional bonding cry.

'Wa-ho,' Queequeeg's men responded.

Kelly, their service mechanic, had already got the *Pequod* warmed up and waiting for them. She was relishing her ten per cent cut of whatever Drake and Colby made from their catch.

Drake was buckling up and doing a systems check when Bazza rushed up to him.

'I forgot to tell you,' he coughed, 'Rangi has shown up an anomaly. A ghost image. One minute there, in the middle of the calving, next minute gone.'

A ghost image? Drake's mouth dried.

Bazza paused, then spoke softly. 'It could be Moby Dick.'

Drake's heart was pumping with dread.

Next time, e hoa.

rake's squadron was first off the helipad. He lifted the *Pequod* and circled the fiord. Behind him, all five rattling rust buckets made it: Starbuck, Flask, Samurai Sam, Czar and Hari were chasing after him. Drake waited for Queequeg in *Daedalus* to get his squadron into the air: still puffing a black plume of smoke, Queequeg led Johnno, Slava, Oscar Bravo, Gayhead and Jenkins along the fiord and over the gates. Silas was waving: Good hunting.

Drake sent a quick prayer to whichever gods were listening, asking that no one should plunge into the deep. And then, 'Let's go,' he called through his com. Out of the fiord the *Pequod* roared, the two squadrons following him and, immediately, they were battling wild, conflicting winds. 'Time to climb,' he said to Colby, adjusting the rotors.

The *Pequod* leant into the wind, Drake and Colby like two people sheltering behind an umbrella as they pushed into the squall. For a long while the chopper had a grim time of it but, miraculously, it didn't break apart. And, checking behind him, Drake saw the rest of the choppers playing follow the leader and, thank God, Queequeg had managed to shut down his smoke trail.

'Hey, Drake,' Colby said, when the worst was over, 'how long have we known each other?'

'Almost two years now,' Drake answered, calculating from the first time they'd slept together. Actually, he'd slept with most of the women at the base. Everyone knew the score and tried not to get attached. They were all fuck buddies. And Colby had no illusions.

Eyes fixed firmly ahead, Colby took a deep breath. 'You asked me earlier if I was married . . . Yes, his name was Jake and, after South Africa, he was called to China to do relief work with the poor. Well, you know what that job's like: shepherding people from one shadow spot in the mountains to the next, from one cavern community to another, before the owners throw you out. And one day, he had around five hundred refugees in his convoy and they stayed out too long . . . and, well, a sun storm hit them . . . and they . . .'

'Colby, you don't have to . . .' Drake tried to give her comfort. Fifteen minutes out in one of those storms was all it took, and all that was left would be black bones melted together.

'I don't need your sympathy, you fuck,' Colby said. She was as closed down inside as he was.

He tried again. 'We all left somebody behind.' Everyone in the squadron had lost someone they'd loved. Maybe that was why they'd applied for one of the most dangerous jobs on earth. They had nothing to lose and nobody would grieve over them.

Bad choice of words. 'Jake wasn't just somebody, he was my life.' She sighed and gave him a forgiving glance. 'I know you always dream of dancing girls,' she said. 'Or is it electric sheep? But . . .'

Suddenly she unclipped her chair belt, leant over and pulled his face around to hers and kissed him. Warmly. Tightly. 'I'm here. I'm real. I've always wanted to do that.' Then she buckled herself in again.

Drake regained his composure. 'What do you dream about?' he asked after a while.

It was as if the kiss had never happened. 'One of these days, I'd like to take a bath. I'd fill it to the brim with cool water. I'd sit in it. And then I'd pull the plug and let that water drain clear away.'

'Room for a friend?'

'Answer me one question. You fart in bed, right? What about in water?'

'Well . . .'

'Thanks for the offer, but I think I'll pass.'

Drake was about to protest, but he saw that Colby had flipped into work mode. 'We've entered the FIZ,' she said.

Small talk was over. 'Okay, radio the rest of the squadron to get ready, and ask Queequeeg if he's okay and to keep his guys in formation. I don't want to lose anybody.' The Southern Ocean was one of the most inhospitable and windswept areas of ocean on the planet; a cyclone wind or water spout could come out of nowhere and take a chopper down. On top of which other companies sometimes liked to get into a dogfight; there was safety in numbers.

'We're right on your tail, boss,' the squadron responded. And Queequeeg came through the headset. 'So are we, and *Daedalus* has still got his wings.'

Relieved, Drake made a visual check. Starbuck and Flask had joined Samurai Sam, Harry and Czar on port. Queequeeg and his guys came up on starboard. With Drake leading, they made a perfect V.

'What about the subs and the tugs?' Drake asked Colby.

'They've just left base and hope to cross the FIZ with an estimated time of arrival in two hours,' she answered. 'They'll await our word that we've planted our flags on whatever we find. Once we've done that and radioed location, they'll be on their way to grapple and take the tow. No doubt Gonzalez will be out there again to complicate matters for us.'

It was a messy business but it got the adrenalin going.

Very soon the grey waves below were dotted with icebergs. Choppers from rival companies were already feasting. Over the headphones was the excited chatter of other companies as they staked their claims. The Chileans had homed in and now the Chinese and Russians were coming. Gonzalez, the pirate, was maintaining radio silence so that nobody would know where he was until, like an eagle, he would drop down from the sky and snatch his prey away before others had time to claim it.

'We'll leave those for the hungry,' Drake said.

The floes on the outer perimeter were always the small ones, eroded away by the waves. The larger bergs of more ancient pedigree were further in. It was just a matter of holding on and finding them.

'Let's go for bigger fish,' Drake radioed the squadron as he peeled the helicopter away. 'Frankly, I've never liked crowds.'

An hour later, and Drake was still not satisfied.

'We'll be approaching our PSR in forty-five minutes,' Colby warned him.

Drake nodded: the point of safe return. The thought never worried him: all choppers worked at the extreme range of their fuel capacities, trying to go farthest out on the assumption that the biggest bastards were just over the next wave, and praying like hell that there was something extra in the tank that would get them back. 'Let's live a little dangerously,' he said, acting nonchalant about it. 'You're not going to get pussy on me, are you?'

'Why aren't I surprised?' said Colby. 'As to your second question, woof.'

Drake radioed the men. 'See those clouds ahead? I reckon our quarry's on the other side, don't you?'

When he reached the cloudbank, Drake pushed *Pequod* up and over.

The aurora came rushing up and out of nowhere, fogbows and clouds of iridescence. Weaving through it was Hine Nui Te Po, the Great Goddess of the Underworld, in a waka of spinning water spouts. 'Welcome to Te Kore, The Void,' the goddess sang, 'haere mai.'

In this place you could imagine a graveyard of ghostly ships, like the *Flying Dutchman* or the *Marie Celeste*. Within this realm lived the mighty kraken, the fabled giant squid, ready to pull the chopper down with its tentacles. Sirens sang men to their death.

Drake shivered. If hell ever froze over, this is what it would look like: a phantasmagoric place of clashing tides, steaming mist and white-tipped waves like a malevolent host on the march, herding all human souls down through the jagged rocks and icy whirlpools into the underworld. He wanted to curl into a foetal position, hugging himself against this place where the darkness was shining and the hands of loved ones were reaching up, pleading with him to save them.

Oh Huppapuppa!

I remember the day you died. I was a teenage boy when you had a heart attack. I found you in the cow yard, amid shit and cow piss, the cows all milling around, mooing frantically; they knew you were going. I yelled, 'Mum! Dad! Something's happening to Granddad!' And when Hemi came, he went down on his knees and cradled your head and moaned, 'No, Dad, no.' You tried to smile, 'At least, son, the sun hasn't burnt me up. I'd have hated to go like that.' And Dad yelled at me, 'Get the cows outta the yard, Francis, for Chrissake, and bring some water so I can clean Dad up.' He was rocking you, wouldn't let you go, and you answered, 'No, son, I'm used to cow shit.'

Then you looked at me. 'The world's not supposed to end like this. I'm sorry, mokopuna.'

They'd all died: Huppapuppa, Hemi, Phyllis, girlfriends, friends. And yes, like Colby, like everyone on the base, even he had left someone behind. Actually, two people: his wife, Georgina, and their baby girl, Mona.

What better place to remember them than here, where souls were screaming and singing waiata tangi, here amid the grinding and crunching of ice, the whistling of winds? The fifth anniversary since . . . the temperature suddenly escalated and the solar deflectors failed in Los Angeles. Drake was stationed there with his family — gorgeous Georgina and happy Mona — and when the order came to evacuate, he was on one of the chopper teams pulling people out and ferrying them to ships, waiting off Santa Monica. Georgina and Mona were on the extraction list.

On the last day they were working against the clock and, as usual, company personnel came last. Whenever he landed to board the next lot of VIPs, Drake kept seeing Georgina with Mona in her arms, waiting in line at Los Angeles airport . . . or what was left of it. The entire city was on fire, the smoke billowing high, and the heat was unbearable. But there was still time before the gauge tipped into the red.

'Soon, darlings,' he would shout, 'soon it will be your turn!' But every time he went back they hadn't been picked up by some other team; they were still in line, waiting.

'Francis!' Georgina cried, 'I'm getting scared, honey.'

He hugged her. 'If you're still here the next time I'm back, damn it, I'm taking you out of here.' He eyeballed the dispatcher, 'Fuck you. Put them on priority.'

But there never was another trip.

A sudden solar flare, blinding, burning, and that was it. The operation evacuation was closed down.

nd Drake began to weep.

'No, no, no . . .' he told himself *don't cry, because you know what will happen, it's always like an invocation, they'll hear you, don't.*

It was too late. Memories shimmered like mirages against the mirror of the sea. *Francis? Is that you, darling? Have you come again?*

Although they were charred beyond recognition, Drake would have recognised them anywhere — Georgina and Mona, a hideous angel with a charred cherub in her arms. With a banshee cry of gladness they came on their drifting wings of flame, ashes in their wake. They flew quickly up towards the chopper, there to knock on the glass, *Let us in, let us in, oh, let us in,* and to gaze through at him, their eyes already burnt from their sockets.

We're still waiting, Francis. And then they fell away from him, down, down into the roaring, extinguishing sea.

Drake dried his eyes. He knew he would see them again . . . and again. They were his cross. His heart was scarred with recriminations.

Yes, by his tears he would bid them appear again.

6 /

THE CHASE

ingo,' Colby said.

Beyond the fogbows and hazy mist the sky brightened, the sun spreading pools of light across the gleaming sea. And below, waiting, was an expanse of dense floes: tabulars, blockies, domes, wedges, pinnacles with one or more statuesque peaks and dry docks with two or more such peaks separated by water-filled channels. They were all extraordinary creations: ice Everests whose glassy surfaces created dangerous reflections that could fool a pilot into thinking he was navigating open sky. Many pilots, not having a spotter as alert as Colby, had crashed into the ice walls of a floating berg.

With relief, Drake saw his squadron, and Queequeeg's, bursting behind him from the cloud cover. 'Okay, fellas,' he radioed, 'we've found our happy hunting ground. Start tagging. Colby? Radio the tugs and submarines the coordinates.' He looked at his watch. 'Thirty minutes max, boys, and then let's head for home. I don't want anybody dropping into the sea.'

The two squadrons began their work, peeling off left and right ... but Drake drove *Pequod* further, and out of sight. 'Sir?' Colby asked. 'We've reached our maximum parameters.' She had a puzzled look in her eyes.

'I hear you,' Drake answered. 'Okay.' Reason took over. With a sense of disappointment, he banked the chopper into a turn but, *wait, what the hell was that?* The sea was boiling on the horizon. 'There she blows . . .' he whispered, *I knew you were out here, Moby Dick*. From the depths began to climb an unholy white colossus, which stared at Drake and then slipped back into the sea.

One moment there. Next minute gone. But Colby had done her job and managed to calculate the mass of the majestic, malevolent ice leviathan. 'You bastard, Drake, why didn't you tell me you were after him? Well, he's too big. We won't be able to take him in by ourselves unless we cut him down to size.'

'No way will I do that,' said Drake. 'How much help do we need to bring him in?'

'Maybe two more choppers to help stabilise.'

The seconds were passing. 'Radio our find to the others,' Drake said.

'No can do.' Bazza had been eavesdropping; his voice came over the earphones from the base. 'You're already too far out and you should be heading for home . . . Jesus . . . are you crazy? Live to fight another day.'

'I can't let him go,' Drake said. 'There might not be another day. I'd rather die out here with him.'

Colby looked at Drake, startled. There was a pause, a crackle and then Bazza's voice again. 'Don't be blackmailing me now. You do that and no more porn or ancient movies. Are you sure it's Moby Dick?'

Colby spoke. 'He's serious, and so am I. And look, here's something that might persuade you: a readout of the berg's mass. Moby Dick's almost a hundred per cent pure! Shit, if we bring this one in, Kuia can buy some better planes and we can all shout ourselves a holiday too. I'm sending the readings to you for confirmation, now.'

They were hovering over the sea, waiting for Bazza's reply.

'Drake!' Colby screamed. Something came growling from beneath the chopper. The sea parted like jaws and vomited from its mouth something huge, something sinister that sang with supernatural force. 'Bank left!' Colby yelled.

And there was Moby Dick, looking in, eyeball to fucking eyeball. 'Yes, I see you,' Drake whispered. This must have been how Ahab had witnessed the whale: *the cyclopean eye, the monstrous frame in all its awful asymmetry.*

The helicopter shuddered, its skiffs scuffing the berg's mountainous tip as Moby Dick tried to lurch into it and throw it out of the sky. The rotors were working hard, creating snowstorms from the drifts streaming off the berg. Suddenly, one of the rotors nicked Moby Dick, slashing that hideous eye, and he roared his deafening and arrogant displeasure at the sky.

'Oh, no you don't,' Drake muttered, not sure where up was, or down until, with a final shudder, he righted the chopper and they gained the horizon.

The berg was already plunging back to the sea, its cliff faces pouring with water. With its accustomed death roll, it corkscrewed into the depths and disappeared from the radar. 'Where's he gone?' Colby asked.

'He'll be back,' Drake replied as he set the helicopter to hover. 'Get the harpoon ready.'

Minutes passed. The sea boiled again and, this time Moby Dick cracked through a sheet of thin ice. *Come and get me, e hoa.*

'Looks like you'll be able to afford that bath of yours,' said Drake to Colby.

Moby Dick leapt with majestic insolence. Oh, he was so beautiful, a kaleidoscope of colours flashing across his skin. There was something wilful and purposeful in the way he turned to the approaching chopper, almost as if he'd been waiting all his life for this day.

'Aye, breach your last to the sun, Moby Dick!' cried Ahab,
'thy hour and thy harpoon are at hand! — Down! down all
of ye, but one man at the fore. The boats! — stand by!'

The airwaves crackled again, but it wasn't Bazza.

'I'm on my way.' It was Queequeeg; he'd been listening in. 'Come on, Bazza, this is Moby Dick, for Chrissake! And Drake's got the motherfucker.'

Bazza's voice came back. 'I need to remind you all of the safety regulations . . . And this is a suicide mission, Squadron leader Haapu . . .'

'Fuck the regulations,' Queequeeg said.

Then, 'Uh oh,' Bazza said, 'Rangi shows a raider coming in on you.'

Colby saw the rival chopper: 'Enemy coming in at three o'clock.'

It was Gonzalez. Even though Queequeeg hadn't arrived, she turned to Drake.

'Post our flag!' she screamed. 'Now!'

Drake's thumb was already on the trigger. The flag, boosted by rockets, sped towards Moby Dick. At the same time, Drake saw Gonzalez let loose with an interceptor. It made contact and the flag was diverted, exploding in the air. 'Flag number two on its way,' Drake shouted, gritting his teeth. From the corner of his eye he saw that Gonzalez had also unleashed a pennant. Which one would claim Moby Dick first?

'We beat the bastard!' Colby yelled as she saw the small puff of snow. At the impact, Moby Dick leapt sideways, revealing the extraordinary chambers shimmering, transforming themselves, creating instability within. But Colby was readying the harpoon. 'Give me a clear shot.'

Gonzalez was dancing around the chopper, making it difficult for her. Colby found a window and pressed the firing button. 'Come on,' she muttered to herself.

The harpoon rocketed away, just missing Gonzalez' landing gear, and a neat little puncture opening appeared on the surface of the berg. 'We're through the skin.' Was that Moby Dick roaring his anger? Colby was too busy steering the harpoon through the berg.

Caught in an updrift of air, Drake was wrestling with the controls.

'Are we locked on?' Drake asked. 'Gonzalez isn't going to give up until we are. Moby Dick is still up for grabs.' And Moby Dick flicked his tail. It was almost black, with stripes of embedded moraine debris, and it trailed the cables of ancient harpoons. The tail's slipstream tumbled the *Pequod* like a toy.

Gonzalez' mocking voice came over the intercom. 'Drown, you fucker! Hey, Drake, gringo, I'm right behind you and if you don't make it, I'm coming up your ass. Give me a shot too?'

'Fuck off, Gonzalez.'

'Oh, but I want to squeeze into him. Open up, Moby baby.' And then Gonzalez screamed at Drake: 'Give him to me! I want to pay him back for my leg.' Drake wasn't the only one with a grudge against the berg.

'No way!' Colby's shout turned to triumph: the harpoon had found the gravitational centre. In a trice it was blasting a shaft and burrowing down. 'What the hell is that?' On her screen, halfway down, Colby saw a mass, an inconsistency. Something dark, like an insect trapped in glass. 'Drake? Do you know what it is?'

'Could be some rock and fossil material embedded millions of years ago. Forget it. Keep an eye on the progress of our harpoon.'

Nodding, Colby began to concentrate on the digital readout and calling out the depth that the harpoon was reaching. 'We're now at thirty, sixty, ninety . . .' She punched some coordinates into the computer, checking the cable left on the drum. 'One fifty, one eighty . . .' There was alarm in her voice. 'Drake, we're at three hundred! Three thirty-five, three sixty-five, three ninety-five . . . and we're only a third of the way through.'

Gonzalez purred over the intercom, 'Lucky me to have more cable than you, gringo. Hasta la vista, baby.'

Drake knew what this meant. The *Pequod* would be pulled down with the cable to crash onto the berg. Or into it.

'We might just make it,' Colby screamed. 'Brace! Here comes the hit.'

On the screen, Drake saw the harpoon break through into the sea below the berg. The spear point flexed, and eight prongs were released, snaking themselves across the bottom of the berg, attaching themselves with small popping explosions, attempting to find the best pattern to maintain the equilibrium.

A sudden snap. 'We're attached,' said Colby.

The hawser took up the slack. Drake felt the whiplash shuddering back up to the helicopter. He battled to keep the chopper airborne as it yawed and flicked through the sky.

Thrashing with rage, Moby Dick was creating mountainous waves around him. *I will never be taken. Never.* Meanwhile, Gonzalez was still hovering. Drake had a sudden chilling thought. 'You wouldn't shoot us down, would you, Gonzalez?'

'All's fair in love and war,' Gonzalez answered. 'And nobody's looking. But, oh fuck . . . this time we gotta bring Moby Dick in, eh amigo?'

'I'm not sharing him,' Drake warned.

'Okay, but I give you just a leetle help?'

Just in time, Queequeeg came in, flying low. The berg was shimmering, changing colour, filling its chambers with water and ready to plunge downward. Queequeeg whizzed past Gonzalez and fired his own harpoon. And now came Starbuck, firing one harpoon after another.

The three choppers pulled. Heaved Moby Dick back from the depths where he was sounding. Back to the surface, back.

Time and time again Moby Dick tried to sound.

Time and time again, Drake, Queequeg and Starbuck pulled him to the surface, the engines of the choppers whining into overload. They had the berg triangulated, keeping the centre of gravity so that no matter how hard he tried to shift the weight within his massive chambers, they corrected.

'Don't let him go,' Drake yelled as he watched Queequeg and Starbuck being whiplashed across the sky as if they were holding on to the end of two ropes.

And when Moby Dick finally submitted, shuddering, riding the tumultuous sea, Drake hovered cautiously. Was that it?

'We're down to fumes,' Colby said.

To come all this way — and crash into the sea? 'Not me,' Gonzalez called. 'Colby, I hate you, you beetch, but I fuck you next time. Go right up your ass with my big Argentine cock and come out your mouth.'

'I love it when you talk dirty, Gonzalez.' Drake grinned. 'Adios, amigo.' There was only one thing to do. 'We're landing on the berg,' Drake ordered. 'Queequeg and Starbuck, join me, and that's an order.'

'What happens if Moby Dick's still got some life in him? Does a death roll?'

'Then land in the sea if you want to,' Drake said. With a shudder, he brought the *Pequod* down. Queequeg and Starbuck alighted close by.

'I'm not getting out,' said Colby. 'I don't trust this berg.'

'Well, if that's the case, I'll stay inside where it's just you and me, and we're nice and comfy, and one thing could lead to another, and it's a long, long way to Tipperary . . .'

'I'm bailing,' Colby said. Together they walked over to the other pilots and harpooners.

'Are we good or are we good!' Queequeeg laughed. He and Starbuck were waltzing together on Moby Dick's back.

Drake was smiling. 'Colby? Radio Bazza. Where the hell are those tugs and mini-subs?'

He should have been ecstatic, but he had a cold feeling up and down his spine.

'This was too easy,' he muttered. 'Way too easy.'

It's not over yet, e hoa.

7 /

EPILOGUE

Even before they reached the fiord, Drake knew that the whole base had turned out to watch. The lights were blazing in the dusk, welcoming them home. This time, Bazza put on Handel's *Messiah*.

Halleluiah! Halleluiah! King of kings!
Lord of lords! Halleluiah!

Tugs and mini-subs came out to greet them, drones were looping the loop and Ralph in the operations centre had raised the solar reflectors to dance on the encircling hills. It was party time for the Yahoos: bungy jumpers and sky gliders trailed colourful smoke in celebration. Bazza, of course, had to save face: 'Squadron Leader Haapu, report to the main office immediately.' When Drake did, Bazza screamed, hopped and yelled and would have continued but for the arrival of Kuia. 'I've broken out the best champagne for you, e hoa,' she said

Truly, the arrival of Moby Dick dwarfed all others that had preceded him. He was enormous, scraping the hell out of the bottom of the fiord and reaching halfway up to the hills, a huge beast come to be moored.

Drake and Colby went up to the water processing operations centre to look at Moby Dick. No matter that his contours were softening — the huge iceberg was still a magnificent sight.

'We knocked the bastard off,' Drake said, holding her close.

Colby looked at him. 'I do believe you're crying.'

Drake shook his head. He still had that nagging feeling. 'I didn't think it would be so easy.'

'Easy?' Colby chuckled. 'The berg fought us all the way.'

'It was supposed to be harder.' Trying to assuage his doubts, he pulled Colby to him and kissed her.

'To the victor the spoils?' she mocked.

'Something like that. Your place or mine?'

Colby considered the invitation, wavered, then screwed up her face. 'I've seen your place but . . . okay.'

They made love, efficiently, careful not to get too sentimental about it. Afterwards, they lay in each other's arms. 'There's a question I've been meaning to ask you,' Drake began. 'How did you know about the hula girls?'

'You sing in your sleep,' she answered, teasing him. 'Sweet leilani, heavenly flower . . .'

'Yeah, well,' Drake countered, 'you whistle through the gap in your teeth.'

'Are you trying to pick a fight, Maori boy? And I was thinking that this was going to be the beginning of an interesting relationship.'

'Perhaps. Hey, I'm not objecting. Doesn't a gap between the teeth mean a lascivious nature?'

She laughed, tossing her head. 'Lascivious? Now that's a long word for a hori helicopter honcho.'

He pretended wounded pride. 'You're not the only one who went to college.' He motioned to his bookshelf.

She picked up *Moby Dick*. 'Looks like you've read it,' she said doubtfully, 'but one book does not a bright boy make. And seeing as we're complimenting each other, did you realise you have one blue eye and one brown eye?'

'It comes in handy for showing my Maori side, and then' — he turned — 'my Pakeha side. So which side do you like?'

'Don't tempt me.'

What are you going to do with your money?' Drake asked. They were snuggled into each other after making love again. 'Are you still planning to buy that bathtub?'

'And bathe in asses' milk? Sure am.' Colby pursed her lips and began to intone, from Shakespeare's *Antony and Cleopatra*, 'The

barge she sat in, like a burnished throne burn'd on the water . . .'
She gave him a look, then kissed him. Of course they had kissed
before, the kind of teeth-grinding, lip-mashing, tongue-searching
kisses that came when they were climaxing. But this one was
tender, sweet, gentle.

'What did you do that for?' he asked.

'I was wondering if you'd like it.' She kissed him again. 'Feel
anything?'

He tried to change the subject. 'So what's in your future, Colby?'

She knew he didn't want to talk serious, so went with him.
'I'll do this for a couple more years. If I'm lucky, I've a hankering to
settle down with the right man and make a baby.' She gave him a
quick glance. 'Correction, seeing as you know my history. Another
man.'

Drake tried to make it easy on her. 'Second time lucky?' He
knew that she was thinking what he was thinking: to start again
and fill the hole that had blown up in her life when her husband
had died in China. 'Not me, I gather?'

She took his hands in hers and flipped them palms up. 'Oh
Drake, one of these days I'm going to see hair growing here.'

He tried to look shocked. 'You wound me deeply.'

In many respects he knew he wouldn't be any good for
her anyway. He'd never get over his other life. He'd always be
wondering: if only he'd taken Georgina and Mona with him on the
trip before the solar flare. And even if he did ever marry again,
they would always be there, waiting for him, waiting.

'What I mean is,' Colby continued, 'I don't think you're one
of those guys who are into commitment with anybody else except
yourself. Apart from which your heart is as big and warm as that
ice cube out there.'

How long was it before the telephone rang?

'Yes?' Drake asked, disentangling himself from Colby's arms.

'Kia ora, Francis,' Kuia began, her voice sounding mysterious. 'Is Colby there with you? You might want to come down to watch your berg being melted. There's something curious in the ice.'

It didn't take them long to get dressed and take the lift down to the ice melting area where Kuia and a crowd of others were watching.

The mass. The inconsistency.

The light was refracting through the berg. The shape within morphed from one image to another: a giant mosquito from an antediluvian era; a *Tyrannosaurus rex*; an ancient artefact from some sunken Antarctic Atlantis; a legendary waka that had missed Aotearoa and ended up girdled in ice. An alien spaceship with its navigator, a thing from outer space, trapped inside.

Maybe it was Captain Ahab himself, wrapped around Moby Dick when he'd gone down to the dark depths of the sea.

'What is it?' Colby asked.

A rotor.

Stop.'

Drake's heart was thudding as he walked quickly through the crowd to the ice wall. 'Turn out the lights.' With the lights off, everyone could see the shape within. Trapped inside the berg was a helicopter. Around it, the hawsers that had lashed around the chopper as it had crashed into the berg and been taken down into the sea.

Drake peered in. Colby joined him: inside, two people, a man and a woman. The man was cradling the woman in his arms.

The name of the helicopter: *Pequod*.

Drake showed not a quiver of emotion. 'The berg was too big,' he said. 'The pilot and crew must have tried to reverse the cable and, when it came back it whipped around the rotors and pulled it down, lashing them to it.'

'Thus, I give up the spear!'
The harpoon was darted; the stricken whale flew forward; with igniting velocity the line ran through the groove — ran foul. Ahab stooped to clear it; he did clear it; but the flying turn caught him round the neck, and voicelessly as Turkish mutes bowstring their victim, he was shot out of the boat, ere the crew knew he was gone. Next instant, the heavy eye-splice in the rope's final end flew out of the stark-empty tub, knocked down an oarsman, and smiting the sea, disappeared in its depths.

Then, on the intercom, came Bazza's voice:

'Get your ass up here, Drake. You think you brought in a big one? Well, there's another just turned up on the horizon.'

Drake looked at Colby.

Destiny.

Don't go out there,' Kuia whispered. 'I've grown very fond of you.'

'We'll be fine,' Drake answered, kissing her on both cheeks. Then she pulled him close and pressed her nose against his in the hongi.

Taking Colby's hand, Drake led the way to the helipad.

The news had travelled fast. As they stepped out, Queequeeg, Samurai Sam, Starbuck, Flask, Czar and Hari were waiting for them. 'This is our date, not yours,' Drake said as he and Colby kitted up.

'Oh yeah?' said Samurai Sam. 'Well, we're coming along just to make sure the date doesn't go bad. You're coming back, you hear?'

'Wa-hey,' Flask said.

'Wa-ho,' Hari responded, punching the air.

Drake could swear there were tears in Samurai Sam's eyes — nah, just spangles of snow, melting on his eyelashes.

Drake and Colby walked out to the *Pequod*. Just before they took off, a sudden radiance shimmered over the sea: an auroral display of such blinding beauty that it took Drake's breath away.

A karanga: 'Haere mai.'

Colby brought him back to the present. 'Say, Drake, do me a favour? Kiss me just once as if you meant to marry me?'

And this kiss was even sweeter than the one in his room. But he was leading, not her.

She opened her eyes, surprised. 'Wow, Drake, you'd better watch out. I might have to think twice about you and the commitment word.'

He kissed her again, this time, more passionately, to shut her up, to stop even thinking about what might be possible.

She laughed, pressing herself against him. 'Just our luck, big boy. You know . . . now that we know the future, you and I haven't exactly got a long shelf life, right?'

'That depends,' he said, jerking his head towards the other choppers, 'on whether or not they can bring us back alive.' Then he smiled, remembering the mangled helicopter in its crystal cave of ice and the two people inside it, cradled in each other's arms. They looked happy.

Really happy.

'Whatever happens,' he said, 'from now on we'll be together all the way.'

No, when I go to sea, I go as a simple sailor, right before the mast, plumb down into the forecastle, aloft there to the royal mast-head.

ORBIS

TERRARIUM

NORTH SHORE HOSPITAL, AUCKLAND, APRIL 1982 —

1 /

Why did old Mrs Travers wake so early nowadays? She would like to have slept for another three hours at least. But no, every morning at almost precisely the same time, at half past four, she was wide awake. For — nowadays, again — she woke always in the same way, with a slight start, a small shock, lifting her head from the pillow with a quick glance as if she fancied someone had called her, or as if she were trying to remember for certain whether this was the same wallpaper, the same window she had seen last night before Warner switched off the light.

Mrs Travers frowned. It was still so dark outside. If it weren't for the night light beside her bed, and the crack of light from the door, ajar to the fluorescent glare of corridor outside, she could almost believe that she was alone in the living, breathing dark, indeed, the only person alive in the entire world. Did the thought scare her? No; at ninety-two, it was such a presumption to be afraid of anything. One was too tired to be scared, if the truth be known, and had no energy to waste on such a silly, vain and superfluous emotion. At this age one just wanted to go.

However, there was going to be a slight delay. 'He won't be long,' Staff Nurse Warner had shouted in her ear. 'Your son Elliot is on his way from England to New Zealand now.'

Elliot was the youngest of Mrs Travers' four children and the only boy. The others were Molly, Kate and Joan, who, over all the years, had dutifully taken turns to go to Mummy's pensioner flat every week and pester her about how was she feeling and was there anything she needed from the supermarket.

Why did everybody shout all the time? Mrs Travers could hear perfectly well. When she was a very young girl of thirteen, her beloved father Cyprian had told Mama, 'The thing about our Essie is that her hearing is so acute. You must have been a bat in an earlier life, eh Essie my girl?'

And, of course, she was never alone. Her sight might be going but she could hear every footfall of the nurses as they walked past her room, every piece of gossip they shared as they came on night shift, every sigh of irritation when Mr Winchester in the next room called out, 'Nurse! Nurse!' (he called out all the time, the insufferable man), and every silly giggle when they went off in the mornings and back to their boyfriends or whoever they lived with.

All except Warner, of course. She never had a boyfriend. Or any sort of friend, man or woman. Warner was dedicated to her job.

It was her middle daughter, Kate, who had found Mrs Travers, two weeks ago, where she had collapsed in her kitchen while making herself a cup of tea. She'd had a stroke. Kate called an ambulance and Mrs Travers was whisked off to the hospital. At first the medical team had thought, once they'd brought her around, that she was making good recovery. But then she took a turn for the worse. Her kidneys stopped functioning.

'Your mother has acute renal failure,' Dr Paterson told Mrs Travers' daughters. 'If she was younger we might have considered the possibility of a kidney transplant, but, given her advanced age and the long waiting list for donors, well, we . . .' His voice tailed off.

'You mean there's no hope Mummy will get better?' Joan asked him, her eyes moistening.

The doctor was evasive. 'What we're talking about is end-stage renal disease. But we would keep her on dialysis until you're comfortable and ready and have had the opportunity to say goodbye.'

Molly exchanged glances with her sisters. 'And there's no chance of any recovery?'

'It's just a matter of your choosing a time to farewell her,' Dr Paterson continued. 'Do you have other family who would like to see her and say goodbye?'

'Our brother, Elliot,' Kate told him. 'He lives in London. He would certainly want to come to see Mummy before she . . . before we . . . before . . . after all, he was her favourite.'

'Perhaps you should telephone him and tell him to come as soon as he can.'

When the doctor had gone Mrs Travers' daughters looked at each other. 'After all, Mummy's had a very good life,' Kate said.

And so they were all waiting for Elliot. Perhaps, for once in his life, he would be prompt. And then, thank goodness, finally, they would let her die.

children? Ha! Molly was sixty, Kate was fifty-eight, Joan fifty-six, and Elliot was the 'baby' at forty-eight. And where on earth had Kate got the idea that Elliot was the favourite? Why would they all think that? Elliot had been mean and nasty as a boy and he'd become mean and nasty as an adult, a stockbroker whose only interest was making money.

And what was all this sentimentality about keeping her alive so that all the family could gather to say goodbye? The children had all taken after their father, Harry, and his maudlin Irish ways. None of them showed a whit of Mrs Travers' disciplined no-nonsense personality. Now her father, Cyprian, with his precise scientific approach, wouldn't have been pleased. He'd have said, 'Waiting for Elliot? Does an old elephant wait for the herd to shake its trunk before it dies? Or a sperm whale wait for a sentimental rub from the other whales before it makes its final sounding? Does a dying albatross wait for some last salute before its eyes glaze over? No! They die when they die. It's only humans who prolong life — and it's all vanity, you hear? Scientists would not think of intervening! Charles Darwin would not have approved.'

Mrs Travers remembered going with her father to a public meeting, and the furore that erupted when he got into a fiery argument with a local bishop about Darwin's theory of evolution. 'The Church's teachings from Genesis,' Father shouted, 'that every species has been created whole and has come through the ages unchanged, can no longer be sustained.' Mrs Travers had just adored watching him in full, passionate, flight. 'Read Mr Darwin! He will give you your answer: evolution by natural selection. The strongest survive, the weak die. Species respond to their environment by evolving to fill any niche available to them. And let us hope that mankind, too, will evolve from strength to strength.'

'They die when they die.' Suddenly, Mrs Travers heard a sound, coming from beyond the window frame, far, far beyond. It was a low, deep sigh, haunting, otherworldly, sibilant, somewhere between a deep hiss and moan. Not a sound to be scared of; rather, one you waited for with breathless anticipation.

Someone was calling her.

When Molly, Kate and Joan arrived later that day, Warner was only too ready to tell them about the 'incident'.

'Your mother was a little unsettled during the morning. She pulled out her catheter. It was probably an accident.'

'But she was so good when we left her last night,' Kate answered. Good was when Mrs Travers was drugged and unconscious; bad was when the drugs wore off and Mummy indulged herself in inchoate sighs and screams and incoherent ramblings.

'You mustn't worry about it,' Warner lowered her voice to a whisper. 'It's what happens. But she's all right now. We've given her something.'

Relieved, they settled down with their knitting, magazines and boiled lollies to keep watch.

17/

Half past four again. Why half past four?

Mrs Travers sighed to herself. The drugs du jour had worn off; ah, clarity for a while! And with it came the urge to be up and about.

Not that there was much chance of that. Even as she shifted

slightly she felt a tightening at her abdomen. That's where the catheter was for the contraption that stood beside the bed, winking at her and giving her the glad eye. She was hooked up to the silly thing — her own personal artificial kidney — continuously pumping into her a special solution to cleanse away all the waste fluids, drain them out and replace with fresh solution. Otherwise the toxins built up in her blood. And the children didn't want them to do that. Not quite yet.

Yesterday had been a good day, lucidly speaking. She'd drifted in and out of consciousness, always aware of Molly, Kate and Joan sitting around her bed talking, knitting, reading magazines and, sometimes, sleeping themselves. She realised she startled them when she occasionally 'woke up'; they would hurriedly ring for Warner to settle her down again. Every hour on the hour other medical staff would come into the room, check her pulse and the dialysis machine, and then make a note on the clipboard at the end of the bed: 'Still Alive', presumably, or words to that effect.

Dr Paterson popped in regularly to check on her. 'Have you heard from your brother?' he asked Molly.

'There's been a delay. He couldn't get out of an urgent board meeting. He won't be arriving for another two days.'

Money before Mummy. Sounded just like Elliot. Really, he was a disappointment. As for Molly, Kate and Joan, they were dutiful daughters, but why, oh why, had they never possessed a life of the mind? 'Expanding our knowledge', Father would have scolded them, 'and using it to advance humankind is what justifies our retaining our niche as a species.'

Actually, at some time in the afternoon, while Mrs Travers' daughters were having a light lunch in her room — they'd brought some nougat to have with their tea — she was prompted by the memory of her father to tell them about him and, in particular, the great moment of her adolescent life when she joined him in the Galapagos Islands.

'Father was the leading herpetologist at the Schwimmer Aquarium,' she began. 'Mother, my sister Gloria and I were accustomed to his being away often, and we were thrilled when he was appointed to lead a scientific expedition to study one of the most intriguing of all reptiles: the giant tortoise, *Geochelone elephantopus*. Our pleasure turned to dismay when we discovered he'd be away for a year. I was thirteen then, Gloria eleven.

'"But the *Artemisia* will be coming back here in three months with specimens," Father said, "and I've arranged for you —" he was referring to my mother "— to come out to me for a month after that. You'd have to make arrangements for Essie and Gloria to stay with relatives, but please, Merle, do say you'll come."

'The trouble was that, as the time drew near, Mother became reluctant. She talked to Father by ship-to-shore telephone in the Galapagos. "I really can't make it, dear," she shouted. "Gloria is sickly again and you know Essie, she doesn't make it any better. She keeps harassing her sister. I really do believe the best option would be for Essie to come to you and I should stay home and look after Gloria."

'I couldn't believe my luck. I skipped around the house, delighted that I was going. To make absolutely sure that Gloria stayed sickly — she had a bad heart — I kept on harassing her, especially at night when she'd weep because she wanted to go to sleep. I only stopped pinching and poking Gloria the night before I went on board the ship and knew, with absolute certainty, that nobody could stop me. Wasn't I a naughty girl?'

At that moment, the effort of telling the story became too

much for Mrs Travers. Instead she lay back among the pillows and let herself drift back to when the visit had begun.

The *Artemisia* approached the Galapagos Archipelago over a pearly sea. Morning mist led to sweeping showers of light rain. It was windy and cold, the clouds hanging low over black porous volcanic rock and jagged cliff formations. Along the shoreline fragmented boulders, lava flows, spatter cones, pit craters, columns of gas-driven steam, blowholes, fissures and uplifted blocks cracked against each other. Every height was crowned with the crater of a shield volcano.

'And the birds were everywhere,' Mrs Travers remembered. 'I'd never seen so many before, crowding the blue vault of the sky — frigate birds, swallow-tailed gulls, albatrosses, brown pelicans, red-billed tropic birds — tribes upon limitless tribes of them. And all so beautiful, so free, that I wanted to fly with them.'

She lifted her hands, trying to follow the flights of the seabirds. Alarmed, Joan asked Molly, 'Look at Mummy. What is she doing? What is she seeing? Do you think she'll last long enough for Elliot to say goodbye to her?'

Waiting for her at an impressive campsite right at the collapsed caldera of an island volcano was Father.

'Essie! Essie, my girl!' he waved.

It was the Eden you found at world's end.

'Poor Cyprian,' Mrs Travers murmured. 'You would have preferred Mother, wouldn't you?'

All the same, Father pretended to be happy to see her and she soon got to know his team of three assistants and four Ecuadorian seamen. The seamen gave her a name: they called her Mi Hija, 'the child'.

It was the mating season for the seabirds, and Father straight away took her to an albatross colony at the top of a sheer sea cliff; albatrosses were balancing on the wind, coming in or leaving to feed on the fish shoals that boiled below. 'They mate for life,' Father told her, 'and see how their courtship is elaborately choreographed.' Indeed, the albatross birds courted for ages, repetitively going over the same patterned ritual. Their long bills circled each other, they made loud, castanet-like clicking sounds and high-pitched vocalisations, their necks arched, and they performed very funny sideways rocking movements — and then they would start again. She could have watched the courting birds for ever.

Father also took her to spy on a colony of blue-footed boobies. It was a different kind of wooing to the albatrosses: the male showed off his nest-building skills to attract a mate. The silly thing was that they didn't use the sticks and twigs to build a nest; instead, they incubated their eggs on the bare ground. Both parents took turns brooding and sitting on the eggs out in the heat of the sun. Two chicks were hatched, two days apart.

'Father showed me Mr Darwin's natural selection in operation,' Mrs Travers recalled. 'The mother hatched two chicks: the second was the "just in case" egg. Once the older chick was hatched, its function was to get stronger, establish domination, and then cruelly peck the younger chick, prevent it from obtaining any food and push it further and further from the nest. The booby parents did not intervene.'

'And neither do we,' Father said.

But was this what Mrs Travers had done to her sister, Gloria — pushed her out of the nest — and if Mother had not saved her, would Father?

The thought bothered Mrs Travers, so she plunged quickly back into her shifting, swirling memories.

Her first swim was unforgettable. The sea was so chill, fed by the cold Peru current sweeping north from the Antarctic. It was green and so clear you could see to the end of forever.

At first she was too scared (aha, at least she wasn't afraid to admit it) to go into deep water. She preferred to stay close by the rocks where she came across a herd of sea turtles, munching away on sunlit seaweed.

'Don't be timid like Gloria,' Father teased.

That made her venture deeper. And there, the true magic opened up to her. She was as astonished at the fish life as she had been at the bird life. The sea was just a liquid sky, and tribes and tribes of fish were in dominion — angelfish, Creole fish, grunts, Moorish idols, blue parrotfish, concentric puffer fish, yellow-tailed surgeonfish, yellow-bellied trigger fish and wahoo scintillated in huge, teeming shoals.

With a gasp she saw a whole group of seals swimming swiftly towards her. She blew bubbles of fear but all they wanted to do was gambol and play, sliding their skins along her body and flirting with her.

Then, suddenly, all around her, the sea was speared by diving seabirds, particularly the blue-footed piqueros. Diving like bullets steeply into the water, their long tails like rudders, they hit the surface with tremendous force. One of them on the way back to the surface with a fish in its beak looked at her, cocking a curious eye: What are you doing here?

Far below her, schools of manta rays and sharks slipped through the dark sea like disturbing dreams.

And so Mrs Travers floated in and out of consciousness in her sea of memories. Before she realised it, night was upon her, and her daughters went home.

She lifted her head and looked out the window. Why, she felt quite light-headed.

What on earth had happened to the view? It wasn't the usual one at all: the sprinkle of city lights, and the familiar volcanic cone of Rangitoto. Rather, she saw a darker, altogether wilder landscape, greying with the morning. A road ran right through the middle of it. Something was moving on the horizon, coming towards her. How very strange! And was that the sound of the sea?

'We found your mother trying to get out of her bed this morning, the naughty girl,' Warner told her daughters. 'Debbie was on duty and, when the alarm sounded, she instantly went to investigate. Mrs Travers was already halfway out of bed. Of course Debbie scolded her, but your mother said, "I want to go now. I want to get dressed and go." It was quite a struggle to get her back into bed and to quieten her down.'

Molly, Kate and Joan looked at each other. 'We noticed Mother doing some rather odd things yesterday. She was looking into the air as if there were people around her. She was talking to them — or, at least, her lips were moving.'

'And do you remember?' Kate asked Molly. 'She started to grope at the air and point and follow things that were flying around the room.'

'She's hallucinating,' the nurse explained. 'It's what happens. I'll tell Dr Paterson. He may increase her medication.'

'No, please don't do that, no,' Mrs Travers tried to say. 'I'll be a good girl now.'

Warner peered into her eyes. 'We wouldn't want you to do any damage to yourself now, lovey, would we? Not before your son gets here, eh?'

⫼ /

Half past four in the morning, on the dot, and Mrs Travers was awake again.

For a moment she panicked. Warner had indeed advised Dr Paterson of her behaviour, and what her silly daughters had said. As he increased her sedation she had tried to struggle and to plead with him, 'No, I don't want extra painkillers', but he didn't hear her.

Had the medication eradicated the memories that had opened up to her about . . . about . . . ?

Mrs Travers moaned into the pillow. It was the same wallpaper and same window, and Auckland was outside as she knew it was supposed to be. But she didn't want it to be Auckland. She wanted it to be that other place. Where was it? What was its name again?

She sobbed with frustration. She thrashed around in her bed, and suddenly she ripped out the tube feeding the sedating fluids into her left arm. Another lunge, and the tower holding her drip twirled away from her in a crazy dance, taking the tube with it. Oh, she didn't even care when Debbie came running in, not at all, because in the interim she remembered —

'You are there, aren't you?' she called through the window.

Thrillingly, she heard the sound again, the low, deep sigh, haunting, otherworldly, sibilant, low, somewhere between a deep hiss and moan.

And it was closer. Whoever was calling her was almost outside the window.

ather couldn't supervise her all the time. 'Time for you to leave the nest,' he jested. Even so, he assigned one of the young Ecuadorian crew to look after her. His name was Felipe and he showed her sea lions lying on the gritty sand and among the rocks. The animals were so close at hand and surprisingly unconcerned by humans.

'They won't hurt you,' Felipe told her. 'You can go right up to them with a club and, bang, you have them before they even know.'

Not far from the sea lions were the lizards of the Galapagos: the marine iguanas. Mrs Travers found them hilarious. They kept on sneezing, excreting salt through special nasal glands. Their heads were encrusted with white salt crowns. They huddled in huge colonies on the rocks to keep each other warm. They were nothing to be frightened of, but they might have been were they larger. How amusing to realise that they only ate seaweed!

Then, near the end of Mrs Travers' month-long visit, the campsite was shifted to another island. Cyprian told her they would be there for the next four days and, after that, the *Artemisia* would be fully laden, and she would return with it to Mother and Gloria.

Two days later Father had to lead an expedition inland, and he left her at the campsite. 'You have some sandwiches, there's lots to see, I'll be back in the late afternoon, okay, Essie my girl?'

'Can't I come with you?'

'No, it's better that you don't. I'll be working, and you'd be in the way.' He had an evasive tone in his voice; he was hiding something from her. 'Don't forget to take your sunhat. Felipe is taking you somewhere . . . he has a surprise for you.'

A surprise?

Felipe took her on a half-day walk. They arrived below the rim of a tall volcano. She saw a wide flat canyon studded with candelabra cactuses.

'Look,' Felipe said.

Far in the distance she saw clouds of dust being unsettled. Then, from out of the clouds, came giant tortoises, five feet tall, lumbering slowly towards her.

'Did you know that some are over two hundred years old?' Felipe asked. 'There were once fourteen different tribes of them over all the islands; oh, millions.' Felipe was prone to exaggeration. 'Now, not so many.'

'Where are they going?'

'They're on their way to bathe in dew ponds that form as a result of the mist,' Felipe said. 'We should sit down cross-legged in their path and see what they do!'

Mrs Travers wasn't too sure of doing that but she wasn't about to be bested by a boy, and a native boy at that. 'All right.'

'You are lucky,' said Felipe suddenly. 'I know this herd. They are the oldest on the island. And look, El Rey is among them.'

'El Rey?'

'The King,' Felipe said in a hushed voice.

Mrs Travers strained to see. Perspiration from the hot sun had dripped into her eyes, making them sting. She took out a handkerchief and wiped the sweat away. Ah, that was better. As they approached, the giant tortoises grew larger and larger. Their faces had a timeless quality, age-worn, and their shells were smooth saddleback carapaces.

But which one was El Rey? They all looked the same to her.

Then they stopped. Just like that. Two hundred yards away. Then, swirling the dust like a cyclone, they began to move apart to form a pathway. And as soon as Mrs Travers saw him moving through their midst, she knew why he was called The King.

He was at least seven feet tall. He must have been six feet across the curvature of his shell. His face was incredibly wizened, his eyes huge and black. When he reached the front of the herd he opened the gash of his mouth and gave a loud, guttural roar.

He came nearer and nearer, a being that blotted out the rest of the world.

'He'll trample me!' Mrs Travers cried to Felipe.

Then an extraordinary thing occurred. El Rey saw her, gave a deep sigh and then, thud, down came his shell, slamming tight around him and sealing him to the ground. The other giant tortoises in the front rank did the same.

Mrs Travers couldn't help thinking with glee, 'And I'm only a girl.' Eyes wide with amazement, she stood up, wiped her dress and looked at Felipe.

He nodded. 'That's what they do! Isn't it funny?' He began to run within the herd, yelling and flapping his hands, and one by one others sighed, and down they went. They looked like huge cowpats.

'But if you approach them from behind,' Felipe said, 'we can have a lot of fun. I show you.'

He sneaked up to a giant tortoise and jumped onto its back. And it didn't even know! 'They may seem mild-mannered now,' Felipe said, 'but you want to see them during the mating season. They roar and bellow and when the males fight . . .' He motioned to her to pick one of the giant tortoises and ride it.

With great deliberation, she walked back through the herd.

'No, not El Rey,' Felipe shouted.

It was too late. Eyes bright and shining, Mrs Travers hopped on The King's back. She laughed in triumph as he rose and walked on, blissfully unaware that he had a passenger. Or was he? The sun had made his carapace hot and the skin under her thighs was burning. His saddle wasn't comfortable at all. Nevertheless, Mrs Travers stayed on him for as long as she could, riding El Rey through the sunlight.

Felipe had become bored. 'Let's go back to the shore,' he said as he dismounted. 'There is still much I can show you.'

She sidled off El Rey's saddle and was suddenly overcome with embarrassment. For some reason, she did a little curtsey. Then she peered into El Rey's left eye and said, 'Thank you.'

And El Rey answered her, *You are not the first and I expect you will not be the last to ride on me.*

Mrs Travers stepped back with shock and fell into the dust. 'What did you say?'

El Rey stopped and looked at her. *Humans come, humans go. There have been many two-footed ones like yourself, child, but taller than you, who have walked among us.*

'Like my father,' Mrs Travers answered proudly. 'He's a scientist. He's come to collect herpetological specimens.'

El Rey's eyes were dark, shining. *I met a scientist once. He was a young Englishman. He also rode on me and, afterwards, like you, child, he thanked me. You are similar to him with your politeness and your manners.*

'His surname wasn't Darwin, was it?' Mrs Travers asked breathlessly.

Darwin? Why, yes! He was so polite that I granted him the gift that only tortoises like myself can offer. We can look back into the past. We can also look at the present and into the future. It is the gift of foresight, and I told him to choose a question and I would answer it. He sat where you are sitting now and he pondered for a long time before asking it. And when he did, the question was — El Rey suddenly withdrew his head and, thump, down came his shell. But his voice echoed from beneath the carapace — *so simple but so terrible, so* sacred, *that I sobbed at the enormity of it. He should never have asked it.* The dust swirled and drifted around Mrs Travers. After a long while, El Rey's shell lifted, and his head appeared and began to weave back and forth.

'What did you tell him?' she asked.

I told him that I would visit him at the moment of his death. And then I would show him the answer. El Rey began to move to one side, as if intending to get past her.

Mrs Travers walked swiftly after him and hopped onto his shell again. Felipe was by now only a speck far away, waving to her. She waved back and he shrugged his shoulders and continued down to the beach.

I did not think I would lose you so easily, child, El Rey sighed. *All you humans have such an insatiable curiosity. It is a hunger in you, but it will be your downfall and you have already taken many of us down with it. It will not be long before the rest of us follow.*

Mrs Travers wasn't about to be put off by a silly old tortoise, even if he was a giant — and a king. 'The rest of us?'

We who live in Orbis Terrarium, El Rey explained, *the Inhabited World, all the birds of the air, the plants and flowers and creatures of the land, and the inhabitants of the sea, sharing our world with you, the greatest predator the universe has ever known.*

'Predator?' Mrs Travers pondered the word, lifting it, weighing it, looking under it as if it were a stone and something was hiding beneath it.

Did you know, El Rey continued, *that hundreds of us have been taken over the centuries, by whalers, pirates and other sailors, for our delicate flesh and our oil? The sailors would come in gangs, some up to eight men, to lift us one by one into their ships, five hundred at a time. Because we could survive without water or food for many months we were an inexhaustible supply of fresh meat. And then we were also devastated by the dogs, cats, pigs and goats man brought to our islands, ravaging the vegetation on which we depend. The black rat pounced gladly on our hatchlings. Since then there have been poachers . . . and others . . . it's the old, old story, my child.*

'But then Mr Darwin came,' Mrs Travers said proudly. 'On the *Beagle*. He saved you all, surely.'

Yes, the young Englishman came, El Rey acknowledged, and then he went. And after him came other scientists. They took hundreds more of us for their museums and zoos. One scientist is no better or worse than the rest.

'My father is not like that,' she said. Abruptly, she jumped off El Rey. 'You should apologise,' she ordered. 'Didn't you hear me? Say you're sorry!'

But El Rey was silent.

In a temper, Mrs Travers kicked him. Hard. She bunched up her fists, pulled her sunhat tightly over her head and began to walk away. 'In that case, goodbye.'

She was halfway along the canyon, heading towards the beach, when she stopped. A venal, greedy look, one tinged with the sense of revenge, came into her eyes. Turning, she stormed her way back to the herd. As she swept by, the giant tortoises thudded and fell, making obeisance to her. When she reached the front of the herd she turned and waited for El Rey to approach.

'Stop,' she commanded.

El Rey looked at her. *Why did you not keep on walking, child? Why?*

Mrs Travers looked hard at him. 'I have a question,' she said. The sun stopped, for just a moment, and the whole of the universe breathed in.

No, child, El Rey answered.

Mrs Travers stamped her foot. 'I'm entitled to it,' she said crossly. 'If you could give Darwin the gift I should have the same right. And I'm not a child.'

El Rey pondered. *Ah well,* he began arrogantly, *I suppose it will not hurt to tell you what Father Christmas will leave you under the Christmas tree. You may ask your question.*

But when Mrs Travers whispered her question into his ear, El Rey was horrified. He gave a roar of such intensity and pain that all who lived in Orbis Terrarium heard it. The sun ceased its passage across the sky. The world stopped still. Then El Rey blinked. *I underestimated you, child. It is the same question that Darwin asked me, the most sacred question of all. No inhabitant of Orbis Terrarium, no bird or animal or sea creature, would ever ask it. Only a human would ever dare to ask the unaskable.*

'I demand my answer.' Mrs Travers compressed her lips.

El Rey nodded. *I suppose I will have to promise you what I promised him. And my promise is this: when you are dying, I will come and give you the answer.*

'But I'm dying now!' Mrs Travers shouted petulantly from her bed. 'You promised.'

And the voice came sighing from beyond the window. *Won't you release me from it?*

'No,' Mrs Travers answered grumpily.

Then she gave a small gasp and put her wrinkled and veined

hands to her face. 'But I can't remember the question now.'

Oh, but I do, El Rey sighed. *I remember everything. My cross is to never forget.*

IV /

At long last, Elliot finally arrived.

He had his little cry with his sisters and dutifully sat by the bedside and looked into Mrs Travers' eyes. He could never hide anything from her. She saw into his soul, and it wasn't love she saw there but horror. Was this old woman really his mother? Is this what death looked like? The silly boy was scared. But then he'd always been scared of his own shadow.

'We will let Mummy go now,' he said.

With a nod, he consented to the dialysis machine being turned off. How long would it take? Molly insisted that a priest come to administer the last rites.

Such sentimental children.

Half past four, half past four.

There was a fluttering sound and, suddenly, a host of doves and finches settled on the windowsill — and then proceeded to come through and perch on Mrs Travers' bed.

Are you coming with us now? they chirped.

'All right,' she said.

What had Father taught her about the finches? Oh yes, they were another example of Darwin's theory of adaptive radiation, evolving into thirteen species.

Mrs Travers felt very strange, very strange indeed. She looked around the hospital room and saw that her daughters were there. And who was the male stranger with them? Why, it looked like Father!

The toxins were flooding freely through her body, poisoning her to death. One by one her organs were shutting down. But she was pumped so full of drugs to alleviate the pain that she was passing in and out of consciousness. She felt very queer.

Mrs Travers looked at her children one by one without any sense of emotion: Molly, Kate, Joan and Elliot. She wished they would go home, put up their feet and watch a bit of telly, and leave her to get on with it.

Oh, and now she did feel quite queasy, and her body was starting to itch all over. She was having hot and cold flushes. She felt sluggish, extraordinarily tired, and she was aware of her heart going thunkety-thunk and the blood banging around her body like old pipes beginning to freeze when winter comes around.

Time was running out. She'd better get going, and follow the finches. *Come along then,* they called to her.

She sat up. At least, she thought she sat up, but nobody in the room seemed to take any notice of her. And when she pushed down the covers and got out of bed, why, they didn't seem to care. Warner didn't even call her 'lovey' and scold her.

Then somebody did bar her way. It was Father.

And she wanted to scream at him, just scream and scream.

He hadn't told her what he was doing in the Galapagos Islands. She only discovered it for herself when she was on the way back home on the *Artemisia*. She liked exploring, and found the passageway leading to the hold.

It was filled with Father's herpetological and other specimens, all nicely tagged and tabulated: birds, fishes, plants. And stacked to the very top of the hold, upside down, hundreds of giant tortoises. Most had been killed; some were still alive, kicking and moving their arms and legs, slowly.

Right at the top was El Rey.

Don't fret, child, El Rey sighed. *It had to happen one day. And don't blame your father. He is no better or worse than all the rest.*

Mrs Travers did scream then. Oh, she had been wanting to scream for years at her father because he was supposed to be better, he really was.

'You told me you didn't believe in intervention,' she accused him.

'I was collecting herpetological specimens.'

'No, you were just as bad, just as culpable as the buccaneers, whalers and sailors before you.'

'I took only specimens from Isabela where the tortoise herds were secure.'

In a fury, she hit him. Humanity had indeed evolved to fill every available niche, even when that niche was already filled by others; humanity, the greatest predator.

She wanted to hit him again, but . . .

Mrs Travers found it so difficult to breathe, and gave a huge inward gasp. She floated, yes, floated over the sill of the window and out of the room, away from them all, away.

The sky widened and whitened and, far away, she could see the sea. Running, she made her way down among the rocks where scarlet-grey lizards were sunning themselves. Then some of the lizards did an extraordinary thing: they leapt into the water, making humorous plopping noises, and when she peered into the water, Mrs Travers could see them feeding on underwater seaweed. The seaweed looked so delicious that she couldn't help herself.

Nightdress and all, she dived into the sea and joined the feeding lizards. Shoals of scintillating fish surrounded her. But they weren't fish at all but rather seabirds coming back to their colony. Mrs Travers walked among them and knelt beside a dead booby chick.

'Oh, I'm so sorry, Gloria, I'm so sorry.'

She wanted to weep, but something lovely, it must have been a tropicbird, lifted her up and carried her to an island — and below the rim of a volcano was a pass studded with candelabra cactuses.

Hello, a voice said. El Rey had arrived. He had kept his promise. Around him, a herd of giant tortoises was waiting. Strangely, there was a windowsill and, on the other side of it, she could see her grieving children beside a bed in which lay an old woman.

Time to go, El Rey said.

She nodded, lifted up the hem of her nightdress and slid onto the carapace. Smiling, Mrs Travers turned to the children on the other side of the window: 'Goodbye.' Then she gasped, 'But I can't remember the question.'

Oh I do, El Rey sighed. *Lean down and I'll whisper it in your ear.*

Mrs Travers heard El Rey's voice and nodded when he told her the question. 'Yes, I remember it now,' she answered.

Come along then, child, El Rey said, *and as I did with Mr Darwin, I will show you the answer.* He gave a guttural roar and, at his command, the herd made way for him as he moved forward. A dark dust cloud rose, radiant, glistening.

There was a moment in the Galapagos, Mrs Travers remembered, just before the sun went down, and the waves were darkening, when the horizon went smoky grey as if many fires were being lit along it. The smoke billowed through oranges and reds, which became pastel shades of cerise, vermilion and blushes of pink within a vault of celestial blue. The reds lasted for a long time. It was the sea that darkened quickly, advancing to the rim of red and, above, one by one, the stars began to appear.

As El Rey turned to face the darkness, Mrs Travers felt a cool wind chilling her.

'Will it hurt?' she asked.

It is only life that hurts, El Rey answered.

'But will it hurt!' Mrs Travers asked again sharply.

Just a little bit.

THE
THRILL OF
FALLING

PRELUDE

CHAPTER ONE —
THE GREAT GOD, 'ORO

When I was born I was very sickly.

My mother, May, told me that I had breathing problems and for three weeks I battled for life in an incubator in Gisborne Hospital. 'Your father and I were told that you might not live and that it was touch and go. We were very distressed.'

Of all the visitors who came to watch over me, none was as vigilant as my grandfather, Koro. He would stand watching me, my deathly pale body wrapped in tubes to keep me breathing. And I know that he prayed incessantly to the great God, 'Oro:

'Almighty One, son of Ta'aroa and Hina-tu-a-uta, come down from the highest heaven, Te Raituitai, and look kindly upon this poor child. Forsake him not, o 'Oro.'

Not only that, but, according to Mum, Koro decided to give me the name of 'Oro's most famous priest, Tupaea, even though that name was reserved for my Uncle Tu-Bad's son, who was instead called Seth.

'He thought that might help,' Mum said.

It must have done because I survived.

Throughout our family history there has always been someone named Tupaea.

Koro's first name, for instance, was Tupaea and he always demanded that people not shorten it.

Behind his back, however, most people called him Big Tu (a few who didn't like his lofty manners would add 'tae' to his name) and me Little Tu to differentiate us — and often they called me Little Tutae in public.

No matter how many times I fought for my honour, the name stuck: Little Shit.

This is the story of the very first Tupaea, the one who came from over the sea to Aotearoa New Zealand.

He's the one to blame for the way I turned out.

ACT ONE

CHAPTER TWO —
UAWA

I /

I struggled into boyhood, an only child with an inhaler as my constant companion.

I became the kind of snotty-nosed eleven-year-old kid with spiky hair and shirt-tail hanging out of his pants who, at our small native primary school, was always on the sideline during school sports days. And although nobody could keep me out of the haka team, I was the skinny brown boy with the big hopeful eyes they tried to hide in the back.

Was I to blame, then, that denied a chance at real life, I would develop a fantastic imagination?

During class, I took to looking out the window so often that my teachers and other classmates worked around me and left me alone to daydream. The main road between Uawa and Gisborne ran past our school, and watching the cars, trucks, motorbikes and buses zooming by kept my imagination busy. 'Where are they going?' I asked myself as I pressed my nose against the window. 'What kind of people are in the buses?'

Wondering who those people were, as they sped by, and what adventures they would have when they reached their destination, was more engaging than listening to Four-Eyes Wilson drone on and on about some dead English poet.

I often fantasised that there'd been a mix-up in heaven on the day I was born and, instead of being delivered to some movie star in Hollywood, I got sent to Uawa. One of these days, though, I was going to hit that road, you wouldn't see me for dust, and go to . . . America, yeah, and bang on the door of some Hollywood mansion and, when Arnie opened the door I would yell, 'Daaaaaad!' Nobody would see me for dust.

'Tupaea, are you with us? On the planet?'

'Oh, s-s-sorry, Mr Wilson.'

Mr Wilson couldn't help himself. 'He's b-b-back, everyone!'

After school was over, I escaped the jeers of my schoolmates.

'Where are you g-g-going, Little Tu?'

I pushed past them and ran out the school gates and down the road. When I got to the bridge, about half a mile away, I opened my schoolbag to look for my inhaler; I was rasping for breath. Where was it? I couldn't find it and in despair I stopped looking for it and leapt onto the railing.

I wanted to forget who I was.

The tide was coming into the channel below as I jumped.

21

ater that day, I arrived at the marae.

There were over five hundred people, seated on chairs facing the meeting house. Oh no, the welcome to the Pakeha guests, sheltering under umbrellas from the hot sun, had already started. And where was Mum? Sitting in the very front, watching the proceedings with the women as usual: no way would I be able to sneak in unseen.

'Why is your hair wet?' she asked when I joined her. 'And have you been home and changed your clothes? No wonder you're late.'

I tried to get my words working, *Come out, come out wherever you are.* 'I-I-I'm sorry, M-mum . . .'

She didn't wait for me to complete my answer. 'He's like his koro,' she said to Mrs Rapaki, who was sitting nearby. 'Always wants to look his best.'

Mum was always speaking for me.

took refuge in my own thoughts. Wouldn't you if you had the choice of sitting in the hot sun listening to long and interminable debates on Maori land or . . . going to Mars like Arnie did in *Total Recall*? Arnold Schwarzenegger was the man.

Koro, however, had insisted that all our family, including the children, be present. The government had sent a ministerial representative today to settle long-standing tribal grievances over confiscated land. That was him, prime steak in fancy duds, trying to smile, pretending to be happy. 'It's important for the mokos as well as for the grown-ups,' Koro had said. 'After all, they will inherit the land we get back.' But all those speeches to listen to as the elders debated whether to accept the government's offer, man oh man! And some of those rangatira were so in love with their own voices that they droned on and on. It was all right for them, sheltering on the paepae, the talking bench of chiefs in the shade of the meeting house, but what about the poor commoners sitting in the blistering heat?

Listening with the rest of the crowd, I counted the elders. Oh, why was I ever born! There were five or six more to go and, because rangatira always spoke in ascending order of importance, Koro was last. The old people on the marae relished the debate, sure, but with my limited understanding of the language I could only understand bits and pieces of what was being said. Nevertheless I did my best to concentrate, closing my eyes and trying to follow the various arguments.

'Te kai o te rangatira he korero,' Mum whispered to me, jabbing me with an elbow when I gave up and started to pick my nose. 'Speechmaking is the food of chiefs.'

The elders were outdoing each other in castigating the government for its offer. They were certainly giving the poor official his beans.

'Sit up,' Mum said. 'It's Koro's turn now.'

Koro always came last because he was from a senior ancestral line. Tall and stately, he liked to wear a hat with a turned-down brim, but he always took it off when he stood to speak, as a mark of respect to the marae. It was also a magician's trick as it revealed his silver hair, combed to perfection; he knew this irritated most of the other elders, who were balding.

Koro was nattily dressed too, in suit jacket and grey trousers. The main reason why he was formally attired was that he was a Maori Land Court official and had a particular station in life to live up to. Some of the other elders, no offence, looked like they'd just arrived from the cowshed. Koro's unapologetic formality and dress was a further affront to them.

'Keeps them in their place,' Mum used to say, 'just in case they're thinking of a making a takeover bid for that final speaking slot on the paepae.'

Koro liked to dress like the true rangatira that he was. If he'd been living in the old days, he probably would have worn a beautiful feather cloak. Slaves would have carried him onto the marae so that his feet didn't have to touch the ground, and he would have been fed by little boys putting morsels of food in his mouth so he wouldn't have to soil his own fingers by touching them; the poor government man would have been on the menu.

He also spoke last because he was renowned for his eloquence and skill in the reo.

'Te toto o te tangata, he kai,' he began, deploying a well-known proverb. 'Te oranga o te tangata, he whenua.' The blood of man is supplied by food, the sustenance of man is supplied by land.

At his words, a loud sigh came from the people. 'You can always count on Big Tu to express how we feel.'

'Without the land we die as a people. Therefore, return it to us.'

No ifs, no buts, no maybes.

'Take that message back to your government.'

And then he sat down.

The official was gobsmacked. I saw him turn to a flunky: 'That's it?'

Yes, that was it. After all, hadn't Koro's . . . er . . . lieutenants already conveyed his message?

I turned to Mrs Rapaki. 'I'm named after Koro,' I said, as if she didn't know.

CHAPTER THREE — WHAT'S IN A NAME?

1/

It's been twelve years since I thought of that day when I jumped off the bridge at Uawa.

That's the Maori name of the place where I was born. The European name is Tolaga Bay, and the bridge is the one you cross if you are driving north into the township. Uawa or Tolaga Bay, what's the difference! The town is still a place nobody ever heard of in a country way down at the bottom of the world. There's no main street; instead there's State Highway 35, which is the road linking Gisborne — or Gizzy as locals call it — with all the small communities of the East Coast.

The place hasn't changed much either: a couple of blocks of shops, Hauiti marae on a road just before the bridge, a war memorial, a pub and a school with a playroom and that's about it. Not far away, Hikurangi Mountain, a strange humpy silhouette that's spoken of in reverent whispers, looms over the land and sea; it's the first place in the world to see the sun.

But I've changed and, sometimes, when I think back to the boy I was, I can scarcely recognise myself. Sure, I was unhappy at school: who likes to be mocked as incessantly as I was? Not that I was bullied in any way — more ridiculed, I guess; I'm not sure which is worse.

I can still see myself running through the school gates that day, and hear my heart thudding as I stood on the bridge. My lungs were hurting; I was trying hard to breathe in. I can remember looking to my left at my arm outstretched and then to my right to the tips of the fingers, and feeling the wind from the sea in my face. And when I took the first step, wheezing heavily, from the bridge into space . . .

One moment I was gasping for breath and then, all of a sudden, my lungs cleared.

And oh, for one moment there was a sense of weightlessness.

I've never forgotten that feeling.

All my life I think I've been trying to find it again, that clarity, as if all the world's air were rushing into me and filling my lungs to the brim.

And that sense of defying gravity before the thrill of falling.

2 /

In those days, my parents May and Wally lived in a small house in Uawa.

Dad was a good-looking dude, quiet, but reputed to be a scrapper; he worked as a truck driver for the forestry. Mum was petite, curvy (whenever she put on weight and her waist disappeared Dad said he didn't mind that she was built for comfort), businesslike and, because Dad was quiet, she often spoke for him too; you didn't have to guess who was the boss in our family. Mum was a nurse in the hospital at nearby Te Puia, about an hour's drive away. Sometimes she would take me there whenever my asthma was playing up, pedal to the floor and watch out anybody coming in the opposite direction. The hospital had been built around natural springs where, in the old days, the Maori would carry people to be healed in the bubbling waters, and it subsequently became a well-known destination for patients with tuberculosis. The hospital had a pool which I'd swim in, and good doctors who put me through therapies to increase my lung capacity and help my breathing.

At school I could well have stayed on the sideline or in the back line, always picked last in school games, but my exercises made me into a trier. At one concert, I stubbornly put my name down to do a breakdance and, billed as 'The Terminator from the Future', I appeared from artificial smoke, spinning and adding a bit of Michael Jackson moonwalking. Although my cousin Seth and others at school may have meant it sarcastically, I was very proud when I was proclaimed a mon-star, and a big hit.

As for Koro, he lived with my nan in an older, established part of the township, in a large rambling house down on the beach: two gables, a verandah facing the sea, and a driveway trimmed with flax. In summer, the pohutukawa grove behind the house blazed with crimson blossoms.

Nan's name was Esther and she had her hair set every Friday at the local salon. She liked to wear floral dresses, never went without lipstick and was totally devoted to looking after Koro: ironing his shirts, pressing his trousers, shining his shoes and sending him off to work with a kiss on the cheek. She was an old-fashioned homemaker and she liked it that way. And she hated my inhaler! Whenever I went to use it, she would rush into the kitchen to boil some water and put some horrible-smelling herbs in it. Scolding me, she would drape a towel over my head and order me to breathe the fumes in.

'Please, N-n-nan,' I would splutter. 'I'm all better now,' even if I wasn't.

Like most of the Mahanas — that's our surname — Nan had shown she had good fertility and produced for Koro three sons as well as my mother, who was the youngest in the family. Actually, our surname should also have been Tupaea, except that Koro was from a female branch: although his mother was a Tupaea and she was the eldest, she married a Mahana, hence Koro's name, Tupaea Mahana. This was always a particularly painful cross for Koro to bear. Though we had good relations with the other Tupaea families along the coast, especially at Anaura, sometimes some upstart would try to put Koro down on the marae by saying, 'You're just a Mahana.'

Koro would swiftly put them in their place. He was known for his devastating use of language, which he brandished as mightily as others might wield a taiaha. You attempted to pull rank on him at your peril. 'That may be,' he would counter, 'but my mother was the first born while all her brothers, indeed, all your male ancestors too, were still in their nappies.'

Every Sunday Mum and Dad took me to family lunch with my grandparents. There, we joined my uncles Tu-Bad, Bo and Charlie and their families for the family roast. Sometimes Nan would set trestles outside under the pohutukawa where there was a breeze, and close to her sons as they tended the earth oven; she loved to get a whiff of the hangi.

I knew that Uncle Tu-Bad's name was really Tupaea like Koro's and mine. 'How did he get the name he has now?' I asked Mum one day.

'Well,' she pursed her lips, 'Koro expected that he would be the one to assume the mantle of our ancestor so when he was a young boy he was sent to Te Aute College. However, he was expelled for skipping class and bad behaviour and, on his return to Uawa people would say, "Oh, that's too bad." They said it so often that the name stuck.'

While Mum had only had one son, my uncles and their wives had spawned sixteen cuzzie-bros between them, including Seth, Abe and Spade, who were my nearest male cousins by age.

I think in the early days this evidence that she wasn't as productive as they were must have been painful for Mum. Koro, however, didn't think that it was her fault at all. As he once remarked, 'I always knew Wally's blood was a bit . . . thin.' He was referring to Dad's ancestry (he came from a lesser tribe that lived 'over the hill') and social standing. However, what can you do when your daughter looks like she's being left on the shelf because all the eligible Maori boys of her class and standing are going to university and meeting Pakeha girls?

As if, anyway, any local boy would marry the big chief's daughter.

Get off the grass.

3 /

Apart from Sunday roasts, there was one other particular day every year that the family reserved for a special feast day and celebration: 23 October.

The annual gathering when I was twelve was typical. We all assembled for the usual fresh-air banquet of roast pig, and Dad and my uncles had been out diving for paua, kina and crayfish.

It was lovely under the trees, with the sun shining on the sea. After we'd eaten the pig, Uncle Tu-Bad leant back in his chair, puku full, and said to Nan Esther, 'Well, Ma, now we can breathe easy. That pig was wandering along the road so if it belonged to somebody they won't know it was me who picked it up because we've eaten the evidence.'

It was a joke (or was it?) but Koro got very upset at the thought that he, a court official, had eaten stolen goods. Beneath his irritation something else smouldered.

'Jeez, Pa,' Uncle moaned, 'lighten up, willya?'

Once Koro had calmed down, the family moved to the usual dessert of sponge cakes, jelly and ice cream, and then the adults shifted to wine, served in Nan Esther's special crystal goblets. My uncles and Dad were more partial to beer but, hey, this was Koro's house and beer was a bit common. As for me and my cousins, we were allowed fizzy drink, but I saw Seth, Abe and Spade switch their lemonade for chardonnay.

Koro stood up, tapped his glass for attention and began his usual toast. 'It was on this day in 1769,' he began, 'that the man who began our clan arrived at Uawa and made himself known to us. He came in his waka from Havai'i, which we call Hawaiki, far across the sea, and he was descended from the original Ancients, the Maohi, who once ruled the world as far as the eye could see.' He was using his arms to indicate, sweeping from one side of the sea's horizon to the other. 'They stretched all the way from Hawai'i in the north, Tahiti and Rapanui, Easter Island, in the west and down to us, Aotearoa, in the south-east.'

'Yeah, yeah,' Uncle Bo muttered, somewhat discourteously.

'Today,' Koro continued, 'that great Polynesian nation has been carved up by the English, French, Germans, Dutch and Americans, and now Hawaiki is known as Raiatea, near Tahiti, in French Polynesia. It was there that Tupaea was born. All the highest and greatest bloodlines of Hawaiki chiefs converged in him and, as a boy, he was ordained as an acolyte in the service of the God 'Oro, Atua of the Maohi.'

My uncles' eyes were getting that glazed 'We've heard it all before' look.

'In our ancestor's day, the great national marae and temple consecrated to 'Oro's worship on earth was Taputapuatea, at Opoa. When it was completed the priests and people beseeched 'Oro to come down from the highest heavens and live among them. Lo and behold, a strong south-westerly wind began to blow and, amid flashes of lightning, 'Oro rode down it. He entered the temple and was acknowledged as the supreme god of the earth and the air. Thus his reign in Tahiti began.'

Koro lifted his glass and we followed him. 'It was 'Oro who sent our ancestor to us,' he said, taking the first sip. 'Thus we give thanks to him.'

'To 'Oro,' we responded.

CHAPTER FOUR —
HOUSE OF MEMORIES

1/

Our family grew up surrounded by stories about the original Tupaea, the one who began our dynasty in New Zealand.

Indeed, Koro took it for granted that we would absorb the narratives by some strange osmosis; he thought that because we had the blood of all the royal kings and queens of Tahiti in our veins that they 'spoke' to us too.

In particular, he felt that his son Uncle Tu-Bad (Koro *never* called him that) would overcome his limitations, now that he was an adult, and carry on the tradition of leadership in his generation. 'When I die,' he told Uncle during our family meetings, 'you will take my place on the paepae.'

Koro had a large study off the front verandah overlooking the sea and, on one afternoon, while the rest of the family adjourned to other rooms to sleep off their kai, I overheard Uncle pleading with him to be set free of this obligation.

'I can't do it, Pa,' he said, holding his head in his hands. 'I've never been able to do it. Bo or Charlie would do a better job.'

The door to the study wasn't quite closed. I knew I shouldn't be eavesdropping, but I was mesmerised as I watched Koro facing his son. A huge Tupaea whakapapa chart entirely covered one wall. Two other walls had floor-to-ceiling bookcases. One was stacked with Koro's genealogy books, carefully numbered and protected in plastic slip covers; open them and you would see his beautiful and clear handwriting. Another bookcase was filled with Maori Land Court records, copies of Hansard and out-of-print library books about the Maori people, especially our famous parliamentarian, Apirana Ngata. On a third wall were photographs, some very old, hand-coloured and in oval frames, of all our family ancestors. Koro also had metal cabinets full of genealogy books, maps and other memorabilia.

It was as if all that history was watching this struggle and witnessing the panic in Koro's voice as he answered his son. 'It has to be you,' he said. 'There isn't any other son to do it.' He had long ago realised that Bo and Charlie had no real interest in living up to the Tupaea legend. 'I know you've always been reluctant to take up the role,' he continued, 'but you're a late developer, that's all. Can't you remember when you were a boy how I would tell you the story of the tortoise and the hare?'

'Yeah.' Uncle Tu-Bad laughed. 'That old story! Well, Pa, this tortoise will never make the finish line.'

'Don't give up,' Koro answered. 'There will come a time when you'll rise to the challenge and when you do that, your family will all support you.' The force of will in his voice was frightening.

I heard Uncle Tu-Bad moaning and saw him shaking his head, no, no, no. He was a big, burly man, fierce looking, but I'd always known him to be kind hearted. With a fierce cry he slammed his fist against a wall.

'All I can say, Pa, is that you'd better not die any time soon.'

21

The news that Uncle Tu-Bad was hanging in there filled the family with relief. 'He's not a natural for the job,' Mum said, 'but I'm proud of my brother for trying to step up to the plate.'

It was in this atmosphere of renewed optimism that we arrived at Koro's for Sunday lunch the following week where he told us of the Order of the Arioi.

One day,' he began, 'the God 'Oro decided to take a wife from among the children of men. He had two sisters, and he asked them, "Could you both help me find a bride?" They agreed and descended with him from their sky kingdom in Te Raituitai. Together the trio travelled throughout the Maohi nation inviting all the women, "Come and dance." Although many of the dancers were beautiful, none of them appealed to 'Oro or his sisters, lacking in femininity and breeding.'

'He was l-l-looking for someone like Nan, eh,' I said.

'Yes,' Koro answered, 'someone who dressed as appropriately as her.' He was referring to Nan Esther's legendary modesty, always trying to keep her family in clothes that covered the entire body from neck to ankles.

'Then,' Koro continued, 'just as 'Oro and his sisters were ready to give up, they found themselves in the vicinity of a red-ridged mountain. There, bathing at the foot of it, was a beautiful girl whose name was Vairumati.' Koro saw that I was entranced by the story and ramped up the description a bit. 'The old documents say that "her face was as the noontide light, and the lustre of her dark eyes shone forth like stars from the deep blue sky". No wonder

'Oro was smitten. Although he returned to Te Ratuitai he asked his sisters to act as go-between.'

I was on a roll. 'That's how the gods b-b-behaved in those days, eh Koro?'

He nodded, approvingly. 'They were always courtly and highly principled. Not like some of the dregs who live in Uawa.'

Seth jabbed me with his elbow. 'Shut up, Little Tutae,' he warned. 'Otherwise we'll be here all day.'

'Anyway,' Koro continued, 'Vairumati was flattered that a god would give her attention and agreed that he could visit her. 'Oro was overjoyed when his sisters took the news back to him and he made a bridge from Te Ratuitai to earth, a rainbow which he could travel down to her home in the red-ridged mountain below.'

'Was it like a slide, K-k-koro?' I asked, edging away from Seth. I was really interested.

'Maybe,' he answered. 'So began 'Oro's courtship of Vairumati. On his first visit he conjured up a cloud to hide his descent and, when he emerged from the vapour and saw that Vairumati returned his interest, he took her as his wife.'

Took? Koro saw me open my mouth to ask a question . . . and he pressed the fast-forward button.

'Every evening 'Oro . . .' Koro decided to accommodate my fancy '. . . slid down the rainbow, and returned to Te Raituitai the next morning. And very soon Vairumati bore a son—'

I opened my mouth again.

'—who became a powerful ruler among men,' Koro rushed on. 'However, two of 'Oro's god brothers became curious about his behaviour. Where did 'Oro go when he went down the rainbow? They set out to find the answer and saw him with Vairumati. Aue, but they should have brought gifts for the happy couple! Ashamed that they had come empty-handed, one of the gods transformed himself into a pig and the other into a bunch of red feathers and they presented themselves, in those ahua, to the two lovers. When Vairumati expressed her delight at the gifts, 'Oro decided to reward his brothers for their ingenuity.'

'C-c-cool, Koro!'

Koro smiled. ''Oro transformed his brothers back into gods and constituted them . . .'

He was looking at Uncle Tu-Bad as he said the word.

'. . . Arioi.'

On our way home that day, Mum and Dad were exchanging glances. Then Mum gave me a word of warning.

'I wouldn't appear too enthusiastic if I was you,' she said.

In subsequent Sunday lessons, Koro told us how the Arioi quickly gained numerous followers and the worship of 'Oro spread quickly through all the islands of the Maiohi nation — and many pigs were gladly dedicated to 'Oro. Their leaders soon built temples and other sacred precincts on Hawaiki, Tahiti, Moorea, Maiaoiti, Huahine, Tahaa, Porapora and Maurua. Only high-ranking men and women were admitted and, because 'Oro and Vairumati had been beautiful, they had to be comely too. An important part of all the ceremonials was the carrying of a young pig to the temples where it was sacrificed and offered to 'Oro with red feathers.

So that was why we ate pork every 23 October.

31

A nd then the shit hit the fan.

Oh, there'd been rumours, but it wasn't until Uncle Tu-Bad was arrested in a police sting that the news came out: he'd been cultivating weed in the backblocks behind Uawa. The operation had actually been the result of a patient surveillance and stakeout on a gang headquarters in Auckland. The police waited until they'd uncovered the courier trail, and it led them to the supplier on the East Coast — and eventually to Uncle Tu-Bad as one of the growers.

The arrests and subsequent trials in Auckland, Hamilton, Rotorua, Whakatane and Gisborne were reported on radio and television and in all the newspapers. The TV newsreader on one channel began the item by saying, 'Among the accused caught in the recent nationwide drug bust was the son of prominent Maori court official, Tupaea Mahana.'

Koro, of course, was devastated. Not just by Uncle Tu-Bad's guilt, but also by the shame of having himself and the family exposed to national scrutiny.

'Why didn't somebody tell me?' he cried when the news broke. He was very angry with the family, especially when it appeared that Uncle Bo and Uncle Charlie and their wives knew about Uncle Tu-Bad's activities, even Dad — I don't think Mum did: if she'd known, she would have told Uncle to wise up.

Koro offered his resignation to the Maori Land Court, but it was declined: he was too good an official to lose. At the initial hearing in Gisborne, some people thought that he might use his influence to obtain a lighter sentence for Uncle Tu-Bad, but he didn't: his eldest son was guilty and should face justice.

Like the other growers, Uncle was sentenced to two years in prison.

'I wish I'd never named you Tupaea,' Koro said to him. 'Your ancestor will be grieving today.'

Uncle Tu-Bad's eyes streamed with tears. And after Uncle went to prison, Koro moved swiftly to find somebody else over whose shoulders he could throw the mantle of Tupaea.

M-m-me?' I asked.

'Sometimes, the mana jumps a generation,' Mum answered, trying to convince herself. 'Now that your Uncle Tu-Bad hasn't worked out, well, you seem to be the likeliest candidate. Ever since you were born, Koro's always loved you. Not only that but . . .' Mum bit her lip, knowing that her spotless reputation was to blame '. . . Pa's furious with your uncles and that makes me, Dad and you flavour of the month.'

All I could feel was absolute terror. I clutched my inhaler, taking a deep draw on it.

'And after all, you bear Tupaea's name,' Mum said.

CHAPTER FIVE—
ACOLYTE OF 'ORO

1/

You know, Koro and Nan Esther's house is still there on the beach at Uawa, No. 5 Pohutukawa Road. I've no idea why they should number it that way as there's no 1, 2, 3 or 4, and the road goes on for a mile before you get to Roger Grant's farm.

Koro still likes visitors. If you're passing through Uawa, stop and say hello for me, eh? Tell him Little Tu sent you.

Don't believe any of the stories he tells about me.

2/

The mana skips a generation?

Well, what can you say when you're only twelve, you want to please everybody and your mother puts the hard word on you? And who was I to disappoint Koro, the man who'd kept vigil over me when I was a baby and given the name of Tupaea to me rather than to Seth? So Koro told (not asked) Mum that I was to stay after every Sunday roast for extra tuition in Maohi history and culture; I think he felt that if he pressed automatic tuning in my head long enough, the ancestral broadcasts would come in loud and clear.

Mum said yes (jumped) and Dad agreed (obeyed) because he never liked being disparaged by the Mahana family and always tried to please his father-in-law.

My uncles Bo and Charlie, and their wives, welcomed the fact that Koro had zeroed in on Mum, Wally and me when it came to what they called 'all that Tupaea stuff'. So did Seth: he, Abe and Spade laughed at me, saying, 'We're glad that we're not called Tupaea.' And when my extra lessons began, Seth constantly asked me, 'Does Koro have anything valuable? Any greenstone or whalebone? Any dollars?' He hoped I'd be able to steal something that he could sell and, with the money, buy stuff to smuggle to his dad in prison.

On those Sunday afternoons, Mum helped Nan Esther clean and tidy up after lunch. Dad turned himself into a dogsbody by chopping Koro's wood and doing odd jobs around the homestead and maybe obtaining a favoured look or two. Koro and I adjourned to the Holy of Holies, the corner of his library where he kept his archives about the Maohi and, especially, Tupaea. In the alcove was a rolltop desk and two chairs and, there, Koro began to seriously induct me into our family history.

The lessons began when he told me the worship of 'Oro became so widespread it reached the extremities of the Maohi nation, even to Aotearoa. So let me set the scene a bit with the day declining into darkness, and the sound of the sea soughing and sucking at the sand.

'From around 700 AD,' Koro began, 'the time when Aotearoa began to be colonised by Maohi from Tahiti, all our tribal histories tell of journeys back and forth between New Zealand to Hawaiki. 'Oro's priests were among that number, travelling the pathways illuminated in the heavens by the stars, not only to Aotearoa but also to other islands of the Fa'atau Aroha, the alliance of nations which worshipped him.'

Mum and Nan Esther were laughing in the kitchen and Dad was chopping wood out the back, but, already, I was putty in Koro's hands.

'They came in slim double canoes, and such pahi could make voyages of up to twenty days without provisioning. They were designed to skim the waves, their sails full before the wind. They would come down from Hawaiki to Rarotonga and thence to Aotearoa, which was in the direction of the morning sun.'

He went out onto the verandah to show me; I joined him there. 'The priests would have come from that direction,' he said; the sun was high above the brilliant ocean. 'However, at some time in the fifteenth century, a comet plunged into seas just south of Aotearoa, creating an immense wall of water that struck the east coast.' Koro made a chopping gesture with his hands. 'Ka kotia te taitapu ki Hawaiki. The sacred seaway of the priests, especially from Hawaiki to Aotearoa and back, was cut.'

'But 'Oro didn't forget us, eh,' I said.

Koro put an arm around my shoulder. 'No, mokopuna, he didn't.'

That evening, as we were driving home, Dad looked across at me and grinned. 'How was it today?' he asked.

I looked up at the evening sky. 'G-g-good,' I answered. There were so many stars up there, eavesdropping from heaven. Good? It was better than that.

Dad was in a mischievous mood. He pretended he was holding a microphone. 'Hello, Little Tu, are you receiving, over?'

Mum scolded him. 'Wally,' she said, 'have more respect.'

3/

ven the spring, with pollen aggravating my asthma and turning it into severe bronchitis, and keeping me in bed, couldn't stop the momentum of Koro's storytelling. When he found me miserably trying to breathe in a room hazy with a humidifier he would kiss me on the forehead, and prop up pillows to support me. 'Are your Maohi ancestors speaking to you today?' He would sit behind me, lift up my pyjama top and start massaging my back. Even though I sometimes protested, 'Puh-lease, Koro', he would carry on regardless.

'What's the matter with you?' he would ask grumpily if I tried to pull the pyjama top back across my skinniness and poking-out ribs. 'I'm your koro. Ever since you were a baby, looking after you has been my job.'

He would resume his lessons whether I wanted him to or not.

'Our ancestor, the original Tupaea,' he began one day, 'must have been born in Hawaiki around 1720. That's when the worship of 'Oro was at its height in Tahiti. The Maohi may have worshipped many gods but 'Oro displaced them all; he became not only their most powerful god but the one God, Te Atua. And the society of the Arioi had grown to thousands of acolytes, sailing in great fleets from place to place, dancing, singing and praising 'Oro.'

I submitted to Koro's rubbing and massaging and his strong hands kneading and opening the cavity in my ribcage so that my lungs would expand. Sometimes it hurt.

'The most beautiful, the most sacred among the Arioi was Tupaea,' Koro continued. 'As a boy he was consecrated to 'Oro. He quickly became high priest and guardian of all the arts of 'Oro and the Maohi.'

'What did he look like?' I asked.

'This is difficult to even imagine, but our ancestor was considered to be without physical flaw. He was tall and handsome, and he was also blessed with great intellectual powers and warrior skills. To mark his status he was given a special tattoo that radiated from the base of his spine, spreading and curving around the hips, and meeting again in the small of his back. One of these days, mokopuna, you'll be as handsome and clever as him.'

Me? Dream on, Koro. And then he hit me sharply, ouch, to dislodge the phlegm that clogged my lungs.

But you can understand, can't you, why Tupaea filled my daydreams?

On those infrequent days when I was well enough to go to school, instead of seeing cars and buses go by, I began to imagine, instead, an Arioi faery fleet, led by Tupaea.

The most famous waka was *Hotu* or Sea-swell, decorated with matiti, long pennants of many colours, and mou, small circular mat sails attached to the tops of the masts. Bunches of feathers tipped each mast. Behind *Hotu* would have been a flotilla of sixty to seventy waka, carrying up to seven hundred Arioi.

'The Arioi,' Koro said, 'drew large gatherings wherever they went, and Tupaea never disappointed the waiting worshippers. *Hotu* and the fleet would come sailing out of the sun like brightly skimming birds. Each waka had a raised platform on which the Arioi danced. To the sound of song, conch shell, flutes and drums, the fleet would manouevre through the sparkling emerald sea, the breaking surf. Then the celebrations would begin: feasting, dancing, singing and exhibitions of athletic prowess that went on into the night.'

No wonder that, while the rest of the class got on with Four-Eyes Wilson's English class, I was locked into my ancestor's story.

But in the 1750s Hawaiki came under attack from nearby Porapora. Alas, the God 'Oro may have been above all others, but humankind, even in Tahiti, was driven by hubris.

'Nothing could save the sacred marae,' Koro told me. 'Therefore, in the middle of the night, when the battle was at its highest peak, Tupaea rescued from Taputapuatea the sacred to'o in which 'Oro resided, a cylinder sheathed in red feathers. Tupaea also took the royal loincloth that symbolised 'Oro's connection with the children of men. While Tupaea's faithful guards fought a desperate rear-guard action, he escaped with the cylinder on *Hotu* and fled to Papara, the royal seat of Purea, the greatest ariki then living among the Maohi. She was regarded as the queen of Tahiti. Safely esconced, he became high priest and adviser to Purea and her husband.'

Koro showed me a small framed portrait of Purea. She was tall, beautiful and her curly abundant hair was bound with a piece of red tapa decorated with tropical feathers and flowers. Beneath a cloak of regal red she wore an ankle-length pare of white tapa patterned in yellow.

'But there was one more task to do. A new marae for 'Oro had to be built. "Would you raise such a marae, o Queen?" Tupaea asked. She agreed, saying, "Let us call it Mahaiatea, and let it be the greatest temple compound in all the Maohi nation." Once it was completed, the God was taken within.'

While Four-Eyes Wilson droned on, I liked to sketch Mahaiatea in my school book. I drew a pyramid with eleven large steps leading up to a sundial. I sketched bird-like figures, heralds of 'Oro, guarding the pyramid. On the middle of the top platform I drew the imposing figure of 'Oro, carved in stone, overlooking his earthly dominion.

The ancient Egyptians may have had their pyramids, and the Aztecs their great complexes and temples to the sun god.

We had Mahaiatea.

4/

Of course my pretence couldn't last.

One day when Koro asked me the usual question, 'Are your Maohi ancestors speaking to you today?', and although I answered yes, I had a panic attack.

Please don't think less of me that I lied to him. I wanted to be an obedient and dutiful grandson and to serve 'Oro, like one of those altar boys at church. My imagination was always playing tricks and sometimes I did sense voices and hear the sound of distant Tahitian drums.

However, puberty kicked in and I realised that all my pretence had led Koro to believe that the ancestors really were speaking through me.

If that was happening, then I must have a particular destiny, right?

And that should be nurtured, right?

Wrong.

CHAPTER SIX —
THE FALL OF AN ALTAR BOY

1/

There was a whole lot of life out there.

I started to rebel, not necessarily against Koro, but certainly against the strictures of small town life in Uawa. In this I was aided by my Uncle Bo who liked to press beer on me and my cousins Seth, Abe and Spade, who, despite my gangling appearance and asthma, soon had me shoplifting with them. I wanted to be cool, I wanted to belong, so while I spoke nicely to Mr Merton in the dairy they ducked behind him and raided the cash register or took cigarettes and sweets.

Very soon, like them, I was skipping school and rebelling against anything that I was told to do. Koro soon noticed. He knew what Uncle Bo was up to, and he grew concerned for me because he'd always harboured a hope that I'd become a lawyer and, maybe, a judge. 'They're the ones who have the power,' he told me, 'not a Maori Land Court clerk.'

Yeah, well, I wasn't the only one with daydreams obviously. Becoming a lawyer was way off base.

Inevitably, there came a time when I wasn't as interested in his Sunday afternoon lessons and, in the end, he rapped my skull with his knuckles. 'Knock, knock, is anybody in the whare? Aue, te hoha o te tamaiti. You're getting to be like your ratbag cousins. And if you don't watch out you'll end up in prison like your uncle.'

Indeed, he became embarrassed by the regularity with which he was asked to intercede on our behalf by Maori wardens who didn't want us to get police records. 'When you appear before the judge,' he growled, 'don't tell them who your grandfather is, otherwise people will know that we're related.'

Everybody began to ask, 'Whatever happened to Little Tu? Where's that nice boy gone to?' They commiserated with Mum and Dad: 'Don't worry, it's just a phase that young boys go through. He'll be back.'

Oh yeah? How easy it is to be a good boy one minute and a bad boy the next.

Egged on by my cousins, I set fires in people's letterboxes, shoplifted, broke into houses and cars, and I took to regularly jumping off the main Uawa bridge, scaring people as they drove across it. I was further encouraged by Seth, Abe and Spade; I was such a trier, probably hoping to show my cuzzies that despite my infirmities I merited their attention. They realised I had no fear and, hey, maybe I might actually kill myself in my jumps and they would inherit all Koro's money. And anyway they could make some dollars out of my foolhardiness.

I was too innocent — or dumb — to disagree when they suggested that I turn my jumping into a money-making operation. They created traffic jams until enough cars had stopped and then pointed me out as I stood on the railing of the bridge. 'Stop him, please, he's going to kill himself!'

There was always some heroic old man who would come running and yelling, 'Don't do it, son!' and try to talk me out of it. I would pretend to go along with him but, at the last moment, I would trip . . .

And that feeling . . . and all of a sudden, my lungs clearing. Then the clarity as if . . . somewhere I would find . . . perfection.

Then, oh, for one moment that sense of weightlessness, of defying gravity before the thrill of falling.

The audience would appear at the railing, ashen-faced, to see if I had survived.

What was I doing? Sitting at the bottom of the river, ho hum, fiddle dee dee, giving them a heart attack.

I would arise like a merman and wave, and my cousins would go cap in hand to ask for money from the now applauding drivers. It was a scam, sure, but my cousins made a lot of money (I got a cut, so I wasn't entirely blameless) until, one day, Koro happened to be in one of the cars. He witnessed the whole charade and watched me jump off the bridge. By the time I reached the road, Seth, Abe and Spade had taken off.

Koro clipped me over the ear. 'Are you a muttonhead or what?'

2/

I was thirteen when Uncle Tu-Bad was released from prison, early, for good behaviour.

All the family welcomed him back except Koro. When he knocked on the door of the homestead, Koro said to Nan Esther, 'Tell him I'm not ready to forgive him.'

His response was stern and implacable but Uncle Tu-Bad took it well. 'I deserve it,' he said.

We all thought that Uncle Tu-Bad would revert to his old ways and resume his plantation activities but he had a few surprises for us.

One day, he really surprised me. I was sitting at the back of his place, smoking weed with Seth, Abe and Spade, when he discovered us. I thought he'd be okay with that but, instead, he hauled Seth off his arse and slapped him over the head. 'What the fuck do you think you're doing, boy?'

He didn't like the idea of Seth introducing me to drugs of any kind.

'Not Little Tu,' he warned Seth. 'Apart from anything else, Pa would kill me if he found out Little Tu was smoking dope.'

Then he looked into my eyes and ruffled my hair. 'You stay away from this stuff.'

That didn't stop my cousins and me from running away from him, laughing our heads off. But I've often wondered whether they liked me at all. Maybe not. I think to them I was a follower, somebody they could order around.

Before anybody could stop us, we'd snatched a little old lady's car while she was in the post office and went hooning around Uawa in it. Then we were squealing down the old wharf to do rubber-burning wheelies at the end.

Not for long. Uncle Tu-Bad must have rung Koro because they both arrived before the cops could put out an alert on the car.

'Thanks, son,' Koro said to Uncle Tu-Bad. They shook hands and then Koro grabbed him in a tight embrace. 'I'm glad you're home among your people.'

Uncle Tu-Bad took Seth, Abe and Spade with him; Koro hauled me into his car and we got out of there. 'Why are you such an idiot?' he yelled at me. 'You'll never get to be a lawyer the way you're going.' He drove me home to Mum and Dad's place. As we went through the township, he pulled his hat down over his face so that nobody would recognise him. I was a bit aggrieved by his action.

'Koro, I don't think I can be a lawyer or whatever you want me to be. P-p-please give up on me.'

He looked at me, astonished, and almost crashed the car. 'How can I do that?' he asked. 'You're the one whose name is Tupaea.'

I pleaded with him. 'Why should his name make any difference?'

My koro stopped the car. He thought I was stupid. Didn't I know? He was always assuming that I knew things and that I never had to be told. What was I? A mind reader?

When he finally answered my question, his voice sounded the way it did whenever he was chanting karakia: hushed, focused, as if he was in the presence of the ancestors.

'Giving you Tupaea's name is like investing you with his spirit. Haven't you learnt anything?'

He knocked on my head again. 'Somewhere inside you his mauri resides and, pae kare, boy, one of these days it's coming out, whether you like it or not.'

ACT TWO

CHAPTER SEVEN —
THE JOURNEY OF THE HOLY ARK

1 /

'We were very distressed.'

I never realised, until later in life, how much my parents had been affected by my infant struggles to breathe. Wally says that the sight of my small body, wrapped in tubes, was almost too much for Mum to bear. I suspect he was also speaking of himself, because my father has always been the soft-hearted one.

When Mum couldn't have any more children, well, that did it: they patiently set about building my body and increasing my stamina so that I could triumph over my debilitating asthma.

So it was that when I was going through my bad ass phase, they built me a home gym in one of our spare rooms. Without realising it — even though they knew that I idolised Arnie — they gave me something that I became really keen on: body building.

The consequence was that I stopped hanging out with my cousins so much. 'Man oh man,' Dad said to me once, 'did we have a lucky escape.'

Dad bought me an inclined bench press. The following Christmas, one of my presents was some barbells. That same day, our outing was to Te Puia Hospital where even Mum got into the pool ('Close your eyes, Wally') and splashed around while Dad and I raced each other from one end to the other. Every now and then Dad pretended to get cramp and let me win: 'Good boy, you showed your dad up, didn't you?'

Koro got into the act on my thirteenth birthday with some parallel bars, and Nan Esther found a medicine ball in a local op shop. Very soon, Dad had stopped parking the car in the garage and converted it into a larger gym space that could take, as well as the above-mentioned items, a pair of rings that he was able to buy cheap. If you were going past our house at six in the morning, like as not the light was on in the garage and there I'd be with Dad doing basic upper-body workouts, including exercises for the chest, back, shoulders and arms, push-ups ('Just one more, Little Tu'), bench presses, back extensions, concentration curls and other routines. If you were really lucky, you might catch Wally hoisting me up onto the rings to exercise my arms: 'Okay, son, now swing away to your heart's content!' All this work was designed mainly to sculpt my upper body so that it would have a large, beautiful fan-like muscle complex. In particular, Dad aimed to give me a V-shaped back so that my lungs would have room to expand and contract like unseen wings, *Come out, come out, wherever you are,* and fly me through the world.

Well, that was the idea.

Sometimes Dad would scratch his head, walk around me

after a session and say, 'They must be hidden somewhere in that body of yours, son.'

2 /

Dad and I could still have been there in Uawa, training, except that when I turned fourteen he made a huge decision.

We were sitting in the lounge watching television when he gave a small cough to draw attention to himself and said to Mum, 'I want to join my two older brothers, Ralph and Tommy, in Wellington. They're driving buses for the city council.'

Now, I think that Dad had expected Mum to immediately veto the idea. If she'd told him, 'No', he would have accepted her decision. Instead, Mum blinked once — Was this really Wally speaking? — and then she must have seen Dad for what he was: a kind and patient man who had followed her throughout their lives but who now wanted to take a chance and prove something, perhaps only to himself. I suspect all those years of being looked down upon by Koro and the Mahana family had marked him and he no longer wanted to be the family dogsbody. Also, there was no more wood to chop.

Although she was upset at the prospect of leaving her beloved father and Nan Esther, Mum decided to support him. 'Okay,' she said.

'You'll come with me?' He didn't quite believe it.

'It will be good for all of us,' she answered.

At the time, I didn't know what Mum meant.

I soon realised that she, also, was making a bid for freedom. For too long the assumption had been that, as the only daughter, she would always stay at home close to the parents and look after them.

Koro and Nan Esther were horrified when she told them of our plans. 'You're going to leave us?' Nan Esther wept. Mum stared them both in the eyes and her gaze never wavered. 'You have your sons to look after you, Tu-Bad, Bo and Charlie and their wives.' Her unspoken message, of course, was: It's their turn now.

Uncle Bo and Uncle Charlie weren't happy about that idea. Having Koro and Nan Esther around their unwilling necks would mean they'd have to sharpen up their otherwise slack lives. 'You're the girl of the family,' Uncle Bo said. 'It's your job to look after Pa and Nan, not ours.'

When my uncles had been children and Mum was unable to defend herself, they'd found it easy to force her right arm behind her back and give it a sharp twist to make her submit. Not any more.

'Oh, is it now?' she flared. 'Time for you lazy sods and your hopeless wives to do some work for a change.'

Mum and Dad's action was desertion and dereliction of duty, but in Koro's case there was more: he didn't want me to leave. 'You and Wally go to Wellington,' he said after one of the Sunday family gatherings, 'but leave my moko here so that I can bring him up myself. How will I be able to talk to him about Tupaea with me in Uawa and him down there in the capital?'

Mum compressed her lips and folded her arms. Leave her only child in Uawa? 'I'm doing this as much for Little Tu as for me and Wally,' she began. 'Maybe he needs some time out from Uawa.'

Time out? I saw Koro open his mouth to say something —

taking a break from your culture was a foreign notion to him — but she ploughed on.

'There are other matters to consider about his upbringing too. You know very well that there are some bad influences on him here . . .' she eyeballed Uncle Bo and my cousin Seth '. . . and Pa, we've been lucky to head Little Tu off at the pass. He was only two clicks away from going bad on us, joining a gang and doing courier work. Don't think I don't know what goes down. Apart from which, specialists in Wellington will give him better help with his asthma and his stuttering.'

Although the arguments were long and furious she wouldn't budge. 'No, Pa. Wally is my husband and where he goes we all go, and that includes Little Tu.'

Seth, Abe and Spade wanted me to tell Mum and Dad I wanted to stay because they were my mates. Sure.

'If you go, Little Tutae,' they said, coralling me at the back of Mr Merton's dairy one day, 'Koro's going to pick on us and we're not interested in that Tupaea shit.'

Did I give a toss? They gave me a black eye, but I didn't care.

On the day that we left Uawa, Koro was distraught.

Our house had been sold, the household belongings had already gone ahead of us and we were ready to leave in Dad's ute. Then Koro arrived, and Uncle Tu-Bad was with him. Was Koro disappointed that I hadn't made any fuss about leaving him? I couldn't look him in the eyes. I was ashamed that I was letting him down.

'Why do you insist on taking my moko away from me, May?' he cried. He was rocking back and forth, tears streaming from his eyes, flailing his walking stick. He couldn't believe she would kidnap me from his presence.

Mum stood her ground. She found an unexpected ally in Uncle Tu-Bad. Something had happened to him while he was in prison. I don't know what it was — maybe it was those Maori language and culture lessons they gave inmates — but something had softened him.

'You go, sis,' he said. 'Don't worry about Pa.'

Still Koro didn't want to let me go. 'Little Tu almost died when he was born,' he cried. 'How will I be able to save him again if something happens to him in Wellington?'

Died? I hadn't known that.

And then, in a temper, Koro uttered some rather choice remarks about Dad. 'And you . . . you were a no-hoper in Uawa and you'll be a no-hoper in Wellington.'

Mum's back went up. 'I will not let you say those sorts of things about my husband,' she said. 'He's been a good son-in-law to you, Pa.' With that she bundled me into the car.

Wally started the engine. 'Thank you, dear,' he said to Mum. He was grateful to her for choosing him, but also disturbed at all the fuss. What if he didn't make better passage in the world and we had to come back with our tails between our legs?

Koro just had time to thrust something through the window at me. 'Take this with you,' he said. 'It will protect you.'

It was a red feather.

My mother's eyes widened. I heard her mutter under her breath, 'And maybe it's time Little Tu had a rest from this . . .'

She shut her mouth before she could say the heretical words 'mumbo jumbo'. Instead, she motioned to Dad.

'Time to go, dear, before anybody says something they might regret.'

And that was that.

CHAPTER EIGHT — DETOUR

1 /

There's a photograph of me with Mum and Dad that must have been taken fairly soon after we arrived in Wellington.

It's a very nice picture of Mum. The camera has captured her side-on so that you don't see that her beam has broadened a bit. And because it was taken without her putting on the usual face she liked to show to the world, she looks very pretty. The wind has blown a few strands of hair across her face and, laughing, she's put a hand up to push them away. It's a film star pose, and she looks good doing it.

What's surprising about the photograph is me. I'm taller than Mum, and even taller than Dad, who was five ten. When did that happen?

Mum and Dad must have bought me a jacket. I'm wearing it, so you can't see how skinny I really am, but the shoulders reveal that I'm filling out. Those wings of mine are folded away in there somewhere.

I've taken a step back and tucked my head in. I'd never thought of myself as good-looking — my hair was too bushy, my eyes were squinty, my nose was too long, my lips were too big — so didn't like having my photograph taken. But those same squinty eyes are bright and expectant.

21

won't say that the move to Wellington was easy.

We arrived during the school break between the first and second term. Mum and Wally settled us into a small two-bedroom flat that Dad's brothers had found for us, up zigzag steps on the slopes midway between Berhampore and Island Bay. From the south-facing windows you could see the sea.

'Well,' Mum said when she stood in the passageway and saw how run-down the place was, 'we've made our bed and now we all have to lie in it.' She was not only referring to us but also to Koro, because no sooner had we moved in and had the telephone connected than he started to call. In the middle of the night.

From my bedroom I would hear Mum answering the phone and talking to him. 'Hello? Yes, Pa, I'm here. Yes, we're fine. How are you? And how's Ma? No Pa, we're not coming home. Please Pa, try to understand. And Little Tu? No, I won't wake him, he's fast asleep but he's fine, Pa, fine.'

We moved our furniture and the rest of our belongings in. Dad immediately went to work for the Wellington buses so that we could pay the rent. I remember watching him battling a southerly as he walked down the steps. He looked forlorn and hesitant and, partway down, he stopped, as if he was about to turn back. 'No, Dad,' I whispered. 'You'll be okay.'

He saw me at the window and waved before continuing down to the street.

My mother has always had hidden resources, a quiet but determined strength.

While Dad was working, she made me help her paint the walls of the flat — she got the rent down by telling the landlord it would increase the value of his place — and, after the paint had dried, I put my posters of Arnie on my bedroom wall. I had three now, and the one of Arnie in dark glasses, wearing a leather jacket and astride a motorbike, was my favourite. On a whim, I sellotaped Koro's red feather to his hair; now Arnie looked like a mean Red Indian dude.

Mum was hesitant at first about what I'd done, then shrugged her shoulders. 'Well, I guess that's as good a place as any.' As for Dad, when he saw the feather on his return, elated, from his first day on the job, I heard him whispering to Mum in a way I wasn't supposed to hear, 'At least Pa didn't go up to the cave in the hills and get that old piece of ironwood.'

Once we had finished the painting, Mum found me a speech therapist. At the same time, she was a whirlwind, organising the house for 'her men', and every now and then she would don one of her smartest outfits and go looking for a job so that she could supplement Dad's income. Success! She was put on a waiting list for nursing staff at Wellington Hospital in Newtown.

Mum also checked out the high schools in the area and took me to Wellington High to enrol because it was co-ed and multicultural. Mum filled in the paperwork, and then we were interviewed by Mr Van Dyke, one of the deans of the school. As soon as he started asking me questions, like 'So, Tupaea, can you tell me what options you were doing in Tolaga Bay?', Mum began, as usual, to answer on my behalf:

'He did Maori.'

'Is there anything else we offer that you like the look of? Food technology maybe?'

'Japanese and classical studies could be interesting,' Mum answered. 'He might go to university after high school.'

University? Not that again.

Mr Van Dyke was looking at me in a quizzical manner. I started to get flustered and turned to Mum. 'I can t-t-talk for myself, Mum,' I said.

Her eyes widened. Obviously things were changing all around her. Then she shrugged, got up, kissed me on the cheek and said, 'He's all yours.'

When she left, the dean smiled at me encouragingly. 'Mothers are like that,' he said.

Not long after that, Mum was called in to Wellington Hospital and offered a position. One of the reasons why she was successful was because, at her interview, she looked around at the Pakeha faces on the interviewing panel and said, 'Well, ladies and gentlemen, looks like your lucky day has just walked through the door, eh?' She knew she had Maori skills that the hospital didn't possess.

Koro kept ringing. It was so sad hearing Mum talk to him. 'Hello, Pa, is that you again? Please stop doing this. We're fine, Pa. And Little Tu has started at Wellington High. Pa, please don't cry. You'll only make yourself sick. Yes, I'll tell Little Tu you called.'

Over the next months, we all began to adjust to the city. I think Mum never really became a Wellingtonian; it wasn't Uawa, but it would have to do. After a while, though, she developed a good social circle.

Dad couldn't have been happier. He was with Ralph and Tommy, and could go skindiving for paua on his days off or when he pretended he was sick and couldn't come with Mum and me to church. Every now and then, he would take Mum to a local pub that was a renowned watering hole for Ngatis, as people from the East Coast were called.

After a while, the telephone calls from Koro began to diminish as he realised we weren't coming home.

3/

Out of sight, out of mind.

I have to confess that the God 'Oro and his emissary on earth, Tupaea, took a back seat to the excitement and challenges of a new school and a new city.

And I was determined to start Wellington High with a fresh slate. I didn't want to be that same young kid with a stutter. My speech therapist was a lovely lady who worked hard on my plosives, and when the second term started I had the stutter under control most of the time. My greatest triumph was to introduce myself on my first day to the English class:

'My first name is T-Tupaea and I come from the . . . East Coast.'

From that moment I was improving all the time.

I also embraced the challenge of becoming a city boy. I was still more imaginative than intellectual, and therefore enjoyed art and music more than maths and science. I also began to revel in languages; all those Sunday lessons with Koro had given me an interest in learning and, more important, the habit of patience.

But I was also filling out and a kind of physical symmetry

came into my life, equalising it in some strange way. Starting in the second term, when friendships had already been formed, made it a bit hard, so I decided to join the kapa haka team. When I began to walk to the back row the tutor, Mr Ropata, stopped me and said, 'What are you doing back there? Come up to the front.' To the front: what was he talking about? I didn't know what to do in the front! I was accustomed to being behind everybody else and copying what they were doing: hands up in the air when they did, and stamping my foot when they stamped their feet.

The next time was when I decided to try for the C indoor basketball team but the phys ed teacher picked me for the B team. At Uawa I'd always been the last to be picked. What was happening? I hadn't realised that, though I was still as skinny as, I'd gone through a couple of growth spurts.

However, my selection brought trouble because I displaced another boy, so his mates decided to rough me up a little, just to remind me of the pecking order. Man, they were big Polynesian guys, and their brother must have been Jonah Lomu. I tried as best I could to fight back with the skills I'd been taught by my cousins in the Uawa Whare Wananga of Fisticuffs where the main law was: 'Fight fair if you can but, if you're in a corner, do down and dirty.'

I was lucky. There were other boys from the East Coast who I was related to, like Horse — already built like a brick shit-house at fifteen — and Bilbo, and they came to my rescue. They allowed me to join their crowd and I came under their protection.

Need I tell you of the second aspect of school that I enjoyed? Wellington High School had lots of pretty girls. A plus was that I could admire girls like Peggy Roberts or Gail Johnson and, unlike in Uawa, they wouldn't turn out to be a cousin, even if five times removed.

And then, one day, I met Thierry. School was out, and I was on my way through the gates when I saw him surrounded by a group of other boys, the same ones who'd roughed me up. They were baiting him and he was crouched on the ground, cowering behind his schoolbag, saying, 'Please don't hurt me.'

Horse, who was with me, said, 'This isn't our fight.' But I'd seen Thierry in my maths class. He was a fair-haired boy, graceful, and I couldn't pass by; I knew what it was like to be picked on. Somewhere in the past few years I must have made a decision that I wouldn't stand for it again — or stand by and watch someone else taking that crap. 'That's enough,' I said to Thierry's tormentors. We began to square off when Mr Van Dyke appeared. 'What's going on here?' he asked. 'Thierry, aren't you late for your gym training?'

Gym training? My eyes lit up. Since Dad had started work on the buses our morning sessions had become almost non-existent. The bullies took off and I helped Thierry up. 'Thank you,' he said. He was already hurrying away and, as I was going in his direction and Horse and Bilbo weren't, I waved quickly to my two mates and followed him.

'I didn't want to get into a fight,' he began. 'I'm not a coward,' he added defensively, 'but I'm competing this weekend and if I'd fought those guys I could have damaged my conditioning. They could have laid me up.'

'What gym do you go to?' I asked.

'My father's,' he replied. 'It's not exactly a gym.'

Curious, I plied Thierry with more questions, but he wouldn't divulge any more information. 'All right,' he said in the end. 'Come next week, bring shorts and a singlet and if you can get past my father . . .'

was unprepared for what I saw when I arrived the following week: a couple of young children were doing floor exercises and some older boys were practising on vaulting apparatus. I realised what Thierry meant: this was a school for gymnasts, and among the athletes were some who were top class and I recognised from television.

Finding the changing room, I put on my black shorts and T-shirt. Gloomily I looked at myself in the mirror: a hick-town hori stared back. When I went back out I saw Thierry exercising on one of two sets of rings. Below him stood his instructor.

'Alley-oop!' the man cried, and Thierry executed a two-and-a-half twist before landing. His instructor grinned and patted him on the back, then saw me waiting.

'You must be . . . Tupaea?' he asked in French-accented English. 'I am Jean-Luc, Thierry's father. He tell me lot about you. I am grateful you assisted him. His tournée was an important one.' Before I could stop him, he was appraising me: gently measuring with his hands my chest, shoulders, forearms and mid-section. 'Strong wrists, biceps good, mid-section good . . . You work out a lot?'

'Just the normal, I guess.'

Without waiting for my reply, he lifted Thierry onto one set of rings and then, before I could say no, hoisted me onto the other. Until that moment my body had been relaxed. But his action caused it to flex, *Come out, come out, wherever you are,* and all of a sudden those wings, folded beneath my shoulders, unfurled.

Jean-Luc was astounded. 'So . . . we discover another body within your body!' he exclaimed. 'It comes out from the chrysalis.'

Then he was all business. 'You have some experience, oui?'

'Oui,' I bleated, trying to keep myself steady.

'You follow Thierry's example? We do a set of warm-ups, so I can consider your stamina, conditioning and flexibility, and you follow the leader, oui?'

'Oui.' I was holding tight to the rings and attempting to keep them from shaking.

Jean-Luc began to issue instructions to Thierry. 'Dead hang, Thierry! Now kip support!'

He turned sharply to me. 'Follow, Tupaea, follow!'

Ugh, aaargh, got it.

Jean-Luc snapped out more orders to both of us. 'Handstand, Thierry! Sustain 1, 2, 3, 4 . . . Sustain, Tupaea! . . . 6, 7, 8, 9, 10 . . . bon! Lower to support, Thierry! Cross pullouts 1, 2, 3 . . . Follow, Tupaea! Good boy!'

Good boy? That's all I get for my effort?

'Fall back to inverted hang, front lever, back lever, front lever, back lever, dismount.'

Thierry flipped off the rings; I followed, crashing to the ground. Thierry looked as fresh as a bird; I was sweating like a pig.

'Okay, Tupaea,' Jean-Luc said. 'You show promise. Tell me why you want to come to my gym?'

'To get fit,' I answered, somewhat lamely.

'Oh, no no no!' he smiled, giving me a knowing look. 'You want more than that, eh mon petit?' He walked to a small desk and wrote an address on a pad. 'You go to this doctor and get thorough examination. And if you pass, I take you.'

Things were happening to me that I didn't recognise myself, but others did.

47

Not long after that, the God 'Oro sent my ancestor Tupaea sliding down that rainbow of his, back into my life. They started messing with my head again.

It happened during history class when Mrs Miller took us for a lesson on Captain Cook.

'The scientific world was buzzing with excitement about the Transit of Venus, expected on the third of June 1769,' Mrs Miller began. 'Three years earlier, the British ship HMS *Dolphin* had discovered an island called Tahiti, renamed King George's Land after the reigning monarch, George III. It was decided that this was the ideal location for making scientific observations of the transit.'

Suddenly, my lessons with Koro came flooding back into my memory. Hadn't he told me about the *Dolphin*?

'When Europeans arrived in the South Pacific,' Koro had said, 'Tupaea must have known that the Maohi world would be changed forever. But for good or evil? There was amazement at first when the *Dolphin* arrived, but then Maohi — and Tupaea and his queen Purea also — realised that Captain Wallis and his crew on the *Dolphin* had come to conquer, and they retaliated against the invader. Of course the *Dolphin* was a gunship, but Tupaea and Purea weren't to know that. It wasn't until the battle at Matavai Bay, on the north coast of Tahiti, that they witnessed the full and lethal power of the *Dolphin*'s guns.

'They sent out three hundred canoes, carrying some two thousand men onto the water. "Attack!" Tupaea ordered. That's when the *Dolphin*'s great guns were brought into action with a savage twenty-four-gun broadside, and another and another.

Within minutes bodies filled the bay, turning the sea blood red, and there were more deaths as further broadsides were aimed at the shore where thousands of spectators had gathered.

'"What is this death-dealing aitua," Purea asked Tupaea, "that can cut our great canoes in half as if they are just floating sticks of wood? Look how it roars and, immediately, people fall around us."'

istening to Mrs Miller, I was almost bursting out of my skin. I wanted to tell her that I knew the story.

'Another expedition was planned under the joint auspices of the Admiralty and the Royal Society,' she continued, 'and James Cook was chosen to lead it. He was given command of the *Endeavour*.' She began to point out on a map the incredible voyage from Plymouth. Then she said the words that made me sit bolt upright:

'Cook established his observatory at Matavai Bay, where the *Dolphin* had anchored three years earlier. He stayed for almost two months, waiting for the transit, and unlike Captain Wallis of the *Dolphin* he was able to make friendly relations with the Tahitians. Among them was a Polynesian sailor called Tupaea, who joined him on board the *Endeavour*. After the Transit of Venus was observed, Tupaea sailed with Cook to New Zealand.'

Tupaea a sailor?

And he joined Cook on the *Endeavour*?

I couldn't help myself. 'That can't be right,' I said.

That night, I rang Uawa. Nan Esther answered the telephone. 'Can I speak to Koro?' I asked.

I was very cross and embarrassed, having tried to explain to the class about our family story of Tupaea — and being laughed at when I insisted he arrived in New Zealand on his own waka.

'I thought Tupaea came to Aotearoa on the *Hotu*,' I said. 'You never, ever told me our ancestor came with James Cook, on the *Endeavour*. Why not?'

'James Cook?' Koro replied, as blithe as a bird. 'Tupaea didn't come with James Cook. James Cook came with him!'

Couldn't Koro understand? My ancestor had just been blown out of the water.

CHAPTER NINE — TUPAEA RESURGENT

1/

Ah well, blame it on my vivid imagination.

I'd assumed that straight after the battle of Matavai Bay, Tupaea had sped back to Mahaiatea, on the south coast. Dismayed by what he'd seen of the *Dolphin*'s death-dealing powers, he'd embarked on a desperate mission: he must, for the second time, save 'Oro and protect him unto death.

Tupaea hastened up the steps of the sacred pyramid and there, under a swollen moon, removed the ironwood cylinder and royal loincloth, spiriting them on board the *Hotu*. Escaping under the cloak of night, he soon had the outrigger skimming like an America's Cup yacht over the jagged reef. No wonder they pinched the design.

Quickly, quickly now, for the white strangers must be close behind! Already the *Dolphin* had opened fire, its shells falling closer and closer.

But *Hotu* surged ahead, into the cloak of night. Relieved, Tupaea looked up at the million stars strewn across the night heavens. Where could he go?

To the farthest ends of the earth, the land at the bottom of the world.

Yes! He would seek the sacred seaway that had long ago been

cut to Aotearoa. Surely, there, among 'Oro's fiercest worshippers, the God would find sanctuary.

As it happened, Koro was due to visit Wellington for a few days, because here's the thing: although he stopped telephoning, he began visiting.

'If the maunga can't come from Wellington to visit Mohammed,' he said, 'Mohammed will have to go to the maunga.'

Every five or six weeks Nan Esther drove him from Uawa to Gisborne, where he boarded the cheap early-morning flight to the capital. He generally stayed for three or four days, as long as his job at the Maori Land Court allowed him.

'We just have to go along with it,' Mum said when the visits started. 'Goodness knows, Pa must have a lot of leave owing. And he loves you, Little Tu,' she added, looking at me, 'and he pines for you.'

Actually, I never found Koro's visits a burden; I looked forward to seeing him. The problem was, though, that as our flat only had two bedrooms Mum said I had to give up my bed for him.

'Don't do that,' Koro told her. 'We can bunk in together. It will be like a sleepover, eh moko, and we can talk all night if we want to.'

Well, though I wasn't keen to share a bed with my grandfather, things have a habit of working out. Although Koro complained on his first visit about my snoring there was something really nice and comforting about nodding off to the sound of his voice, like surging waves coming across the midnight sea.

I almost blotted my copybook, however, on a subsequent visit. Dad had gone to collect Koro from the airport, and they were coming up the zigzag steps when Mum gave a small scream.

'Quick,' she said, 'you forgot to take that red feather off your Arnie poster and put it in the wakahuia.'

She was referring to its more appropriate location in the small carved box which we kept in the sitting room on what I called 'The Altar', the ledge above the fireplace, where it was surrounded by family photographs.

The reason I had forgotten to remove the feather was that the poster was no longer Arnie looking like a mean Red Indian dude but Tupaea looking like Arnie. I was almost tempted to leave the feather there.

No, perhaps not. Not yet.

21

I was surfing after school with Horse and Bilbo when Koro arrived. Mum had told him where to find me, and he caught a taxi to Lyall Bay where we were sitting on our surf boards, waiting for waves just beyond the causeway. The planes were soaring from the airport, close by, into the wild blue yonder. Although I was more focused on my studies, I'd never lost the wonderment of a Uawa schoolkid pressing his nose hard up against the window, except now I was watching planes, not cars and buses.

When I saw Koro get out of the taxi and pay the driver, I felt a rush of joy and told my mates, 'I'm going in now. See ya.' Although he was wearing a hat and three-piece suit, Koro took off his shoes and socks and rolled up his trousers. He couldn't wait for me to come ashore and waded out to his knees. 'Still got some leave left, I see,' I said.

He laughed, embraced me as if we hadn't seen each other

for centuries, and then appraised me. 'What's happening to you? You look a different boy. Where's my skinny mokopuna gone? Well, whoever you are, are your Maohi ancestors speaking to you today? They were riding on surf boards, too, when Cook arrived in Tahiti.'

'Yeah,' I said sarcastically, 'just before Tupaea joined him and c-came to New Zealand on the *Endeavour*, eh Koro.'

'And your stuttering's not so bad now. Good boy!' Koro followed me back to shore. 'Anyway, Cook's not important. He should count himself lucky that Tupaea came to New Zealand on the *Endeavour*. It was such a tub, and not as militarily equipped as the *Dolphin*. Nevertheless,' he added enigmatically, 'Purea and Tupaea had already let one Pakeha boat go and they weren't about to let a second slip through their fingers.'

3/

It was always Koro's habit, on the first night of his visit, to take me out to a special dinner. In preparation, Mum laid out a pair of good trousers and a shirt. She couldn't wait to get rid of us.

'Why don't you and Dad come with us this time?' I asked her, as she primped and prodded and smoothed me down.

'You know that we're banned,' she answered. 'And me and your father like to have the flat to ourselves sometimes so that we can be ay-lone.'

'Oh, Mum, puh-lease.'

Koro was such a sharp dresser and I like to think that we turned heads whenever we entered a restaurant. Our waiter asked him, 'Would you and your son come this way?', no doubt figuring that flattery would get him a good tip.

We took our seats and Koro gave the menu to me: if he didn't allow me to take charge, how was I going to become a gentleman like himself in polite society? I asked the waiter about the specials, then ordered Koro's favourite chardonnay. Because he was always channelling Tupaea — when did he ever stop? — I made a silent bet with myself that we would start talking about our ancestor before the mains were served.

I won.

'Yes,' he said, sipping his wine, 'our ancestor did depart with James Cook from Tahiti. It happened five weeks after the transit had been observed. Of course Tupaea would have known that Kopu — the Maohi name for Venus — was due to make its voyage across the sun, but when Mr Green invited him to look through the main telescope, I think even he was shaken by what he saw.'

Venus, moving like a waka, bucking in the blazing eye of Rangi, its timbers smouldering and its sails bursting into flame, before it sailed into the cool universe beyond.

'He would have cried out, "Make haste, o waka, go quickly!" and shared a telling glance with Purea. And from that look must have come Purea's decision:

'"Yes, great priest, when the *Endeavour* leaves our shores, you must go with it."'

Let's cut, then, to the evening before the *Endeavour*'s departure. Tupaea went with Purea to Mahaiatea to pray to the God 'Oro. Some people say that something staggering occurred: the God commanded Tupaea to take him from Mahaiatea.

Thus, when he and a young acolyte, Taiata, went on board

the *Endeavour* some say they had with them not only priestly clothing, conches, drums and flutes but also a secret cargo: a large ornate chest that was immediately taken below.

'As the ship sailed away,' said Koro, 'the shimmering water was alive with canoes. Tupaea climbed to the topmast head and waved farewell. From the shore, Purea and thousands of the Arioi were chanting prayers for him. He put the past behind him and set his face northward. That was where England was, and where he thought he was bound. But . . .'

'But?' I asked, my fork hovering. I never liked Koro's buts.

'The Transit of Venus might have been the stated purpose of James Cook's voyage,' Koro said, 'but the unstated intention was to find the great southern continent — Terra Australis Incognita. Our ancestor, Tupaea, found himself hostage to the desires of the empire. Instead of sailing north, the *Endeavour* turned south.'

4 /

We returned from the dinner to find Mum and Dad's bedroom door closed.

Koro gave me a look. 'Still sleeping together and doing you-know-what at their age. Disgusting.'

In my bedroom, although I was tired, I saw that Koro was warming to his subject. I put earplugs into my ears. 'How are you going to hear with those things blocking me out?'

'I've got training at Jean-Luc's in the morning,' I groaned.

You try to go too fast,' Jean-Luc was always complaining. 'Slow down. Concentrate on conditioning and stretching first. Then get your basic skills into your body so that it does the work without thinking.'

However, he'd allowed me to do some floorwork — flares, dive rolls, handsprings, aerial cartwheels — and, sometimes, if I was a good boy, some work on the vaults. 'Shows promise,' he kept saying, knowing that I was champing at the bit and that I wanted to get back on the rings. 'Before you go there, Tupaea, we must still build strength into your arms and mid-section. But it is not enough to attain physical perfection. There are many others who also do that. You yourself must contribute your . . .'

He was flailing for the right English words.

'What sets you apart, Tupaea? What makes you different, comprends?'

'I don't understand,' I answered, puzzled.

He tried again. 'What is the essence, the personality, that makes everything you do yours? It must come from your head and heart as well as your physique. From your histoire, too, mon petit! It will give you the grace and originality to triumph, the thing that only you, Tupaea, can do!'

Koro wouldn't be stopped. When I switched off the light, turned my back on him and closed my eyes, his voice came rolling over me, more surging waves travelling through the moonlit sea.

Ah well, may as well ride them in.

'You know that Cook hadn't wanted Tupaea to come on the voyage?' Koro began. 'It was only at the request of Joseph Banks, who paid for Tupaea's and Taiata's berths, that Cook agreed to have them aboard. Banks thought of Tupaea, initially, as a curiosity — like a pet lion or tiger.'

Koro was massaging my back, sometimes giving it short hits with his open palms. Even though I no longer required it, he couldn't get out of the habit. And I was too blissed out to tell him.

'I think James Cook's attitude was more personal,' Koro said. 'He was probably affronted by Tupaea's mana and didn't wish to acknowledge that a Maohi was equal to him. Apparently our ancestor's proud and austere attitude did not make him popular with the *Endeavour*'s crew.'

I hated the thought of Tupaea being isolated on the English ship. 'He did have friends on the voyage, didn't he?'

'Banks, despite his attitude, yes,' Koro conceded. 'The artist Parkinson perhaps, as well as the astronomer Green and Banks' two black servants. Who knows? Tupaea and Taiata may have taught them how to coax Maohi rhythms from the conches and deep-toned drums they'd brought on board, eh?'

On that chuckling thought, I finally succumbed to tiredness.

'But how can I find Tupaea?' I murmured sleepily. 'Tell me, Koro, where should I seek him?'

'Yes, Little Tu, we have to acknowledge that the *Endeavour*'s story belonged to Cook and Banks and, therefore, why should our ancestor have a place in the documents? Nevertheless, Tupaea *is* there. You must look not at but *through* the documents, moko.

'Beloved grandson, look also past the written to the unwritten. Put yourself into the spaces between the words on the page. Go past the spoken to the unspoken. Seek the priest in our own language, not the language of the coloniser.

'Mokopuna, be your own navigator.

'Your ancestor is waiting.'

CHAPTER TEN —
THE ARRIVAL OF THE ARIOI

1/

Through various karakia and chants the Arioi priest was able to recognise the ancient star clusters — there they were as of old! — and by the position of the sun on the horizon, plot the way ahead. When Tupaea noticed the myriad passages of birds in the sky, he knew that land was nigh.

'There came a sunset when the young watch, Nicholas Young, sighted a promontory. Cook called the land New Zealand but your ancestor Tupaea knew otherwise: this was the fabled land of Aotearoa. And Tupaea realised 'Oro — or destiny — had a different purpose for him: to reinstate the connection that had long ago been severed.

'He saw tall mountains, white cliffs, fertile land and then a village, with smoke coiling from many cooking fires. For the first time, he glimpsed the people, descendants of the Maohi voyagers.

'He knew he would be the first priestly visitor for over three hundred years. But would the people remember?

'He said to Taiata, "Bring me my robes."'

Hello, Little Tu, are you receiving, over?
This is what I saw.

2 /

The sky was a strange colour that day, with the sun a fiery glowing ball, sending sunbursts from its surface.

The Maori, watching from the shore, were struck with wonder at what they saw. What was that moving across the blazing eye of Rangi? It was a strange magnificent waka, bucking amid the solar flares, its timbers smouldering within the raging solar sea.

'Make haste, o waka, go quickly,' they cried. With a roar of relief and acclamation they saw the canoe negotiate the transit and sail through to the cool universe beyond. Then it tipped and plunged headlong from the highest heavens like a fiery comet. Through the atmosphere the waka flamed, into the foaming sea.

What wonder was this? The canoe emerged newly born from the waves. It was like a huge island, with wide bluff bows, a raised poop and a square stern. The large sails made the island look like it was carrying its own clouds above it.

A brilliant rainbow arched from the highest heaven, and birds shrieked and flew from one end of the earth to the other. 'O iwi, bow down,' the birds commanded. 'The Arikirangi is coming.'

And Tupaea slid down the rainbow, landing on the strange island.

The people gasped, for he was a man without physical flaw.

On his head was a circular cap, like a woven helmet, and from it sprouted a tall headdress made of beautiful red, yellow and black feathers. His body glistened with oil, and around his midriff and thighs he wore a girdle of red feathers. A shoulder cape reached down to the waist and was tipped with a fringe, this time of yellow feathers.

He had not come alone. A small boy child alighted alongside him, draped in pearls; they stood on the floating island, shining in the rainbow's holy light.

Once Tupaea was satisfied that all the people had gathered, he began to chant:

> *A hee mai te tua, e ia papama 'ehe*
> *No te tai a tau te po . . .*
> *The sea rolled, the tides mounting*
> *For a period of nights . . .*

As he chanted the small child took up a great conch-shell trumpet, a putaiiteaeha, which brayed from horizon to horizon. Then he beat out intoxicating rhythms on some drums, and the whole universe swayed as Tupaea began to dance:

> *E po fanaura'a atua, o te po Mua Tai'aroa;*
> *It was the God's birth night, the night of Mua Taia'aroa*
> *O 'Orotaua atua i fanau mai i te reira po . . .*
> *'Oro taua was the God born that night . . .*

Dipping and swaying, Tupaea lifted his arms to the sun, lowered them to the earth. When he twirled and gestured, the feathers he was wearing gleamed like a cloak of many colours.

> *'Oro atua o te Reva e te whenua nei;*
> *'Oro, god of the Air and Earth;*
> *'Oro haia; 'Oro atua o te Arioi*
> *'Oro manslayer; god of the Arioi.*

Then Tupaea revealed the beings which had come with him: goblins of ghastly white, in red skins, tricksters and devious. The people marvelled when Tupaea bade the goblins bring him to shore on smaller waka, for as they rowed they had their backs to the land, which meant that their eyes were at the backs of their heads.

There, on the sand, the small child brought forward a cylinder.

Tupaea unveiled the ironwood that had been stored within a sacred canopy covered with feathers, and offered it to the Maori people. 'Do you remember?' he cried.

With tears of gladness, they nodded their heads. Oh, it had been such a long time since 'Oro had been among them!

'Then bow down before the great God, bow down!'

From that moment onward, all the people honoured the priest: 'Arikirangi! Tupaea! Haere mai! Greetings, captain of the *Endeavour*!'

— INTERLUDE —

CHAPTER ELEVEN — TUPAEA IN AOTEAROA

1 /

Tiwhatiwha te po, ko te Pakerewha!
Dark, dark is the realm of the spirits!
Ko Arikirangi tenei ra te haere nei.
Red and white strangers are coming!
Arikirangi, high chief, he is coming!

Tiwhatiwha te po, ko te Pakerewha!
E mokopuna, you may wonder why Maohi of Aotearoa thought Tupaea was the captain of the Endeavour. Well, his arrival had been foretold long before by Toiroa, a tohunga from Mahia. 'Arikirangi, high chief, he is coming,' the tohunga said. 'He comes with red and white strangers.'

Now, with Toiroa's foretelling in mind, it may appear contradictory that the Endeavour was strenuously opposed by Maohi when it attempted first landing. Tupaea, however, wouldn't have been surprised by this! Even in his own homeland of Tahiti, this was how the people traditionally responded to strange visitors.

What were the circumstances? A fifty-strong warrior group attacked Cook's landing party. The aggressive warriors did all they could to repel the floating island. A Maori warrior was killed during the beach encounter.

Tupaea, in fact, stopped further bloodshed. He spoke in the language of the Maohi to the attackers. It was the first korero between Maohi priest and Maohi iwi of Aotearoa for more than three centuries. And they understood!

This only confirmed his status as captain and, therefore, it was to Tupaea that all questions were directed:

'Is the floating island yours?

'Have you come to re-establish the Fa'atau Aroha and the sacred seaway to Hawaiki? If so, welcome, we have long awaited your arrival!

'But who are these red and white strangers who have arrived with you? Why are they so transgressive of Maori custom, not responding to our challenge by acknowledging our rangatiratanga, and, instead, coming onto the land without our permission? We will leave you, o great priest, to punish your goblins and tricksters.'

From that moment, the news spread throughout Aotearoa that the Arikirangi had truly arrived.

During all the initial, and tense, encounters that followed — for, oh, the actions of the red and white strangers were sometimes sacrilegious, belligerent and hostile — it was with Tupaea that we wished to korero, talk. Indeed, Tupaea was so desirable that one of the tribes tried to steal away Taiata, presuming that if they did so Arikirangi would be compelled to stay among them!

Tupaea captained the Endeavour onward, and he arrived at Anaura on 20 October 1769. There he was invited by the paramount chief, Whakata Te Aoterangi, to his palisaded kainga. He was offered hospitality and he begat the dynasty that takes his surname in Anaura.

2 /

Ko Arikirangi tenei ra te haere nei!

E mokopuna, three days later, on 23 October, Tupaea arrived in Uawa on the Endeavour.

A welcoming party called him from the shore, 'Haere mai, e Arikirangi, nau mai, kua tae mai! Come among us, great lord, you the physical manifestation of 'Oro, come under the cloak of love!' War canoes were sent out to his waka, and he was garlanded with flowers. When he set foot on the land, over a thousand men and women greeted him with song and haka.

For six days, we of Uawa were determined to show our greatest hospitality. Great feasts were organised for Tupaea, together with marvellous entertainments, reaching far into the night. Of course, his goblins and tricksters were sometimes like irritating children, but we put up with them for the privilege of having Tupaea in our midst.

He was the guest of honour at Te Rawheoro, the great Maori house of learning in Uawa. Can you imagine the scene, Little Tu? Great crowds gathered to greet him, some having travelled from other tribes to the north and to the south. Sometimes, sessions were limited as tohunga and other sacred priests met him in whare wananga to try to close that gap of three hundred years. We invited Tupaea to travel throughout Uawa, and he consented. We were *moved by his ancient tales of Hawaiki and of the current politics and culture of the homeland we had left many centuries before. He thrilled us with his stories of Mahaiatea and his queen, Purea. Wherever he went he was treated with great reverence. Valuable cloaks and ancient ornaments were given to him to take back as tribute to 'Oro's marae and its sovereign lady.*

Why? We knew it was not his destiny to stay.

There was one inspiring event when Tupaea escaped the rain by talking to us within a high-arched cavern. Thenceforward, the cave has always been known as Te Ana no Tupaea. Even today, when you visit it, people say that if you put your ear to the walls you can still catch past echoes of the liturgies of 'Oro which he intoned and the blessings that he gave to the people.

It is written that during the farewell arose the sound of acclamation, a thunderous haka and women in karanga.

'Haere atu ra e te rangatira!' the women called. 'Hoki atu koe ki a Hawaiki nui, Hawaiki roa, Hawaiki pamamao! Return safely to our ancient homeland, Hawaiki, the proud land, the long land, the land far away.'

Children were named after Tupaea. Places were called after him.

Mokopuna, he begat our dynasty in Uawa.

Ka haruru te moana!
The sea mounted, the tides rolled
Ka haruru te whenua
Thunder roared across the land
Hail to thee, Arioi, hail!

ACT THREE

CHAPTER TWELVE —
THE THRILL OF FALLING

/ /

I turned seventeen and, one day, when I was taking Koro to catch his plane to Gisborne, he gave me a quizzical look.

'You once asked me, when you were a boy, what our ancestor looked like.' We were standing at the gate before he boarded. 'Looked in the mirror lately?'

I should have been more self-aware but, yes, I realised what he meant. I'd now reached my adult height and for some time had wondered why everyone around me had shrunk: Koro, Mum and even Dad; I'd filled out too. I was in my final year at Wellington High where, wonder of wonders, something clicked into place: from being a trier I'd come through to the A team and my grades had improved as well. If only things were like that at home.

Koro was a mindreader. 'Be kinder to your parents,' he said.

'Dad's all right,' I answered. 'It's Mum who's a pain in the arse.'

'I won't have you using that kind of language,' he reprimanded. 'And you mustn't say those kinds of things about May. She's worried about you all these years and, now that you're becoming an adult, she finds it hard to let go. We all do. You may have grown up, but to us you're still that little baby in the incubator struggling to breathe.'

'Could you tell her to cut me some slack?'

'Well, maybe she would if you weren't so secretive. Where do you go when you sneak out the window at nights?'

Uh oh, so Mum knew. And was I about to tell Koro, with his old-fashioned morality and attitudes towards modesty and . . . everything?

'Perhaps if you asked her nicely,' Koro said, 'and told her where you were going, she might say okay.'

I did; she didn't.

21

One thing was for sure: the dream that I go to university seemed possible after all. I wasn't unenthusiastic and, as Dad used to say, 'It beats working on the buses.'

Mum started to give me a lot of unsubtle hints. 'I was speaking to Mrs Samasoni in community services and she says that your mate Alapati [alias Bilbo] and some of the other boys at Wellington High are going to Victoria University next year.' Or, 'One of the medics, Dr Granger, you know him, he tells me there's an open day at the university next weekend. Do you want to hop along and take a look?'

One afternoon, I caught her on the telephone to Uawa. She had the decency to blush before saying, 'Koro wants to speak to you,' and beating a hasty exit.

'Is that you, Little Tu? Your mother tells me you want to do law at university. I'm proud of you for making that decision. Don't worry about those application papers. I'll get them for you and we can look at them together when I'm next in Wellington, eh?'

Once upon a time I'd have had a panic attack and reached for my inhaler. Although I felt that Mum and Koro were ganging up on me behind my back, most of all, I was glad that I was fulfilling Koro's wishes, even if I wasn't sure that they were my own.

was also loving Jean-Luc's gym, and closing on my friend Thierry.

'You start gymnastics later than most,' Jean-Luc said, 'but you already have un physique d'ange when you come to me, so that makes up for lost time.'

It wouldn't be long before I would join Thierry on the rings. Meantime, for preparation, Jean-Luc put me through sessions at the pool close by the gym. From the low dive board he had me practising pikes and tucks into the water. He was really firing my core but 'Shows promise' was all he would say after each session.

Shows promise? I showed much more than that! And I was earning my body shape and mid-section as Jean-Luc sculpted me with his punishing exercises.

'Do you know how to carve an elephant out of stone?' he asked me one day, as I was sweating with the exertion. 'It is not only achieved by chipping the elephant out of the granite but sometimes by chipping away everything that is not the elephant.' I think he meant that as a compliment.

Along with my physical reshaping came something else.

Jean-Luc had mentioned that physical perfection was not enough. What was my essence? What was my personality? What set me apart? Certainly my self-confidence was developing and, with it, fearlessness. Is that what Jean-Luc was looking for?

Here's one example of how it showed itself.

3/

There was always rivalry between Wellington High boys and Scots College boys, not only in sports events but also out of school.

One day, Thierry, Horse and Bilbo and I discovered that a bunch of Scots guys were meeting every Saturday to show off by jumping from a superstructure of four levels and zigzag pathways that took you down to the harbour, into the water below. 'Let's go and spoil their party,' I said to Thierry.

From that day, a duel developed as we challenged the others to jump from the lowest level and then by degrees upped the ante by ascending for other jump-offs from higher points; if you were the last man jumping, you were the winner. Passers-by liked to watch and applaud. After a while word got around and people came every weekend especially to watch.

Nobody from either school, however, had attempted to jump from the fourth level because it was set back from the other pathways. You would have to clear the three levels below by jumping out twice as far and, if you misjudged the circle of plungeable water below, splat. To make matters riskier, that circle of entry was not large — maybe three metres wide — and you couldn't even see it from the top.

What the hell. Both sides had been talking of doing it for a while and, on the last day before our schools broke up, I thought, It's now or never.

'I'm going for it,' I told Thierry, Horse and Bilbo.

Actually, Thierry was the better contender but he said, 'My father would kill me if I did something like that. And you . . . well, you don't have a father like him!'

Came the day, and I'd decided against it, but some Scots College boys arrived and . . . what's a guy to do? Backing out was not an option.

'You've got to jump five metres out to even clear the superstructure,' Thierry warned, 'and how can you guarantee you'll make the deepest water?'

The only way to do this was to run at speed up the stairs, change into second gear when you got to the ramp leading to the fourth level and then kick into third gear so as to obtain enough propulsion to make the leap. But . . . if you put on too much speed, you would end up overjumping the target.

Was it my fault that the local newspaper had sent a reporter and photographer? Well, I'd developed into quite the showman, and (excuse me, Koro) was buggered if I was going to risk my life for nothing. Taking my example from those times when I jumped off the Uawa bridge, I told Thierry, Horse and Bilbo to start working the crowd for dollars and bets. 'Yeah, we've got a contender here,' they jived, 'so put your money down!' And Thierry showed off some backflips and double somersaults that were part of his repertoire, and the crowd oohed and aahed.

No business like show business.

I put on a show too. I made a great play of chalking my take-off point on the fourth level and seeking the advice of sightseers. 'Hey, maybe I should move the chalk mark to the left?' I measured out my approach, pretending to be anxious about the uneven surface. 'If I trip, kiss me goodbye, folks!' I encouraged some of the Scots College boys to jump with me and, getting into the act, they made a few run-ups before shaking their heads and leaving me to it.

By the time I made my final sprint I had the audience in the palm of my hand. As I ran, somebody in the crowd called, 'Don't do it, son!'

It was too late. My heart was thudding as I approached the take-off point. I crossed my fingers, hoping that I'd chosen the right spot. I saw the chalk mark.

Nailed it.

Took a step into space. Counted to three and prayed. Looked to my left at my arm outstretched and then to my right to the tips of my fingers.

The air rushed into my lungs.

Oh, my body flexed and for one unbelievable moment there was more than a sense of weightlessness. With great clarity I felt that defying gravity was indeed possible and . . .

In that moment I could find the perfection I was seeking.

Then came the thrill of falling.

There I am, in a photo on the front page of the *Dominion*, watched by alarmed sightseers, leaping for my life:

WELLINGTON HIGH STUDENT CELEBRATES LAST DAY AT SCHOOL WITH DAREDEVIL DIVE ust a dive? Didn't the photographer see the pike, half-pirouette and somersault that I executed to stop myself from overshooting and to ensure that I entered the circle of water feet first?

When I got home, my pockets brimming with dollars collected from the grateful punters, Dad patted me on the back. As for Mum, she was always on my case and she went blue in the face telling me off. 'You could have been killed!'

To be truthful, I almost shat my pants and, soon after, the city council banned all jumping from the spot.

The photograph was published in Uawa. When Koro saw it, he sent me a brief note: 'Still a muttonhead.'

Jean-Luc wasn't happy either. He harangued me for at least ten minutes in front of everybody at the gym, before passion drove him to his own language.

He may have been looking for self-confidence and fearlessness — but stupidity?

No, he wasn't looking for that.

CHAPTER THIRTEEN —
THE FORCE OF DESTINY

\| /

Not long after my daredevil dive, the phone rang for Mum late in the evening. Calls that come after midnight are never good news.

It was Uncle Tu-Bad. 'Could you come home, sis? Ma's died. I'm with Pa right now. He'll need all of us.'

My beloved Nan Esther had slipped away in her sleep.

Mum, Dad and I went back to Uawa immediately to support Koro. 'Those brothers of mine,' Mum said, 'couldn't organise themselves out of a paper bag.'

She was wrong. When we arrived, Uncle Tu-Bad had already taken charge. He'd sorted out the death certificate and selected a casket. The only thing he hadn't done was to dress Nan before she was taken down to the marae. 'I thought I should leave that to you, sis,' he said to Mum. 'Ma would have preferred her own daughter to put a lovely dress on her, comb her hair and make her pretty.'

Uncle had even organised the ceremonial aspects at the marae and got all the relatives on the job catering for the many visitors who were expected to arrive to farewell Nan.

'Do you see what your eldest brother is doing?' Koro said to Mum after she had embraced him and cried on his shoulder.

During the funeral, Koro was formal, dignified and strong. After all, he was a chief and his people — there must have been over six hundred on the marae — expected a certain restraint in the face of death. Tall, stately, his silver hair combed, he was the proud rangatira receiving everyone with immense generosity. They cried; he didn't. They wanted comfort; he gave it. A loud sigh came from the people. 'Yes, you can always count on Big Tu to show us all, by his example, how to rise above our grief.'

Behind the scenes, however, Koro found fault with Uncle Tu-Bad even when there was no fault, sending him and Bo and Charlie out on more expeditions to catch fish, hunt pigs and find succulent forest roots so that the visitors would have extra delicacies to praise.

'Pa,' Uncle Tu-Bad would say to him, 'could you let me handle it?' Since his return from prison he'd got involved with the community and the marae, and people were looking up to him.

Mum didn't escape Koro's critical gaze either. 'Tell the women more visitors have arrived at the gateway,' he would say to her. 'I won't have anybody complaining that they had to wait in the hot sun. And make sure the young girls in the kitchen have lunch ready and on time. It was late yesterday.'

As for my cousins and I, we were on constant clean-up duty: the showers, the latrines, the grounds and so on. Seth, Abe and Spade eyed my height and shoulders with some respect, but that didn't stop them from trying to put me down. 'You d-d-do the latrines, Little T-T-Tutae,' they mocked. 'That should be s-s-second nature to you.' They laughed and laughed as if it was a great joke.

'I wouldn't go there if I was you,' I said, deliberately articulating my words and squaring off. 'You clean those latrines, because if you don't you'll be down them.'

They got the hint.

Yes, in public Koro presented the perfect image of a chief.

However, late at night, when everybody was asleep, I would catch him weeping on Mum's shoulder. She was looking after the budget for the funeral, balancing the outgoings with the koha the mourners would leave to help pay for the tangihanga.

'What will I do without your mother?'

I found these private revelations of Koro's vulnerability surprising, almost shocking. How would he cope when we put Nan into the ground? Uncle Tu-Bad had led a crew up to the graveyard to dig the hole. 'You boys too,' he said to me, Seth, Abe and Spade. I was only too willing to do that for Nan; after all those times she made me breathe her herbal fumes, I owed her.

Watching Uncle as he directed the work, I couldn't help but think how proud Koro should be of his eldest son. Later, when we buried Nan, I heard him say to Koro:

'We'll be all right, Pa. Don't worry, we'll be all right.'

2 /

The question was what to do with Koro, now that he was a widower.

Soon after the tangihanga, Mum, Dad and Mum's brothers got together. They all looked to Uncle Tu-Bad to chair the meeting. 'May will have to move back to Uawa to look after him,' Uncle Bo said. 'She's the girl in the family.'

'Just because she's the daughter,' Uncle Tu-Bad answered, 'doesn't make May the one to take sole responsibility.'

'Pa's a pain in the arse,' said Uncle Charlie, 'and he'll get worse now that Ma's not around. He'll need a housekeeper to keep him in the manner he's accustomed to and we can't afford to hire one. May's the best person to do the job.'

Mum was glaring at Bo and Charlie. 'You brothers have got this all sorted out, haven't you. Don't I have a say?'

Wally made it easier for her. 'I know you think I like my job in Wellington, dear, but family is family.'

None of us heard Koro joining us. 'Talking about me behind my back already?' he asked. 'Well, I've made my own decision about what I want to do. May can't move back to Uawa. Are you all stupid? She and Wally have got good jobs down there and I'm not going to ruin Little Tu's chance of going to university.'

I thought he was going to claim his independence and tell the family that he was quite capable of looking after himself. Instead:

'So, if the maunga can't come to me . . . I will go to it,' he said. 'I'm moving to Wellington.'

'We'd love to have you, Pa,' said Mum, 'but we haven't got any room.'

'Esther and I had savings,' Koro answered, 'and I've had a good pension plan for years, so now that I'm retired that will ensure my financial independence. I'll rent the homestead out and we'll buy a house in Wellington together.'

I could see the wheels turning sluggishly in Uncle Bo and Uncle Charlie's minds. Pa spending his money and not leaving any to them? They didn't like that either!

'You go for it, Pa,' Uncle Tu-Bad said.

The proposal meant a lot of travelling back and forth between Uawa and Wellington.

Mum, Dad and I returned to the capital, and Mum started

looking for a property with at least three bedrooms and space for Koro's library. When she'd narrowed down the choices, Koro flew to Wellington and, finally, he and Mum settled on a big old place in Island Bay: two double bedrooms overlooking the sea, one single room at the back, a huge basement, double garage and sleepout.

'You'll like it here, Pa,' Mum said. 'You can have one of the bedrooms in the front. Wally and I will fix up the basement for all your books and whakapapa, but some of your precious things will have to go to a storage unit out at Porirua.'

'And will Little Tu have the room at the back?' he asked anxiously. 'I think he's old enough to sleep by himself now.'

Gee, thanks, Koro.

'Oh, him,' Mum answered, as if I didn't matter. 'Can't you see that he's got his eye on the sleepout? At least if he goes in there he won't wake us up when he goes training in the mornings and he won't have to sneak out the window any more to be with his mates or those girls who keep hanging around him.'

As always, I zipped my lip. If I protested Mum might present evidence and I might not be able to refute it.

Once the sale was settled, we drove back to Uawa to help Koro to pack. Ralph and Tommy came with us, having hired two huge moving trucks for the job.

Uncle Tu-Bad organised a big farewell for Koro at the marae. People from Uawa know how to throw a good party, no matter what the occasion, and Koro was extolled and honoured for his leadership and generosity. During the celebrations, he revealed another reason why he was coming to Wellington with us.

'Look at those elders,' he said to Mum. 'They can't wait to see me go so that they can move one up on the paepae!' He cast a proud glance at Uncle Tu-Bad. 'Well, they'd better not do that too soon because it looks like the tortoise has put on speed and is coming through. Maybe I should have left sooner to leave him space to do it, eh.'

Came the day we were supposed to leave, there was no sign of Koro.

'I think I know where he's gone,' Dad said. 'Probably to see Esther and say goodbye to her.'

We drove out of Uawa to the family graveyard and, sure enough, there was Koro's car, parked at the bottom of the cliff face that rose starkly from the bush. The cemetery was lovely in the sunlight; the cliffs behind were tapu, sacred, like palisades climbing to the sky and honeycombed with potholes and tunnels.

'There he is,' Dad pointed.

'He's been up to that bloody cave,' Mum groaned when she saw him emerging from the trees.

He had something wrapped in a blanket. 'What's that he's carrying?' I asked her.

'Don't,' she warned me, knowing I was teasing. 'You know what it is.' She wound down the window and yelled, 'I'm happy to have you in the house, Pa, but that ironwood and whatever or whoever is in it is going straight into the storage unit.'

When he came to the car, Koro looked at me, puzzled.

'What is your mother talking about?' he asked.

CHAPTER FOURTEEN —
SLIDING OUT OF THE SKY

1 /

Koro came to stay.

At first Mum, Dad and I were concerned that he would be lonely staying home by himself. What were we thinking! Two weeks after he arrived in Wellington the phone began to ring.

'Hello, Uncle. Why didn't you let me know you were in town? Could you help me out? I have to attend a land meeting with Ngati Awa and you're just the right person to go onto their marae with me. I'll send a car to pick you up.'

'Tena koe, rangatira. I have to talk to some bankers today: would you come with me as my elder? The car will be there in half an hour.'

Again, the phone. 'May I speak to Mr Mahana? Oh, Mr Mahana, I've been given your name. We're looking for a kaumatua for the proposed heritage pathway around the eastern bays and I've been told you'd be perfect.'

'Will you be home for tea?' Mum would ask, as Koro smoothed his hair and tightened his tie.

'Better not wait for me,' he would answer. 'I should have realised that my poor nephews and nieces would want someone from Uawa to be on their paepae. Had I known, I would have moved down earlier.'

21

Meanwhile, I was successful in obtaining one of the places for Maori in law at Victoria, and also got a Maori scholarship to help pay for my fees and give me an allowance.

How could I possibly fail? Koro had strong-armed every Maori politician he knew.

Bilbo decided to join me at university ('Could you call me Alapati now, mate?') but Thierry went to work with his father at the gym, and Horse decided to go overseas for a gap year. While I was in the line enrolling, I met a cute Maori girl, Marama Te Puni.

'You're not from the East Coast?' I asked.

'No,' she said, puzzled. 'Why?'

'Oh, nothing.' In private, however, I was thinking, Yay, not a cousin. As well, I needed to know somebody who looked like they had brains and could help me out; it was an added attraction that Marama was also pretty.

My university studies began well.

First-year law required me to take a general course — I chose arts: Maori, history and philosophy — plus legal studies. I gave English a miss; if I'd paid attention to Four-Eyes Wilson that might have given me the confidence to tackle it. Despite my anxieties, I took to my arts subjects as to the manner born. Much to my surprise, Koro turned out to be a help rather than a hindrance, mainly by doing his 'homework' at the same time as I did mine. Whenever he wasn't helping out somebody in Parliament he liked to bring home piles of books on Maori and Polynesian culture.

'Gee, Koro,' I would tease, 'how many of those did you steal from Wellington Public Library this week?'

'Concentrate on your homework,' he would growl.

To help pay for my studies, I got a part-time weekend job cleaning windows, but, hold on, these weren't just any old windows and not from the inside either. No, they were high tower buildings and some of those windows were thirty storeys high.

Bilbo — sorry, Alapati — got me the job. You may have seen us, lowering ourselves down the buildings on scaffolding, hooked on safety lines like mountaineers. Alapati knew I had a good head for heights, and he and I liked to swing like monkeys across from one side of the building to the other. On my part, the big plus was the money, so, after I got my certification, there I was, earning more than most of my mates and, as well, doing law.

Jean-Luc saw me one day. 'You are fearless too?' he asked. 'Are you not afraid you might fall?'

The thought had never entered my head.

Yes, and sometimes, something arose at university to remind me of Tupaea. During a history lecture, for instance, while the professor was talking about Captain Cook's voyages throughout New Zealand, I was looking *through* his words and wilfully reading the history my way, Koro's way.

'Throughout the rest of his stay Tupaea captained the *Endeavour* on a circumnavigation of Aotearoa. Wherever he went the people cried out, "Tupaea! Tupaea! Welcome Tupaea, ariki no Hawaiki!"

'Sometimes he tried to warn them about the red and white strangers. He often succeeded. On occasion, he didn't. But they were magnanimous in their forgiveness; after all, the goblins and tricksters were under his protection.

'The circumnavigation proved that there was no great southern continent. Cook's masters in Great Britain had thought that the eastern coast of Aotearoa was its edge; they should have asked Tupaea as he would have told them it did not exist.

'Near the end of the voyage, while the *Endeavour* lay at anchor in the sparkling waters of Waitangi, Tupaea invited Ngapuhi chiefs on board. The chiefs exchanged gifts of cloaks and mere with their visitor from Hawaiki.

'Then came the time when Tupaea told them, "E'oa ma, e 'aere ana au." His sojourn among them was ended.

'The news was carried from one height to the other across Aotearoa, and a huge ululation of sadness and grief sounded even unto Te Raituitai, the highest heaven, as they beseeched 'Oro: "Will you not allow your priest to stay with us?"

'War canoes accompanied Tupaea's ship *Endeavour* to the horizon. There, flocks of birds were hovering, ready to accompany the priest onward and away.

'Tupaea set his face northward. Finally, he was bound for England.'

I thought my version was better.

And, another time, the God 'Oro suddenly popped into my head during a philosophy lecture.

We had a guest from Europe who was talking about ancient myths. I thought of Four-Eyes Wilson — if he could see me now.

Then the lecturer said something interesting. 'Of course, today, there are still many societies for whom the myths of Olympus or Valhalla, of gods, goddesses and one-eyed monsters, are still as real and as relevant as they were in ancient times.'

The lecture hall rippled with amusement. 'What or how,' the lecturer continued, 'would they feel if Cyclops, say, had survived the ages of man and lived in a cave on Mount Olympus . . . or even here, in New Zealand, near Invercargill! Our rational mind would refuse to admit that possibility, but what if?'

As the laughter rose I thought to myself:

'Mate, you don't know the half of it. Maori still live with their own versions of Cyclops. Mine had his house in a cave at the back of Uawa where he slept in an ironwood cylinder and was kept warm by a royal loincloth of red feathers. Now he's in a storage unit in Porirua.'

3 /

Then, one evening, I went to train at the gym but discovered a CLOSED sign on it and the words CONFIDENTIAL PRIVATE SESSION. Puzzled, I shrugged my shoulders and turned down the corridor. As I was leaving I saw Thierry. 'What's this about?' I asked.

'My father is taking a special clinic for a gymnast from overseas. He arrived this afternoon from Europe and he returns tomorrow.'

'He's here for just one night?' I was accustomed to visitors turning up at the gym. Some of them were world-class athletes who were perfecting some routine. Others wished to train for a routine that was beyond them, and wanted Jean-Luc to help them achieve a breakthrough. Or, more seriously, they required remedial work after some injury.

This secrecy was different. 'I can ask Father if we can watch if you like,' Thierry said.

I followed him past the sign and into the gym. Jean-Luc was taking the visiting gymnast through some conditioning and stretch exercises. Thierry spoke to him and pointed me out. Jean-Luc hesitated and asked the gymnast. At first he shook his head, but then he made a small moue, okay.

The gymnast went back to the conditioning and stretching, Jean-Luc speaking quietly and insistently to him. 'No, you must continue! Thirty more repetitions! No, is still not enough! Fifty more stretches so that when you pump up you can reach maximum chest expansion! Your body is not at the level it needs to be to guarantee the excellence of your performance! Comprends?'

Not until Jean-Luc was satisfied did he allow the gymnast to complete the warm-up. And as he stood, Jean-Luc was measuring the gymnast's chest, biceps, thighs and manipulating his feet and massaging the ankles. 'Okay? We get in the harness now and you show me what you do.'

The gymnast turned, lifted his arms, and Jean-Luc fitted the harness to him. 'Yes, Maître,' he nodded. It was that action of lifting his arms that allowed me to recognise him:

He was the famous aerialist, Maurice Sernas, of Le Cirque du Monde, one of the most spectacular international circuses in the world.

'What is Sernas doing in New Zealand?' I asked Thierry, as I watched the aerialist approach a hanging rope. I'd noticed the rope many times before, but it was usually rolled tightly within the rafters.

'He's halfway through a tour with his new act, *Boléro*, for the Grand Chapiteau, the big top, and he has struck trouble with the performance. Circus acts depend on split-second timing and if one performer is out of synch he can destroy the entire choreography of the others. So Sernas has come to Father for a diagnosis.'

'Why Jean-Luc?' I asked.

'Sernas is a former student of my father's,' Thierry answered, looking at me as if I was stupid. 'Jean-Luc is the world expert in the corde lisse.'

The corde lisse!

It is considered the finest and bravest of all the aerial disciplines. Although the trapeze is still a main attraction, no circus today would even think of putting on a programme that did not have on its bill the best corde lisse exponent it could afford.

Climbing the suspended rope by a series of fluid wraps, hoists and pulls, and every now and then executing beautiful release moves and fluid acrobatics, the aerialist reached the top of the rope.

And then, down he (or she) would come. The suspended rope was an axis by which the aerialist described angles on a vertical plane. The vocabulary depended on the theme of the performance, and this was where the corde lisse reached the heights of athleticism and enchantment: anything was possible as the aerialist wrapped and unwrapped from the cord and described astounding arabesques in the air. You could be as athletic, artistic and imaginative as you wished.

The rumours were true, then: Jean-Luc had once been an aerialist. In France he ran off to join a Russian circus, and as a young man attained fame for his daring and virtuosity on the corde lisse. The circus had toured the world, including Australia.

The troupe had taken a flight to Auckland, one of the cities scheduled in the tour.

You must have heard the story, it was in all the newspapers: they were stranded when one of the directors ran off with the takings. Jean-Luc and the other performers managed to get back to Europe but he never forgot his sojourn in New Zealand.

Ah, yes, New Zealand had always been regarded as a place where Baby Austins and planes with propellers went to die. At the end of his career, still a young man, Jean-Luc drifted down to that well at the bottom of the world, married a New Zealand girl and settled in Auckland. He had never been forgotten by circus colleagues who continued to send him their budding aerialists.

Or, as in Sernas' case, sought him out when they were in trouble.

We begin,' said Jean-Luc.

Sernas gripped the rope, the gym resounded with Ravel's *Boléro*, and, to the insinuating and insistent rhythm of a snare-drum, Sernas went into action: he hoisted himself up with a front flip, snapped into a hip wrap knot, and by a series of other manoeuvres he kept climbing.

I'd never seen anything as masculine and beautiful. As Sernas hoisted himself further — sometimes deliberately unwrapping himself so that he fell a few metres, causing me to blanch — Jean-Luc shouted approval and guidance. 'Yes, Sernas, good! No, Sernas, inhale! Yes, Sernas, excellent body extension! No, Sernas, tighten the solar plexus! Yes, *parfait!*'

The music mounted, seeming to climb with Sernas, and it was at the height of its passionate and percussive rhapsodic zenith when he reached the top of the rope and then . . . oh . . .

He launched himself down into an increasing wider and

wider number of revolutions, toe drops, holds and spins.

My heart was in my mouth, the routine was so . . . spellbinding and breathtaking.

I happened to look at Jean-Luc and saw him give a slight shake of his head. 'He pushes his technique. Why?' Even so, Jean-Luc greeted Sernas exuberantly. While Sernas was recovering, they went into a huddle and I knew that Jean-Luc was giving him notes.

'But what is wrong then, Maître?' Sernas asked. 'Why do I feel this great sense of—' He couldn't find the words.

Jean-Luc interrupted him. 'Two problems only. The first is easily fixed. You must extend the time you take for your warm-ups. After all, ten years have gone by in your career, oui? What you came by naturally as a boy must be worked harder for, now that you are a man. The warm-ups are two-thirds of the iceberg that the audience do not see. But you need the conditioning for the one-third that they do see!'

He chuckled, patting Sernas lightly on the back. Then his face became serious. 'Regarding the second problem, I am not sure . . . But go through your routine again and I will try to locate it.'

As he spoke, his eyes gleamed, yes, as if he'd realised how to find it.

The music began again, provocative, demanding. Sernas gripped the rope.

Jean-Luc turned to Thierry. 'Switch off the lights,' he said.

Sernas looked at Jean-Luc, shocked. 'I won't be able to see what I am doing,' he said.

'Sernas,' Jean-Luc commanded, sharp, peremptory. 'Pay attention! Carry on.'

While Sernas went into his routine, Jean-Luc moved about

purposefully, setting small arc lights — maybe four or five — on the floor of the gym, training them on Sernas. Then I saw that they were not focused on Sernas, but on the rope itself.

During the run-through, it was not Sernas that Jean-Luc was watching but the rope.

What was that? I thought I saw something. The second problem: the rope quivering, as if too much stress was being put on it. And when Sernas reached the top, the quivering was still visible, as if he and the rope were fighting each other.

Sernas descended; Jean-Luc handed him a towel. Sernas looked at the older man and I thought he was about to weep, but Jean-Luc smiled reassuringly at him. 'I bow to you,' Jean-Luc began. 'When you first came to me you had the heart of a cub and now . . . you have the heart of a lion. You are the greatest exponent of the corde lisse in the world. And now I will tell you what the second problem is . . . and it is more serious than the first.'

'This is why I am here, Maître.'

'You no longer have a partnership with the rope,' Jean-Luc said. 'As soon as I switched off the lights and you cried out, "I won't be able to see what I am doing", I knew it.'

I looked at Thierry, not daring to breathe.

'I was watching the rope and I could see the pressure you were putting on it, the way it trembled and shivered, as if it was carrying the weight of two people not one . . . And, to some extent, it is. The rope supports you, but it also supports the great expectations that you have of your performance. Thus you do your spectacular work but you expand the arabesque a little wider, you hold the lean-out a bit longer, you establish a different centre of gravity for the piston, you reach further in the hang, you delay the transition between the crucifixion and the dive, comprends?

You are performing on technique, you are imposing on the good will of the rope. Before you know it, pouf, your timing has gone up in smoke, pouf, your technique goes into the danger zone, pouf, you are micro-managing your performance, pouf pouf pouf! No wonder the rest of your cast are bewildered, because they take their cues from you and, if you are even a few seconds out . . .'

'I understand, Maître,' Sernas answered.

'Good,' Jean-Luc said. 'So my remedy is this. Return to Le Cirque du Monde. You will get through the season all right, but . . . once it is over, come back to me. We must find the heart of your performance, the essence, and offer it to the rope! What is it, Sernas? What is the histoire that the rope can lovingly embrace? The "you" which you can give the rope so that you and it can work in balance and harmony as you fly in the great and splendid darkness that is our world.'

Jean-Luc hugged Sernas. 'Thierry will take you back to your hotel now. We will have another session tomorrow before you go back to Europe. Sleep well.'

I waited until Thierry and Sernas had left the gym.

'Still here, Tupaea?' Jean-Luc asked. 'Why am I not surprised?'

Βut . . .

Can you see, now, why I did what I did?

I told Koro, Mum and Dad that I was quitting university. Of course they were all upset, especially Koro and Mum. 'But you've only just started your studies,' Koro said.

Mum turned to Dad. 'This is what happens when you take care of your child when he's coughing his lungs out. When he grows up, he throws it all away.' Then she turned to me. 'Oh, well, it's your life.'

'Yes, it is,' I answered, holding my ground.

And Koro angrily asked, 'How will you become a lawyer? How will you fulfil the dreams of your ancestor? You're ruining your career.'

'There are other ways,' I said.

'Like what, mokopuna?' He was losing his temper.

I wasn't sure yet. Oh, and don't think that I couldn't have made it in law: my grades were pretty good. Was I making the right decision?

'I won't have it, Little Tu!' Koro shouted. He began to bang his walking stick on the floor in a temper. 'I will not let you leave university.' I looked at him tenderly. Oh, he'd never been afraid to resort to melodrama, using emotional blackmail. I knew his tricks inside out.

'All my life you've taken it for granted that I would become what you wanted me to be,' I said, as I kissed him on the forehead. 'I only wish I could do that for you, but I can't any longer.'

'Don't speak to your grandfather like that,' Mum exclaimed.

'You have to let me go now, Koro,' I continued. 'Trust me, and let me be who I want. Not what Mum wants. Not what you want. But what I want.'

'And so you think you know what that is now, do you?' he asked.

Come out, come out, wherever you are. 'I think so,' I answered.

'Not good enough,' he thundered.

'All right then, Koro,' I said. I took a deep breath. 'I want to be my own navigator.'

For a moment there was silence. Then Dad gave a slight cough. 'Well, Little Tu can't be clearer than that, eh dear?' he said to Mum.

POSTLUDE

CHAPTER FIFTEEN —
ONE YEAR LATER

1 /

I live in Marseilles now. The winter quarters of Le Cirque du Monde are on the outskirts of the city.

I've been training hard. Jean-Luc is my choreographer, and together we have created an aerial act. I've practised each element of the act, the combination of held postures and drops — arabesques, hip wrap knots, crucifixions, dives, lean-outs, pistons, windmills and miracle splits — over a thousand times, but it feels more like a million.

Koro has been staying with me.

Letting me go? Well, it helped that Uncle Tu-Bad finally made it to the end of the race. Koro has begun to talk to him again about Tupaea; he is the rightful heir. Even better, Koro's planning to return to Uawa soon.

Not that I could rid myself entirely of Koro. Do you think Mum would have let me come over here without a chaperon? Get off the grass. And Koro had, of course, been bereft at the thought of my leaving New Zealand. 'It was bad enough when your mother brought you to Wellington, but now you are going to France?'

He had acted as if we would never see each other again. In a moment of passion, I said to him, 'Come with me, Koro.'

I really meant it. He's my best friend. I'm glad he came.

21

On our trip over here I wanted to give Koro a surprise.

'We're stopping a few days in Tahiti,' I told him.

The flight arrived around midnight, and as soon as we'd checked into our hotel, all Koro wanted to do was look at the starlit sky. 'There they are, mokopuna,' he said. 'The directional stars and constellations still looking as they must have in Tupaea's time.' He was in the grip of deep emotion as he pointed out Matari'i, the Pleiades; Ana muri, Aldebaran; Ana mua, Antares; Te matau a Maui, the hook of Scorpio.

I knew he was thinking of his ancestor, for, you see, Tupaea never did get to England.

On the return home the *Endeavour* dropped anchor in Batavia. There, Cook set to repairing the vessel as well as allowing time for those crew who had scurvy to recover from it. But Batavia was an unhealthy city criss-crossed with canals filthy with litter and excrement and, all around, swamp filled with clouds of malaria-carrying *Anopheles* mosquitoes.

'Some of the ill were kept on board,' Koro said, 'but others were carried onshore and put into tents. Nobody knew anything about malaria in those days and didn't realise it was carried by the mosquitoes. Multiple bites made the sick get worse and they succumbed to the fever. Dysentery, from contaminated local water, also weakened them, and the ship's surgeon himself was the first to die.

'Aue, Tupaea and Taiata also must have been bitten. Some desperate and kindly attempts were made to find fresh fruits for them both, but it was too late. Taiata died, racked by fever and attacked by a cold and inflammation on his lungs. Tupaea was unconscious at the time and didn't even know the boy had gone until a few days later. When he was told, Tupaea was inconsolable, crying out for him.'

A star fell from the highest heaven, Te Raituitai. Together, Koro and I watched it trailing across the night sky.

'Can you imagine,' Koro asked, 'our ancestor bewailing his fate? He knew that he would be next to go. Who would mourn him and prepare him for the journey to Rohutu noanoa, the Tahitian paradise, to meet 'Oro after his death? Who would administer the last rites? Where was the grand temple where he would be surrounded by his relatives and friends? Who would come for his bones to take them back to Raiatea? How would they find him? When he did, indeed, succumb to death, he and Taiata were both buried on the island of Eadam.'

'I wonder,' I said, 'how Purea felt when she heard that Tupaea had died?'

'I imagine she took the news very badly,' Koro replied. 'She would have ascended to the topmost staircase of Mahiatea and looked across the sea towards Batavia, attempting to invoke a pathway for his spirit and Taita's to return to Hawaiki.'

Then I asked the question that had long been bothering me. 'Why did Tupaea decide to join James Cook on the *Endeavour* in the first place, Koro?'

'Don't you know?' he answered. 'When he left Tahiti he was on a diplomatic mission for Purea.'

Between the arrival of the *Dolphin* and the *Endeavour*, Purea had suffered a huge defeat at the hands of the fighting chief Tutaha. At one of the battles, the sand had been covered with the bones of her defenders and Tupaea himself had been wounded by a spear tipped with a stingray's tail; it pierced his chest.

'When you reach England,' Purea said to Tupaea, her eyes burning bright, 'I want you to be my ambassador and petition King George to support me to regain control of the Maohi nation. An alliance with such a rich and powerful king could help me to oust Tutaha and take back sovereignty. Ask King George in my name, as one sovereign to another of equal standing to me, to give me waka as powerful as the ships I have seen and fill them with cannon and arms so that I might fulfil this task.'

'And Tupaea too,' Koro continued, 'had his own vested interest in obtaining Pakeha arms. With them he could return to Raiatea and take the island back from its conquerors and for 'Oro. Who knows, Tupaea may have realised that the Pakeha would be back in Tahiti again and that, at some point, the Maohi might need to go to war with the pale strangers, using their amazing armaments against them.'

There was one other stop before we resumed our journey to France.

I took Koro on a plane to Porapora and then a small vessel across the lagoon to Hawaiki — or Raiatea, as it's known. There was mist on the water, but as we approached the island it lifted, and a beautiful rainbow appeared.

I should have known that Koro would be reduced to tears. 'Thank you, mokopuna,' he said.

We found the local rangatira. 'As soon as the rainbow appeared,' he smiled, 'I knew somebody was coming.' We shook hands and pressed noses. Koro was weeping with joy and, for the first time I could recall, speechless.

'My grandfather and I are descendants of Tupaea, the Arioi,' I said on his behalf.

The rangatira called a huge meeting, which lasted into the night. Above, the stars were dancing, eavesdropping.

But all that Mum wanted to know when I rang her from Tahiti was: 'Did Pa give that ironwood and red cloth back?'

'You'll have to ask him,' I said.

CHAPTER SIXTEEN — ARIKIRANGI INCARNATE

1/

Tonight's the night.

The unveiling of the Cirque's new production, *Oceania*.

Mum and Dad have arrived after a long trip from Aotearoa to Paris and thence down to Marseilles. At the airport, the first thing Mum asks me is whether or not I have a girlfriend; she still harbours a hope that I might come back to New Zealand and to Marama — but Marama has found someone better.

'Yes,' I reply, 'her name's Odile Dessaix.'

She looks at Dad. 'Oh no, what happens if we have French grandchildren!'

He smiles at her. 'Actually, dear, it's about time Little Tu started thinking of marrying and . . . any moko will do.'

The traditional Grand Chapiteau has now become an arena show so that it can play in cities where the big top can't go and where more people can be packed in. There's no ceiling however: the darkness is criss-crossed with wires and aerial equipment of the kind that is usually behind the scenes — and the stunts are more perilous.

I'm able to spend a little time getting Koro and Mum and Dad to their seats. They're sitting with Odile; Mum is telling her lies already, you know, about what a difficult baby I was and all that kind of stuff.

Koro arrives with hair combed to perfection. The women sitting in the same row are overwhelmed by his handsomeness. Mum growls him. 'Don't get any ideas. Our plane goes back in three days and you're not staying in France any longer.'

I leave them because I must start my conditioning. Things go wrong only when you don't allow enough time to warm up.

Half an hour later.

Good, the daylight has completely faded and the night has fallen. I'm still stretching, limbering up, conditioning and will continue to do so right up to my appearance. While I'm doing this my dresser and make-up personnel are getting me ready: body paint, spandex, costume. 'Do not forget to check the rope when you are up on the platform,' Jean-Luc says. 'Otherwise—'

'I know.'

The sound of the deep bass comes rumbling throughout the arena. I watch the beginning of the show from the wings. Not an empty seat in sight. The audience is silent, expectant. The announcer's voice projects through the inky space. 'Ladies and gentlemen, bonjour and welcome. Come with us as we take you back to the ancient islands of the Maohi.'

I am still warming up. 'More stretches,' Jean-Luc says, 'more.' Suddenly the strobe lights are everywhere, creating a kaleidoscope of colour. To the sound of a thousand drums, faery waka begin to enter. They're in the form of a flotilla of brightly skimming birds, and aboard are beings of exotic and incredibly beautiful appearance.

The crowd erupts into applause. The beings are the Arioi, wreathed and garlanded, they gyrate and dance on the platforms as they skim across the floor of the arena. 'Homai te tahi mata'i na matou,' they sing to the great God 'Oro, "ei ahi na muri. Give us a breeze to encompass us from behind so that we may sail as smoothly as upon a bed. Let our prayers take us safely, O God, even into the harbour of the land to which we are going. Look kindly upon us; have pity upon thy shadows. Forsake us not.'

They are quite a spectacle, in their extravagant costumes with tall headdresses. Some are tumblers, others are acrobats, a few are flame-throwers, and they're all dancing, back-flipping, tumbling and rolling.

Others fly in on aerial silks, ethereal, spell-binding, weaving the colours of the Pacific Ocean together.

'But the world is changing for the Maohi,' the announcer interrupts. 'As foretold by the ancestors, wizards and goblins and strange apparitions are coming to change their world.'

Down go the strobe lights, and up comes that deep rumbling bass again. The audience watches agape as from out of the starlit sky appear two death-defying Russian swings. And from either side of the arena come acrobats to fly across the night like comets, trailing long tails of fire.

The rumbling sounds grow louder, reverberating through the space and juddering every seat. A huge blazing sun begins to rise above the arena. Shimmering behind it, the shadow of a waka.

'Your conditioning okay?' Jean-Luc asks me as he prods and pokes me; he's as bad as Koro. 'All right,' he nods, satisfied, 'up you go.'

I nod as he presses the button and the winch begins to pull me up to the highest point of the arena.

'Take your position.'

I hear the roar from the crowd as the dazzling globe rises higher and cantilevers over the audience. It's almost above them, on top of them. If something should go wrong and it should fall . . .

It's horizontal over the arena now, and that menacing ghost image hovers on the other side.

The waka punches through the incendiary sun. The timbers are smouldering and the sails burst into flame as the ship falls through the blazing eye of Rangi. Descending slowly, its sails taut, the waka tips.

The crowd screams as it falls, ready to crush them. Their fear turns to relief as, all of a sudden the waka swings and begins to circle the arena. The gun ports open and from them come volley after volley of cannon fire, broadsides that deafen the audience.

The audience put their hands to their ears. Smoke, red-tinged, obscures the waka but . . .

There it is! Applause greets it as it settles into the centre of the arena.

It is the *Endeavour*.

Strobe lights hit the waka again and again. The image it presents is of one of power and domination. Submit to me, oh you who look upon me.

Silence falls. The smoke drifts away.

'm standing on a platform high above the arena where the audience can't see me. There's room for only one person. But I can see the audience far below, the thousands who have come to today's première.

It's a strange life up here in the dark. You're alone but the darkness is filled with expectation. Things can come alive up here. You can daydream. Let your imagination soar.

It is, indeed, a great and splendid darkness.

2/

All these years, my ancestor had been waiting.

Come out, come out, wherever you are. Jean-Luc had helped me to find him. 'It is not enough to achieve physical perfection. What is the essence, the personality that makes everything you do yours? It must come from your head and heart as well as your physique. From your histoire, too, mon petit! It will give you the grace and originality to triumph, the thing that only you, Tupaea, can do!'

Koro had been unconvinced and I had to show him. I took him to the gym. He watched in the darkness as I coiled and unwrapped myself.

'To see you wrapped up like that . . . You looked like the baby in the incubator again with cords in your arms and down your throat. And now . . .'

The announcer cuts through the silence again.

'In the southernmost part of the Maohi nation, the people gather to confront the goblin apparitions.' Three carved Maori war canoes appear on the stage, confronting the shimmering ship. It is such a powerful moment, this first encounter of Maori with the invaders.

I settle my headdress. Among its feathers is the red feather that Koro gave me many years ago; it's my lucky charm. I wait for the rainbow, the colour of black pearls glowing, through which I will slide down to the great god ship below.

'But this time,' the announcer continues, 'the Maohi people do not need to worry. The God 'Oro has sent his emissary, Tupaea.'

'Time to go to the rescue,' Jean-Luc says into my face mike.

'Count me down,' I answer.

'Ten, nine, eight, seven . . .'

What's this? Some interference.

'Six, five, four, three . . .'

Hello, Little Tu, are you there, over?

'Two, one, and you're on. Open your wings, Tupaea.'

They've been resting, relaxing. Now they begin to flex, and the wind is rushing up beneath them, and I lift.

The strobe lights hit me. I am the Arikirangi incarnate.

The rainbow bridge begins to glisten. Ancient voices call through the sound system. The audience gasps.

Nobody has ever negotiated the corde lisse from this enormous height before, but the rope and I are in partnership. Here in my own Te Raituitai, I look to my left at my arm outstretched and then to my right to the tips of the fingers.

I grasp the rope and take the first step into the dark air. From below, I know that my entrance is spectacular. All the spotlights catch me as I glitter gold in their glow . . .

All my life I've been searching for this perfection.

The air rushing into my lungs . . . and oh . . .

Then comes the sense of weightlessness and, yes, it is possible to defy gravity.

Up here, I'm in perfect suspension between heaven and earth, slowly twisting and turning and tumbling and unwrapping myself.

litter explodes like silver rain across the audience.

Ancient drums and conch shells raise fanfare after fanfare as I slowly descend the rainbow bridge to the *Endeavour* below. The audience applauds my beauty.

Hovering above the prow, I unroll at the horizontal, spinning, spinning, spinning down.

At the last minute I release the rope.

The audience screams.

Oh, the thrill of falling.

The screams turn to applause again as I alight on the prow of the *Endeavour*.

I bow to the three Maori waka.

I make a further bow to the audience and, in particular, to the place where my Koro must be sitting. I'm wearing a circular cap, like a woven helmet, and from it sprouts the tall headdress of beautiful red, yellow and black feathers. My body glistens with oil and around my midriff and thighs I wear a girdle of red feathers. A shoulder cape reaches down to the waist and is tipped with a fringe, this time of yellow feathers.

And then I begin to dance.

I was named after the man who was the captain of the ship called the *Endeavour*. He brought the God 'Oro to Aotearoa.

Can you see, Koro? Can you see?

My name is Tupaea.

AUTHOR NOTES —

MAGGIE DAWN /

A few years ago I saw a young Maori girl in a Porirua mall minding her small brother and two sisters. She was buying them an ice cream: one ice cream to share. I bought a second one for them and gave them some money so they could see a movie. She said that she would pay me back, and that one day she was going to own her own mall. I'm looking forward to meeting her again on that day.

WE'LL ALWAYS HAVE PARIS /

Film buffs of 1940s films will immediately recognise the title of this story, which comes from the classic 1942 Warner Brothers film, *Casablanca*, produced by Hal B. Wallis, with a screenplay by Julius J. Epstein, Philip G. Epstein and Howard Koch, and directed by Michael Curtiz. The film starred Humphrey Bogart, Ingrid Bergman, Paul Henreid and Claude Rains.

'When I Fall in Love' is one of many songs composed by Victor Young. Lyrics reproduced here courtesy Alfred Music Publishing.

ONE MORE NIGHT /

In 2007 the prize-winning and very successful playwright Albert Belz (Ngati Porou, Nga Puhi, Ngati Pokai) approached me for permission to use my first collection, *Pounamu, Pounamu* (1972), as the basis for a playscript. At the time *Pounamu, Pounamu* was the subject of another adaptation proposal, so I suggested to Albert that he should use my second collection, *The New Net Goes Fishing* (1976). He set to work on a play, *Whero's New Net*, which expanded one of the main themes of the collection — the urban migration of Maori from the East Coast to Wellington — to a depiction of the New Zealand diaspora and the migration of Maori to London.

The play was premièred by Massive Theatre Company in Auckland in 2009. It was provocative and intriguing and it gave me an idea: Albert had turned my stories into a play and I thought it would be interesting to turn the play back into fiction; among his other plays are *Awhi Tapu* (2003), *Yours Truly* (2006), *Te Karakia* (2007) and the highly acclaimed *Raising the Titanics* (2010). My thanks are due to Albert, and James Kyle Wilson and Sam Scott of the Massive Theatre Company Ltd, for allowing me to use the script of *Whero's New Net* as the basis for the novella.

The lyrics are from the song 'Kingfisher Come Home', which I wrote for Charlotte Yates, and the words were first referenced in my short story 'Halycon', *Te Ao Hou* magazine, 1971. The song was one of twelve original lyrics put to music by well-known New Zealand singer-composers and premiered in *Ihimaera* at the 2011 Auckland Arts Festival.

Lyrics quoted from '*Home and Away* Theme', words and music by Mike Perjanik, are quoted courtesy of Mike Perjanik Productions Pty Ltd.

Red is the English translation of the Maori name, Whero.

PURITY OF ICE /

The story itself goes all the way back to my 1950s childhood when, as a boy living on a farm, I would write stories on my bedroom wall at night. Most were about being the captain of a spaceship or submarine, and one of them was accompanied by a small pictograph: the lassoing of an iceberg and towing it to a base in the fiords of New Zealand. Fast-forward to 2011 and the bones of the story are still there, a genre piece of science fiction-fantasy, mixed up with the effects of global warming.

Herman Melville's *Moby Dick* (1851) is one of the world's greatest novels. As well as giving the white whale's name to the giant phantom iceberg, I have used chapter headings from the novel and extracts from it are featured in the story.

Readers will note the reference to Apsley Cherry-Garrard's *The Worst Journey in the World*, Chatto & Windus Ltd, London, 1922. There's a passage in the book that has always haunted me:

> *'Our problems are not new: they are as old as the men who hunted the prehistoric hills. When they hit one another on the head with stones the matter was confined to a few caves: now it shakes a crowded world more complicated than any watch. Human nature does not change: it becomes more dangerous. Those who guide the world now may think they are doing quite well: so perhaps did the dodo.'*

And Cherry-Garrard wrote this ninety years ago.

For those interested, a US patent (6616376 — Bagging Icebergs) was issued to Richard Fuerle, on 9 September 2003, covering a method and apparatus for bagging an iceberg. One edge of a large, flexible, waterproof bag, with floats at the open end and a drain at the bottom, is sunk and drawn under an iceberg by a ship. When that edge is refloated, the iceberg is inside the bag. The edges of the bag are tied over the iceberg and salt water is pumped out of the bag from the drain. As the iceberg melts, the bag fills with fresh water and can be pulled by the ship to where the fresh water is needed. The water can then be pumped out of the bag through the drain.

ORBIS TERRARIUM /

The only story in this collection to have been published before, 'Orbis Terrarium' is the result of a commission from Italian editor Marco Sonzogni for a story for *Second Violins* (2008). New Zealand authors were given introductory paragraphs from unfinished stories by the great Katherine Mansfield and invited to use the paragraphs for the creation of their own stories. In my case, I had just returned from a trip to the Galapagos Islands, where I had fulfilled one of my great ambitions: to look into the eyes of the oldest living creatures in the world, the giant tortoises of the Galapagos.

The first paragraph is from Mansfield's unfinished 'Such a Sweet Old Lady', 1923.

I have set the story in April 1982, the centennial month and year of Charles Darwin's death.

THE THRILL OF FALLING /

I decided to write this novella to commemorate the latest Transit of Venus, in June 2012, and the special conference and celebrations held in Uawa. The spelling of Tupaea is the Maori one. In Tahiti he is called Tupaia. Other sources call him Tupia.

'A hee mai te tua . . .': this version of the origin of 'Oro was dictated in 1840 by Tamara of Tahiti and Pati'i of Mo'orea, as cited in Donald S. Oliver, *Ancient Tahitian Society, Vol 2: Social Relations*, Australian National University Press, Canberra, 1974. It is the source of most of the information about 'Oro and the Arioi.

Other works consulted were J.C. Beaglehole (ed.), *The Journals of Captain James Cook, Vol I: The Voyage of the Endeavour, 1768–1771*, Cambridge University Press, 1955; Te Rangi Hiroa (Peter H. Buck), *Explorers of the Pacific: European and American Discoveries in Polynesia*, Bernice P. Bishop Museum, Hawai'i, 1953; *Captain Cook in New Zealand: Extracts from the Journals*, A.H. & A.W. Reed, Wellington, 1951; Alistair Maclean, *Captain Cook*, Collins, 1972; Sir James Watt, 'Medical Aspects and Consequences of Cook's Voyages', in *Captain James Cook and His Times*, Robin Fisher and Hugh Johnston (eds), Douglas & McIntyre Ltd, 1979, pp. 138, 140; Alex Calder, Jonathan Lamb and Bridget Orr, *Voyages and Beaches: Pacific Encounters, 1769–1840*, University of Hawai'i Press, 1999. Joan Druett's *Tupaia* (Random House, 2011) was also consulted and is an excellent biography for those seeking further information.

When the ships of James Cook's second expedition arrived in New Zealand, Maori clamoured for Tupaea. The news that he had died was received first with disbelief, and then with deep mourning. 'Aue, Tupaea!' James Cook himself acknowledged the topic when he visited Queen Charlotte Sound. Here are extracts from his journal of 4 June:

One of the first questions these strangers asked was for Tupia:
and when I told them he was dead, one or two expressed their
sorrow by a kind of lamentation, which to me appeared more
formal than real . . . It may be asked, if these people had never
seen the Endeavour, *nor any of her crew, how could they become*
acquainted with the name of Tupia, or have in their possession
(which many of them had) such articles as they could only have got
from that ship? To this may be answered that the name of Tupia
was so popular among them when the Endeavour *was here, that it*
would be no wonder if, at this time, it was known over great part
of New Zealand, and as familiar to those who never saw him as
to those who did. Had ships of any other nation whatever arrived
here, they would have equally inquired of them for Tupia . . .

In New Zealand, 'Oro is comparable to Rongo, God of Agriculture, and also to Koro, patron of dance and desire.

ACKNOWLEDGEMENTS /

As always, grateful thanks to my publisher, Harriet Allan, and the staff at Random House New Zealand, and to Anna Rogers, my editor, for our collaboration and her advice and work. Thanks also to Ray Richards, my agent, my employer Manukau Institute of Technology, and the New Zealand Arts Foundation for a grant in 2009 which enabled me to write *The Thrill of Falling*.